Also by Stone Spicer

Deep Green
Hidden So Deep

Visit author's website at
Novels-by-StoneSpicer.com
Like me on Facebook

Unforgivable
DECEPTION

STONE SPICER

Order this book online at www.trafford.com
or email orders@trafford.com

Most Trafford titles are also available at major online book retailers.

Print information available on the last page.

ISBN: 978-1-4907-9948-3 (sc)
ISBN: 978-1-4907-9949-0 (hc)
ISBN: 978-1-4907-9947-6 (e)

Library of Congress Control Number: 2020903596

Cover design by Pamela of Delaney-Designs.com

Photo of Bellows Field Beach Park, Waimanalo, Oahu, used
for chapter headings taken by Kekoa Ornellas

Trafford rev. 02/29/2020

 www.trafford.com

North America & international
toll-free: 1 888 232 4444 (USA & Canada)
fax: 812 355 4082

Close your eyes and listen in,
I'll whisper lies with a daggered grin,
And while truth dies, I'll spin and spin,
And play upon the fear within.

—Robert Scott

A NOTE TO MY READERS

*M*y story contains a real-life experience that a dear friend and I were an integral part of. The circumstances of the rescue off the island of Molokai described in chapter 7 as well as the surrounding area are quite factual. It was early in 1983.

Other than this tailored rewriting of history, the balance of the story is just that—a story that has emerged from imagination onto the printed page. Place-names and locations mentioned, however, are not imagined but are or were real in every sense of the word, like Ahalanui the warm pond of Kapoho on the Big Island, which, regrettably, disappeared forever beneath a flood of lava in 2019.

Chapter One

A small cabin high on the southeast slope of Haleakalā, island of Maui; 6,000 feet above the sea

It might have been a dream with the deep blue of the ocean's surface stretching out far below reaching out to the horizon. It was a home sellers' fantasy and an acrophobia's worst nightmare. But it was neither. It was Annie Gaines' and Taylor Gordon's newly acquired view from their new home high on the slopes of Haleakalā. Their view looked down the expansive slope to the ocean on the south side and the city of Kahului toward the west.

Actually, it was theirs and their landlord's, but at that moment—looking out through the large plate glass window at the ocean far below, morning coffee held in one hand while holding their partner's waist with the other—no one else in the world existed.

Annie and Taylor, partners for the past fifteen months, had been very fortunate to find this small quaint cabin being offered for rent. The rent was far more than they would have liked to spend and considerably higher than they could easily afford, but that view . . . It was their love nest, and they'd find the means to keep it.

The elevation above sea level was high, along with the rent they paid. But sometimes in life, you have to overlook a few things, and they toasted their decision each morning with coffee as they gazed out over the slope of the mountain that was the key point tourist attraction in Maui.

Their home occupied a small footprint on the mountainside, which pleased them. The small cabin adequately covered their needs. It offered sufficient room for their sparse furnishings, but a gift of a potted plant would have created a challenge in finding floor space. A wide area off the living room was their kitchen, but since neither enjoyed cooking, the size was adequate. There was available space for coffee makings, and that, alone, covered 80 percent of their needs.

The single bedroom had a built-in bed platform with drawers beneath, which took up most of the room. A tiny bathroom covered all the essentials, including an economy-sized shower stall. *Economy-sized* being the operative word—adequate for its purpose, provided they didn't get amorous and decide to shower together. If they did, and they often tried, they discovered a crowbar along with a quart of Vaseline were both essential components.

The cabin had been built over a century ago, during the missionary era, according to their landlady, ostensibly to take advantage of the view and the solitude of the mountain. She speculated that the used barnwood cabin had possibly been the remote escape for some person of wealth. If old secrets were known, perhaps even a place for an illicit rendezvous as it was far enough removed from the community, observing eyes, and the forever-loose lips.

A tenth-mile driveway reached out from the cabin to the main road leading up to the summit or down to the city of Kahului. A few exotic silver swords adorned the property with *naupaka* bushes edging the drive.

The young couple loved the cabin for its uniqueness. Annie had grown up in the Koko Head area of Oahu on Papio Street. Plywood houses and pig farms in the area were her playground.

Taylor's upbringing was in the cattle country of Wyoming with rolling, empty prairie land and grazing cattle as his.

The early morning water around the crater-shaped isle of Molokini, clearly visible through the cabin window, beckoned boaters to come and play, much like a mermaid waving a red flag to garner a sailor's attention.

Its pull was working well this morning; Taylor could feel it. Taking a sip of coffee, steam rising around his face, he proclaimed in his customary brief use of words while pulling Annie closer in a conspirator fashion, "We need to join all those other boats, snorkelers, and sun worshippers out there. Why don't we finish our coffee and drag the boat down to the ramp?"

Annie was accustomed to Taylor's impromptu decision-making tendencies, so she wasn't the least surprised at his suggestion. Since first meeting him, he possessed what she had come to think of as a reactionary inclination toward life. If he ever actually gave a degree of prethought when he came to these sorts of decisions, she had never been aware of it. For the most part, she embraced that impromptu quality and loved him for it. It was an attribute she was not used to in her own life but found she enjoyed the energy of doing things on the spur of the moment. Their time together had not been stagnant but rather filled with fun, excitement, and pleasure. Taylor had the capacity to look at life without the hindering fogbank that life often handicaps people with.

With the proclamation having been made on how their day should unfold, both felt the need and excitement to get on with it.

While Taylor readied their boat, Annie gathered the necessary ingredients for their day: food, water, towels, some sunscreen, a cold six-pack Primo beer, and a myriad of other things deemed appropriate and already stuffed into her Tutu Annie travel bag. The bag was her favorite, a never-leave-home-without-it accessory. It was a carry-all made of bright, colorful Hawaiian print material—red hibiscus in this case, with pink plumerias printed helter-skelter on it. She had decorated a small cooler to match.

While Annie was going over all the things they would need, Taylor was outside hooking *Kalia*, their boat, to the car.

Taylor loved their home but could have easily done without the steep, long road that led up to it. His car, an older model Ford Explorer with three-hundred thousand miles and counting clocked on its odometer and a myriad of worn parts, could generally make the trip down without mishap, but the return trip was, at times, quite iffy. He had gone to the extreme of taping a tow company's business card to the dashboard—a precautionary move.

A newer car was needed, and Annie continued pestering Taylor about getting one, but he was unwilling to consider it and appeared to become upset whenever the issue came up.

"I don't want to draw any attention," he'd tell her when she insistently asked why. Their choice of such a remote location to live was also an integral part of Taylor's chosen lifestyle of *invisibility*. Annie perceived his actions as a need to be inconspicuous to the world and his fellow man, something she failed to understand but nevertheless accepted because she loved him—it just wasn't who she, herself, was, though.

Taylor had just finished checking all the lines and tie-downs when Annie joined him. She carried their small cooler and had her bright red-and-pink-flowered supply bag slung over her shoulder, and she had a big, excited smile lighting up her face. It was the beginning of a perfect day.

Chapter Two

*B*efore Taylor unexpectedly showed up in her life, Annie Gaines had been working as a bartender-waitress in a cocktail lounge on the mezzanine floor of a downtown Honolulu office building. It was appropriately named the Perch; however, most regulars referred to it simply as the Lounge or the Watering Hole. In many minds, calling their favorite and frequently visited place the Lounge carried a softer impact, especially when confessing to loved ones who were at home looking at dinner getting cold on the table.

The Perch was always quite busy in late afternoons, drawing a regular clientele from among the mass of lawyers and accountants who populated the twenty-seven-story office tower. Most were there looking to fortify themselves for their coming jam-packed, bumper-to-bumper drive home, but many others were there drowning an especially tough day experienced in court or recovering from being routed by an angry client.

While enjoying a Knob Creek on the rocks at the Perch, they could sit and converse with clients or fellow workers in the relatively subdued and pleasant atmosphere. Or if alone, they could simply gaze through one of the multitude of windows facing Honolulu Harbor and the iconic and historic Aloha Tower, once the magical, almost fairy-tale, symbol that greeted Matson Cruise Lines twin ships, the *Lurline* or the *Mariposa*.

Besides the view, the atmosphere, and the convenience the Perch had to offer, Annie herself had become a major drawing card. Her tallness and leaness and her flawless brown-skinned features lent authority to an attractive Hawaiian background. She had a mane of rich black hair with a tinge of red that cascaded to her shoulders.

Her resilient, always-positive attitude became a strong magnet to the bar's patrons who had come to know and appreciate who she was. And she unintentionally provided many overworked, overachieving corporate climbers with a breath of fresh air along with a subliminal need to make love to their wives as soon as they stepped through their front doors, cold dinner waiting on the table or not.

The main clientele that made the Perch a second home was 90 percent testosterone-loaded lawyers, power brokers, and CPAs—a challenging crowd for any attractive woman.

Working alone most of the time, Annie had become aloof to the constant interest she generated from those hoping to gain her attention and possibly her affection. She made a conscious effort to keep emotional and physical entanglements from coming into her workspace. In the evenings, Alex, a young local man of regal proportions, worked beside her until closing time and did an exceptional job of keeping any would-be aggressors at bay until the door was locked.

This separation of work from her private life had been working successfully for her until one particular day when a tall, ruggedly handsome man walked in late one afternoon and smiled at her.

Taylor Gordon was a name she soon came to know. He carried an air of soft sincerity, an unpretentious bearing, and an inviting smile that totally disarmed her. She learned that Taylor worked in an office within the same building that afforded him the convenience of coming in to the Perch in late afternoons, ostensibly for a cold Primo before leaving for the day. Annie naturally assumed he was married—as were most of the clientele who floated in and out—but he quickly dispelled that notion, and before long, they had developed a comfortable, in-lounge friendship.

Taylor always managed to make her laugh, and she found herself anticipating his visits and the lightheartedness he brought in with him and very quickly began feeling the day was incomplete when he didn't walk in the door.

He had a habit of writing short notes or poems on bar napkins and slipping them onto her tray as she passed by and often wadded up paper money, leaving it piled on the table as a tip. It was a frivolous thing to do, but Annie enjoyed the playfulness of it. If she was too busy to unravel the bundle he'd left, which was often the case, she'd shove it all into her apron pocket, then laughed when she pulled it back out later at home and reread some of the notes he'd written crumpled up with the cash.

An avid swimmer, Annie loved going to the historic natatorium, the old WWI memorial, jutting out into the water at the east end of Waikiki Beach. The open-air structure was a salt water–fed swimming pool of Olympic proportions. It was the very same pool that Hawaii's ambassador and surfing champion Duke Kahanamoku used to swim in as he practiced for the Olympics, and it was Annie's favorite place to swim laps. It was often devoid of other swimmers sans a few tourists hanging off the edges, and the openness and emptiness of it suited her.

She had arrived on a Sunday afternoon one day and noticed the familiar face of a man exiting the pool at the far, opposite end. It took her some time, swimming two laps, before she figured out that the familiar face belonged to Taylor. Taking people out of their familiar surroundings often affects memory and recall, but she knew this man was a friend even if his name escaped her. It was one of the hazards she'd discovered from working in a popular place—so many people knew her by name, but she knew them only by their faces. *Besides,* she rationalized, *the lounge is dark, and people don't walk around barefoot and shirtless in just a bathing suit and looking so hot.* She realized exactly who he was while swimming her laps and felt quite happy when she found him still sitting there when she emerged from the water after finishing her laps.

They sat together and talked in the waning sunlight on one of the cement bleachers before they graduated to the nearby Queen's Surf Barefoot Bar. Neither was willing to bring the time to an end. They sat at the bar and talked into the night as Kui Lee sang, Varoa Tiki danced and the venerated Sterling Mossman engaged the audience in music and laughter. It was a memorable evening in a magical setting and created the ideal stage for romance.

Chapter Three

$\mathcal{F}$or the past six years, Taylor Gordon, the man whom Annie was starting to think of as a very dear friend, had been working for the financial investment firm TGL & Company. Their offices occupied the entire twenty-fifth floor of the same building where the Perch was located. Its proximity to Taylor's office made it a very convenient stopover at the end of the day and his work complete, or as complete as Taylor chose it to be. For the most part, he worked unsupervised and made his own hours. If one was to ever ask him, he would have cheerfully offered that, this very moment in time, the moment he walked out of the office and closed the door, was the *very best* time of his day—a workaholic he was not.

He had no formal title at TGL & Company. It was a position that was created specifically for a person who possessed his unique abilities. He enjoyed an uncanny aptitude for numbers and attention to detail, and because of that, he acted more or less as a *funnel* for all the financial business TGL handled.

He was, in part, responsible for making sure that anything regarding clients and the financial paperwork that accompanied them was properly handled—all the i's were dotted, t's were crossed, and alternatives considered. Anything that had the potential of getting TGL in trouble, financial-wise speaking, was his responsibility to keep them out of. Because of his financial expertise, he was expected to scan paperwork to see if various financial pathways a client's money could take had been looked at and evaluated and the path chosen that best fit with the clients overall monetary objectives. He was in the unique position to recommend further action that the CPAs and counselors of the firm may have overlooked. This status caused him to be shunned by most of the employees. They viewed him as a threat to their well-being. This same element was the very thing that the company's owner and CEO liked best about having him there.

Taylor's formal education was at the University of Hawaii. He graduated with honors and went on to complete his master's degree in finance. He'd done all this within a time frame that astounded the dean and impressed most of the professors who instructed him.

Born and raised in Sheridan, Wyoming, he'd followed his heart and the desires of a young man and enrolled in the University of Hawaii soon after graduating from high school. He'd heard intriguing stories of the coed season that occurred in Hawaii each spring break and decided he wanted to experience that annual two-week nonstop, often risqué, booze-filled beach party for himself. Also, on the positive side, depending of course on what values you were using in choosing which side was deemed the positive one, the UH had a reputation as an excellent institution for financial education.

Upon graduating with a master's degree, he talked with counselors at the University Placement Center about potential employment. It turned out they had only one job available to offer him. It was with TGL & Company. It couldn't have worked out any better.

He wasn't a CPA. He had never wanted to go that route being content with the knowledge and abilities he possessed. He was young and enjoyed an aptitude that allowed him to look at financial matters and view them under an entirely different set of spotlights than CPAs were trained to do for decades. In a very short time, he had become an indispensable asset to TGL.

His undoing, though, began when he made two spur-of-the-moment blunders. The second blunder, taking them out of sequence on the scale of importance to him, came about when he met and fell in love with Annie Gaines. In his quest to get to know her and, hopefully, find a combination of words and deeds that would steer her to his bed, he'd lied and introduced himself as Taylor Gordon, the name of a second-grade buddy he'd known. He was never exactly sure why he'd done that.

TGL & Company had, of course, hired him under his legal given name—Jason Baker, the person he'd been all his life. Why he had blurted out the name Taylor Gordon to Annie or why that name was even part of his brain was a puzzle, but he had stuck with it instead of correcting it and making himself appear to be the fool that he suddenly felt himself to be.

Initially, he hadn't taken the potential relationship with this waitress very far forward. It was intended to be a one-night stand—maybe two, if he worked it right. Perhaps he had become too used to the bar scene and the associated one-night stands that were synonymous with many bars. His expectations regarding Annie weren't too high. Very quickly, though, the relationship with her became something serious, something he didn't want to see come to an end. He was starting to care deeply for her, which meant he would eventually need to figure out a way of explaining to her what he'd done and then pray she wouldn't head for the nearest exit.

The first biggest mistake you already know the second—and probably the greatest mistake he'd ever made came a year and a half into his six-year career with TGL & Company. His shortsighted actions came from not thinking clearly and not taking those thoughts very far into the future. This error in judgment had the potential of putting him behind bars at Oahu Correctional facility for a very long time.

It happened while searching for some critical information late one evening. Jason stumbled onto some previously unknown files. Anthony, his boss, had always insisted that he alone, as CEO, be the only person to handle certain clients. As it happened, though, some information that Jason was hunting for was needed for one of these off-limit clients. His boss had been called to Sicily for the funeral of one of his brothers, and he must have forgotten to replace the files in his locked drawer before hastily rushing from the office to the airport. His boss would be gone for a week, maybe longer. Jason didn't want to leave the client waiting and saw no reason he shouldn't try to help.

While trying his best to take care of the client, Jason uncovered a rather large discrepancy—one that had the notable appearance of being quite deliberate. Looking further into other similar accounts while searching for answers, he noticed the usual sums of money being deposited to the client's business account. There was nothing extraordinary about that, but then he became aware that not all of what should have been deposited was getting to where it was supposed to go. The precise amount of what was unaccounted for showed up on a private ledger under his boss's own name. It took Jason several days looking through other clients' account ledgers in the usually locked drawer before discovering a pattern with exacting percentages of cash that were being routinely redirected to a single holder's account, an account owned by none other than Anthony Gravello, his boss. All the funds in this private account were being held in trust by a bank in Sicily.

It was a shock at first. Jason didn't have any personal experience with this sort of money-diversion scheme, but he knew enough to know precisely what he was looking at. It was very simple in its overall operation: his boss was skimming large amounts of money from clients while amassing a sizable net sum neatly tucked away in Sicily.

It had taken Jason several weeks and much soul-searching before he began forming a plan to create his own *hidden* account by squeezing funds out of his boss's pilfered funds prior to the deposits being made to this hidden account. He began shortchanging every other deposit and adding those moneys to his own hidden account. With the way his boss operated, Jason was positive he wouldn't discover the discrepancy until the time came when he begins withdrawing the money for his retirement—hopefully, a day far in the future. On that day, Anthony Gravello would discover he had much less money than he thought he ought to have and would immediately suspect foul play, but by then, Jason would be just a distant memory.

Something that Jason didn't know at that moment—and if he had, it would have been enough to scare him straight as a stick—was that his boss was intimately connected, albeit currently estranged, with a well-known crime family in Sicily, a family that one didn't dare mess with if they cared about remaining healthy.

At the time, though, it was a thrill even though it scared Jason to his core. He knew he'd have to be long gone by the time his boss got wise to what had taken place. He just hoped his boss was sufficiently arrogant that he would not think to look at his hidden account's bottom line until he is in the position to begin using it. Even if he did, he'd still see it growing in value and would hopefully not take the time to add up any of the numbers. The more he thought about what he was doing manipulating these sums of money, the more at ease he became with doing so—*it had become the proverbial piece of cake.* He was soon shortchanging every deposit made into Gravello's hidden account, not just every other—a dangerous step forward.

* * *

When he met Annie that night he walked into the Perch, not having any thought of a future relationship, a feeling of mutual attraction quickly began developing, and Jason began to change the timing and the scope of his money scheme. He became a little less careful, upping the percentage he withdrew from his boss's deposits. He also decided that he could be very happy with far less than the megamillions he'd first envisioned. A lesser amount meant he'd be able to leave TGL's employ much sooner than originally planned and still have enough money to fund the beginning of a good life. His original objective, before Annie, was to accumulate at least two million and then disappear. With feelings for Annie strengthening, he began liking his knew, albeit lessened, objective.

Four months had elapsed since the hours they spent talking on the cement bleachers of the natatorium and enjoying their time at Queen's Surf Barefoot Bar. He'd stuck with the name Taylor Gordon throughout the time he'd spent with Annie. The fear remained that the truth would quickly end the relationship that he had come to love so much. He despised himself for having started the name charade in the first place and spent long hours trying to develop words that would set things straight without losing the woman he knew he was in love with. But he could never find those words.

How long can I keep this up? How much longer can I keep this falsehood in place and allow it to cripple anything decent that's going to come in the future?

They were having a quiet dinner at the Royal Lanai Restaurant in Waikiki when Taylor finally found the gonads to tell her, but as the evening wore on, he hadn't done so and decided another week or two wouldn't change anything.

During their dinner, he dug the hole deeper for some inexplicable reason, and his lie became more unretractable when he told her he had a large inheritance that would soon come to him, and when it did, they could move in together and find their perfect home. Suddenly, he was even more ashamed for adding to the lie, which was destined to bury the man he'd always been so proud to be.

Their relationship had become very close, and Annie drifted between her apartment by the zoo and Taylor's apartment behind Punchbowl with its view over the city. She bought the inheritance story and loved the thought of moving to Maui, something they'd often talk about, and starting a life together. The idea of going off-grid and moving to an isolated spot in Maui was Taylor's ultimate dream, and he seemed overly anxious to do so. Annie was ecstatic.

* * *

A year had passed since Taylor left employment with TGL & Company, and they were living together in Maui. The embezzled funds, Taylor's supposed inheritance, were securely entrenched in a bank in Denmark, except for a stack of cash he'd put into a bank's safe deposit box in Kahului, Maui—*fallback* money he called it. He put the box's key in a hidden spot for safekeeping, along with some information he'd collected while at TGL that he hoped he'd never have to divulge but that could be his ticket out of jail if push ever came to shove.

During the lapsed year, there had been no Honolulu Police Department officers from the Metro Squad or goons imported from Sicily knocking at their door. Taylor was feeling secure in their cabin home on Haleakalā as each week became a little easier to hold on to his secret. Although it also added to a mounting difficulty for him—it was making the hole he'd dug deeper than he'd ever imagined it could get if he ever had to explain the truth. He wasn't a stupid man and knew someday he'd be faced with revealing the truth.

Chapter Four

$\mathcal{W}$hen Taylor finished hooking the boat to his old car, he and Annie climbed in for their day in the water.

Taylor's old Ford Explorer got them and their boat to the launching ramp at Kihei without problem. They were excited with the prospects of the day and pleasantly surprised to find the ramp was almost vacant. They had been prepared for the normal lengthy wait, but they found only a woman and her two kids preparing to step onto a waiting boat as a man held the boat tight against the pier and offered his other hand to help her and the kids get in. It immediately powered up and rapidly pulled away from the pier, leaving it open to Taylor. He made fast work of getting *Kalia* into the water, getting the car and trailer safely parked, and getting the boat's motor warmed up, ready to go.

They were on their way for a fun-filled day. The magic of being out in the water surrounded by the ocean's intoxicating environment quickly enveloped them. The inescapable scent of marine life, salt, and seaweed was a magical part of the attraction they both enjoyed. It had succeeded in exerting its pull on them, like a magnet beckons to a piece of metal.

They had been so engrossed in the energy of their plans when they first talked of them at the cabin they failed to heed one of the prime directives all boaters were aware of: the need to *always, always* check marine weather reports before venturing a foot into the water.

Their failure was perhaps understandable but still inexcusable. Their favorite radio station had been playing the sort of music they both loved as they had gone about preparing to leave the cabin. The station unfortunately employed an announcer who possessed a seriously flawed monotone voice incapable of garnering the briefest of audience enthusiasm much less attention. He played *their* music, so they endured his announcing just to hear the tunes.

While they had been preoccupied preparing for their adventure, the announcer was in the process of issuing a detailed weather warning advising his audience about pending strong trade winds, relatively nonexistent at present but destined to increase in strength as the day progressed. If conditions continued, he cautioned anyone listening, small-craft warnings would undoubtedly be put into effect. Neither Taylor nor Annie heard any of that. Getting out onto the smooth water was all that they were interested in, not listening to the voice of someone they were convinced would put them into a coma were it not for his rhythmic, make-you-want to-move music.

Had they been listening to his words and alert to the warnings, they might have opted for a drive around the island to Lahaina for a glass of wine instead of heading out into the water. Maybe they could have tried out the new zip line in Iao Valley. But that was not how things went.

The boat was new to them, and their desire to use it was keen. Obtaining the boat in the first place had been luck mixed with an unplanned act of kindness.

Quite soon after moving into their cabin, the topic began coming into their conversations. With the vastness of the ocean constantly in their view, possessing a boat became paramount in their thoughts. They talked at length about all the places they could go, the sheltered coves they would find to dive or snorkel, and the secluded beaches they could make love on.

Part of the difficulty of deciding on a boat was a matter of what each of them wanted. Annie was looking for something big enough to spend a night on whenever the opportunity arose. Taylor was looking for something small and unobtrusive. He was almost adamant in his desire for nothing splashy, his exact words, just something they could enjoy without drawing attention. Like his thoughts on having a new car, he'd told Annie he didn't want anything that couldn't blend in and go unnoticed.

It was the one difficulty Annie had to overcome in their relationship. Taylor loved life and embraced it all to the hilt but only if he could be invisible while walking through it. She often thought that if she didn't know him better, she would suspect him of being a wanted man, hiding out from the law.

* * *

As it often happens, when the desire for something builds in intensity and frequent thought is given to it, the universe acts by providing it—the law of attraction hard at work.

They had been sitting late one afternoon in the dining room of the old Pioneer Inn in Lahaina, enjoying a dessert of *zuppa di inglese*, something they'd heard about and wanted to try. It was a place they often frequented because of the ambience of the old historic inn. In bygone days, a century earlier, the inn catered to the infamous whaling ships and rowdy crews that made Lahaina their favored port of call. Today, there were too many developers with their sights set on its perfect location, nestled beside the famous harbor and the two-hundred-year-old banyan tree that was bigger than a city block and photographed more often than a hula dancer and almost as frequently as Diamond Head. They felt compelled to frequent it, cementing memories of its grandeur before it succumbed one day to a bulldozer's blade.

It had been an enjoyable day, and feeling charitable, they decided to prepay the dinner tab of a man in uniform who was sitting alone at a table close by. It was a gesture of kindness, and thanks to the uniform and the man who was wearing it, they were soon engrossed in a lively conversation with him. Midway in their conversation, they realized they were being offered a boat at less than a penny's cost. Capt. Lane Davis, a marine pilot stationed at Kaneohe Marine Corps Air Station in Oahu, told them of his pending transfer back to the mainland. "Texas," he explained. He told them it was too difficult to take the boat with him. He mentioned having been given the boat by another marine, a friend who was also being transferred home. Captain Davis said he wanted to give the boat to them in like fashion. "Passing on the kindness," he'd said. They were ecstatic.

The boat was not what Annie had envisioned as well as being considerably showier than what Taylor had hoped for—but it was a gift, and they accepted it. They had flown to Oahu the following week, picked it up at the marine base in Kaneohe, and placed it on a Young Brothers barge headed for Kahului, Maui.

Two weeks later—today—they were skimming so quickly across the smooth ocean water their hair stood straight out behind them in the wind. They were sitting comfortably on a thickly padded white center console bench seat in their eighteen-foot, open-bow Boston Whaler. A large ninety-horsepower Johnson outboard motor was roaring with life behind them with a promise of more power waiting for their command—it would have been impossible for either of them to be happier.

Changing course partway to Molokini, they took aim for the island of Molokai. It was an easy decision after looking out over the water in amazement at the mass of boats and people already accumulating around their initial destination—and it had yet to reach 7:00 a.m. The island of Molokai was not too distant, but they had to travel almost the entire length of the island to reach the harbor that was at the extreme end, the place Taylor had in mind to go.

The wind had picked up appreciably and was causing a chop on the water's surface. Frequent small whitecaps tumbled across the surface and slammed into their bow. The conditions, though, were nothing their boat couldn't take in stride. "Boston Whalers," as Taylor proclaimed, "were designed for this kind of water."

Annie would later reflect on Taylor's words with deep regret, realizing she'd had too much faith in his knowledge and capabilities and failed to question the decisions made or question the unspoken dragons Taylor seemed to possess and wanted to keep hiding from the world.

From Annie's perspective, Taylor had always demonstrated a confidence that she had come to lean on and rarely question. This thing that had anchored itself in Taylor wasn't just about the boat but was a combination of the simple decisions he would make. She harbored a concern that if he wouldn't open up and bring her into his confidence to enable them to work together on the issues he was concerned with, a chain of subtle events could be initiated that would hurt their chances of living as partners.

Chapter Five

They were headed for a little-used anchorage on the southwest edge of Molokai, Hale O Lono Harbor. Their journey went quickly, thanks to their new boat, but they arrived a bit dampened because of the spray generated by the boat's bow and speed.

The anchorage was originally dredged and created to be a working harbor but now was a lonely place left abandoned by the State of Hawaii, destined to battle the elements on its own. It was several miles west of the island's main town of Kaunakakai with the small community of Moanaloa just a few miles distant. For years, the harbor had been very active, serving as the main supply center for sand destined to replenish the rapidly eroding beaches of Waikiki, but the need ceased after stone breakwaters had been put in place on Waikiki Beach.

Now the harbor was a solitary, mostly deserted, place left for use by ocean-traveling yachts, local fishing boats seeking shelter for the night, and a few weekend fun-seekers looking for a secluded getaway place to anchor. Fishing was good in the harbor, and the *opihi* on the breakwaters plentiful. For the most part, though, it sat in ignored silence. Even people living on the island, for the most part, left it alone since it was difficult to get to and offered little attraction and sparse shade as reasons to go.

Taylor was in full control as he guided the boat through the impressive-sized breakwaters, handling the increasingly larger entrance swells with ease. He opted to drop anchor along the left edge of the harbor instead of tying up to one of several old cement pylons that remained standing in quiet testimony to days gone by.

The water was warm where Taylor had elected to anchor and a short, easy swim to an overhanging steel ladder. Since they were both good swimmers, their choice of anchorage was ideal. Taylor figured that being anchored a short distance out, instead of being tied to the pier or pylons, would help keep sand and debris from tracking onboard from the bottom of their feet, making cleanup once they got back home much simpler.

"We have about two hours, Annie," Taylor proclaimed, just as she was about to jump overboard. "By then, we'll need to *hele on* back to Maui. Any later and that boat ramp will be jammed with so many boats waiting their turn to haul out, it'll look like a beehive at lunchtime in a flower patch, and it'll take forever."

Acknowledging his words with a wave of her hand, Annie went over the side into the water. She looked back up at him still standing on the deck of their boat. "I'm going to walk out on the breakwater," she explained, pointing off to her left. "I want to see if there are any glass floats that might have found their way onto the rocks without breaking."

Annie was forever on the lookout for the green fishnet glass floats that were once so numerous populating the drift-line of every beach fronting the Pacific Ocean, along with everything else that drifted on the water. At a time long past, they were used extensively by Japanese fishing boats as an integral part of their fishing before the advent of plastic and Styrofoam. Fishing boats, at that time, were often outfitted with kilns and had employed onboard glass blowers for the single purpose of creating fish floats to replace those that continually broke loose from the nets. Some of those now-treasured glass floats still drifted on the ocean, finding their way onto beaches throughout the Pacific basin. They were becoming quite rare though. Annie had a collection of many of them and of several different sizes and shapes.

Prior to diving off the stern, Taylor acknowledged her words and said he was going to take a walk over to an abandoned scout camp that he'd read about.

Annie knew of the camp Taylor mentioned. He'd talked about his interest in wanting to explore the old Boy Scout campground and was anxious to make use of this opportunity to do so. She knew he had been hoping she would choose to go with him but knew he also understood her need for some alone time and glass-float hunting.

They each headed off in different directions. Each enjoyed having their own personal time and looked forward to the fun they would have sharing experiences on the boat ride back to Maui.

As Annie enjoyed searching the breakwater, Taylor was discovering that the hike to the camp was a lot hotter and much drier than he had anticipated. He passed through scrubby forests of *kiawe* trees, which kept his enjoyment of the hike in check. But then he hadn't intended this hike to be strictly for enjoyment but more for space or time away from Annie and familiar surroundings so he could do some good, old-fashioned soul-searching—still trying to come to terms with himself and what he'd said and done. More than that, he needed to figure out what he must do about it. Stealing and lying were not the behaviors of the person he ever envisioned himself becoming. His life had been almost perfect, and he was messing it up pretty badly.

He had forestalled the inevitable for longer than he should have—on both accounts, the name and the money. Both were beginning to have their impact on his relationship with Annie and with himself and he was beginning to dislike who he had become for creating such a cloak-and-dagger cover up. He and Annie were investing themselves in this relationship with the full intention of getting married and hopefully having kids. None of that was going to happen unless he spoke up and begged forgiveness—and received it!

Also, he couldn't help reprimanding himself, *how stupid could I possibly get? Stealing money from a member of a Mafia family. What on earth was I thinking?*

Hiking the obstacle-strewn trail, course vegetation and dead-falls scattered far and wide, he was having trouble with his rubber flip-flops, and his feet were beginning to suffer. The sharp points of the needles growing from the kiawe branches were irritating, but his determination was not going to allow him to call it quits.

Deep in his thoughts, he resolved to be prepared to accept whatever verdict Annie would pronounce on him. He decided that when he got to the camp, he would simply take a fast look around so he could at least say he'd been there, then hurry back, and join Annie on the breakwater and get this mental ordeal over with and behind him and let the future unfold on its own course. He hoped there'd be other days to come back here and explore the camp and surrounding area—with Annie.

If things went well with her when he got back to the harbor, he'd go for a cooling swim with her; and then, hopefully, he'd have time for a cold brew before they found some shade to sit and talk.

* * *

It was closing in on 10:00 a.m. Out on the ocean, the trade winds were steadily increasing in strength, and the size of the waves, commensurate with the winds, were building up to become quite a powerful force. Not aware of any of this, being sheltered by thick vegetation and having finally made the plan for his talk with Annie, he felt good about the direction things were taking, so he let his thoughts return to nature.

He briefly gave thought to the problems he would need to contend with in facing the increasing wind when time came to head back to Maui, so he simply decided to enjoy the cooling effect the increased wind was having as it pushed through the trees—it was helping ease the weight of other thoughts.

As he continued his quickened pace to the scout camp, he became aware that the surrounding brush he'd been working his way through was opening to a large clearing surrounding a collection of collapsed buildings and split-wood fences. He knew he'd found the scout camp. His curiosity peaked as he busily began exploring the place he'd read about.

He was starting to think that there may be a way out of his money predicament, right his wrongs with TGL. It was worth a try. He was smart, and knew he could work out a plan to return the funds to TGL, to Gravello's private account, and if discovered, to hope for forgiveness. He was certain his boss would not find it easy to forgive him, but the man certainly wasn't in any position to call the authorities—a thief can rarely point a finger at another thief. He just hoped Annie's love for him was strong enough that she could find forgiveness as well.

As he became increasingly excited about correcting his wrongs, he relaxed and was aimlessly wandering around the camp, taking it all in before heading back to the harbor. Feeling good about his decision and feeling relaxed, he failed to notice a tree root that grew above the ground next to an old wooded water trough. His foot caught it and he went down, hard, landing face-first in the old trough.

He quickly became aware of a swarm of bees his sudden arrival had startled from their work and were swiftly surrounding him, striking at any bare skin that showed. His eyelids and face were the worst. Try as he did, he was unable to get his feet under him to stand free of the wood trough. Something, the string of his bathing suit, was caught on part of the splintering wood of the trough and holding him in position. The pain of stings soon became a blur before he succumbed to unconsciousness.

* * *

On the other side of the harbor, Annie was paying attention to an entirely different surrounding, one she wished she could go back and re-do what ultimately led up to her current predicament. She was conscious but panic was slowly exercising its grip.

A distance off the coast of Molokai

*W*hile Taylor was facing potentially fatal circumstances, the love of his life, Annie, several miles away, also faced an ocean full of potentially calamitous conditions. She was on the sheer edge of panic.

She was quickly discovering the extreme depths to which panic could push a sane person who, under normal day-to-day living, would have denied even the existence of the word *panic*. She was shocked by her reaction to the life-threatening circumstances she faced. She was having flashbacks of past events in her life and was beginning to realize that her life could come to an end very rapidly.

Why now when my life has become a rose garden? Why today when there is someone in my life who loves me beyond question?

She had no answers, only questions.

Until meeting Taylor, she had felt like her whole life had been placed on hold waiting for that special person, a man like Taylor, to show up and hold out his hand to her. She sensed the sting of guilt knowing he'd had something very troubling weighing on his mind lately, yet she had done nothing to encourage him to voice it, to share it with her, to ease the burden he was obviously shouldering, desperately trying to shield her from it. She was certain that, together, they could make everything better but felt that chance quickly being drowned out by the waves and the chill that was beginning to rattle her nerves.

Young and athletic, taking life on the edge whenever she wasn't at work in the bar, she didn't fully understand this fear that was building within her. It was something very strange to her thoughts and decided she didn't like it at all.

Last weekend she hadn't felt any panic when facing off with a tough-as-nails rugby team in a scrimmage game. The group of women was a go-for-broke team that wanted nothing more than to pummel her into a shapeless pile on the playing field. She'd faced them without fear. Nor had she experienced any panic a few weeks earlier when she was forced to dodge a moray eel's unforgivingly sharp fangs while body surfing at Queen's Beach. She'd stepped on a coral head that the eel apparently considered as its home.

So why was she feeling the sharp ridge of panic now? *If it hadn't been for that surfboard,* she lamented!

"This darned surfboard," she said to no one but the turbulent wall of water that surrounded her. She struck her fist down on its surface in frustration.

She had found the surfboard washed up on the breakwater lining the entrance to Hale O Lono Harbor while looking for glass floats. It was in near perfect shape even though it appeared to have been stuck in the rocks for a goodly length of time judging by the marine life already making home on its surface.

With the found surfboard in hand and nicely formed surf rolling in, she had decided that those were good enough reasons to catch a few rides. *No more than three or four rides, and I'll go find Taylor and spend the time with him.* It was her plan, anyway.

With abandon and some difficulty, she had pulled the board from the rocks, threw it into the water, and dove in after it.

Unfortunately, she'd been enjoying herself so much she had let her attention to time and surroundings wander, Taylor temporarily forgotten, and had allowed herself to get caught in a swift-moving current that rapidly transported her away from the safety of the shore.

Waves and currents can be deceiving when not paying particular attention to them. Massive waves, beautiful to behold, parading toward shore often camouflage swift currents running below the surface. She knew this like she knew the shape of her nose. She also knew that in contests of life or death, when the ocean is competing, the ocean always had the superior ability to win.

Shaking her head, bringing her awareness back to the present, losing unwelcomed thoughts of the past, she looked into the distance to where the harbor was supposed to be but could no longer see it nor see the breakwater. In fact, the entire island of Molokai had become simply a dark silhouette showing through the mist left by the passing waves. It was immediately evident she had drifted a very long way.

She had no idea how long she'd been floating, but she knew she was drained of energy. Her arms were weak from the exertion of paddling against what suddenly seemed to be enormous amounts of unrelenting water. She had nothing left of her energy. There was no way she could manage to paddle the distance back to shore against the strong current.

She was too tired to think of Taylor and of what she was leaving behind, and she was beginning to accept the sad fact that this may be her fate.

She was familiar with hypothermia and knew it was now staking its claim on her as drowsiness flooded through her mind. With effort, she jarred herself awake and sat up straighter on the board.

Shivering uncontrollably, she shouted into the wind, "What a stupid thing to have allowed to happen!" As if in aid to bring her mind back to the present, a cresting wave crashed over her board and smacked her hard on the side of her face. In her numbed state, she sadly smiled at the absurdity of the whole situation. She was an athlete with a positive outlook—she wasn't designed to get into this sort of mess and not find the back door to get herself out.

As she rode up and over the crest of a wave, one in a very long, unending progression of wave crests, her mind slowly registered something her eyes had caught sight of. She held her breath as the milliseconds of time stretched long as she waited to ride up the face of the next wave, anxious to confirm what she thought she saw.

And there it was—her mind hadn't been playing tricks—no make-believe mirages. It was a long way off, but it was definitely a boat, and in Annie's exhausted mind, it was bigger than life itself. A warmth spread through her body in response to the encouraging sight. Her thrill at knowing it was there was matched only by her immense frustration at having to wait for each wave to pass under her before being elevated up for another look—they couldn't come quickly enough as each glimpse continued to confirm her prayer.

Finally seeing it clearly, her heart abruptly plunged in despair. It was a boat, of that there was no doubt, but it was aimed in the wrong direction and was traveling away from her.

She could just make out a person standing on the stern gazing out, seemingly looking directly at her. She started to wave frantically, screaming in the loudest voice she could manage. Unfortunately, her waving was a one-armed affair, having need to keep a tight hold on the surfboard with the other, not daring to let go, her voice hardly beyond a whisper in the immense outdoors of the ocean. She made up for any perceived shortcomings with as much enthusiasm as she could muster; but with the action of the waves, like clockwork, consistently burying her from sight behind towering walls of water, there was little more she could do but pray and continue to wave.

Chapter Seven

Fishermen on the horizon, midday, Kaiwi Channel, midway between Oahu and Molokai

"*F*ish on."

The words were loud and clear—notably loud and overflowing with customary excitement. Make it *loud and clear* was a standing order between these two friends since half their words would be immediately swallowed up by the wind, the white-capped waves, or the sound of the boat's twin engines growling beneath the boards of the deck they stood on.

Stone's *shaka* sign of approval was quick in response as they both cracked into broad smiles catching each other's excited expressions. With a quick high five, each man vaulted into a well-practiced symphony of motion necessary for boating their catch.

The captain of the boat was Stone. He was christened Kensington Kuokoa Stone many decades before, but not a lot of friends knew him by his full name. Acquaintances likely weren't very sure what his full name actually was—he was simply Stone.

His closest friend, fishing buddy, and the other side of the high five was Lloyd Moniz. They had been friends since their freshman, wet-behind-the-ears days at the University of Hawaii as they'd studied for their bachelor's degree in business and marketing. They had shared many of the same classes during those years and had spent too-numerous-to-count sleepless nights cramming for finals. They were both enjoying their fifty-fourth year of living and had been close friends for well over half that time, supporting each other through the toughest of times and the purest of life's joys.

Game fishing was one of those joys. They were away from land, in the salt air, the hustle and bustle that accompanied their time out on the water. That was where they found their nirvana. Here, in the middle of nothing but ocean swells and frigate birds, their only connection to civilization was a dark shadow of one of the islands rising above the water over a distant horizon. It was the serenity they craved, unequaled anywhere else they could possibly conceive of being.

The abrupt shattering of that serenity when a fish took one of their lures only served to elevate the pure enjoyment and the instant adrenaline rush that came with their time together on the water. It also served as a signal to a delicious meal they could look forward to when they touched land.

In many respects, each man was an opposite pole of a magnet and gave their friendship an even balance. Stone—a tall, toned, and muscular man from a daily weight-training regimen—looked at life from a positive point of view, a rose-colored-glass perspective. He was conscious of the foods he ate, often spending considerable time in food markets reading the complexities that was the list of ingredients, avoiding anything he considered a not-going-to-eat-any-of-that sort of food. He also went by the rule of thumb that said if the list of ingredients was too voluminous or whose printing was too tiny to read, it went right back on the shelf. At six-foot-two, he had a quiet nature and thoroughly enjoyed *alone* time whenever it presented itself.

Lloyd went in the opposite direction, leaning toward learning and mind improvement versus physical activity. He had a mind for details and excellent recall. If he became involved reading a good biography, the day could easily come and go before he'd think of moving from his favorite chair. At five-foot-six, he was thin in stature, drawing heavily on his Portuguese heritage. As he was outgoing and extroverted, you would often find him at the center of a conversation taking place with friends over a big steak cooking on his open-flamed barbeque or entertaining them with his litany of jokes.

The exception to all the general rules of behavior for both of them came to the surface when an opportunity for a fishing venture present itself. Exercise and reading were quickly put aside and forgotten, replaced by a fishing pole and boat.

They had already spent the early hours in the waters of Kaiwi Channel between the islands of Oahu and Molokai and were becoming exhausted fighting against the strength of the building waves and strengthening winds. As usual, they were on Stone's yacht, *Wailana Sunrise*, and had fishlines dragging through the water behind them in hopes of attracting a fish curious enough to swallow one of their lures.

Game fishing was the universal term for what they were doing, but that term was thrown about quite casually aboard the *Wailana*. If anyone had asked them, they would be told, with straight faces, that any fish they caught was a game fish—further distinction wasn't necessary unless it had to do with taste and the preference for the breed of fish they wanted right then. They had already boated three *kawakawa* since beginning their adventure early that morning, so they were already happy with the day's take and willing to pull in the lines and head for land, home, and calmer water. This new fish tugging on one of their lines abruptly revived all their anticipation and excitement—the increasing weather was quickly, but not completely, put aside for the time being.

They had six lures in the water that morning. Normally they would have had eight lines out with two running high and wide on special outrigger poles, but that day, with the hard trade winds blowing over the water's surface, they chose to keep the count down to a more manageable number. The outrigger poles had intentionally been left behind. Strong winds and breaking surf combined with too many lines in the water usually meant a very strong possibility of facing a massive line tangle followed by hours of tedious work to untangle them and a loss of a lot of fishing time.

A few hours earlier, when first becoming aware of how quickly the ocean swells were increasing in size and the strength of the wind building, they seriously contemplated pulling in all but their hand lines and turning around to head for home. There was comfort to be found back on shore, poolside at the yacht club in Kaneohe, observing the latest fashions in women's bikini wear—a pleasant pastime enjoyed by both. They'd listened to the weather report before heading out and knew the possibility existed this would be the case and their day would end early. They were prepared for what they may have to do for a quick return to land.

Just as their decision was made to turn and head for home and they were reaching to retrieve the poles, that was the very moment one of the poles, its Penn International reel with its 130-pound test line, began to sing its song. Whatever was straining on the other end of the line was big and muscular; there was no mistaking it. It had been drawn in and encouraged to take a bite of the lure that Lloyd had recently created. He was quite pleased with the fish's choice of lures to digest—he would certainly make more of them now.

Plans of returning to land were temporarily placed on hold as the game of deep-sea fishing began.

The song coming from the reel, more a high-pitched whine than a song, created by the rush of line being pulled off the reel, was causing so much friction the reel began smoking from the buildup of heat—a sure sign of the muscle power of the fish on the other end.

They quickly hauled in the other lines, and Lloyd reached for the pole that was now bent over like a twig in a stiff breeze. He clipped himself into a safety harness, sat down, set the reel's drag a little stiffer and began his tug-of-war fight against the exceptional strength coming from the other end. After helping pull in the other lines, Stone resumed control of his yacht. Not much more than two minutes had elapsed since the reel first begun to play out. The two of them were very proficient and well-rehearsed.

Stone was competent at handling the helm, doing what he could to keep the boat's stern aimed in the direction the fish was determined to swim. He slowed the boat's speed hoping to lessen the strain on Lloyd's arms.

After thirty minutes of pulling against the fish, Lloyd was searching for his second wind—the effort was exhilarating but exhausting. The fish had yet to break the surface of the water, choosing instead to head deeper, but suddenly, they saw color flashing in the water less than a hundred feet behind as the fish broke surface, jumping and shaking in a futile attempt to dislodge the two-inch hook firmly anchored in its mouth. It was a *mahi-mahi*, an easy fish to identify, and the only fish in Hawaiian waters with a habit of flashing a beautiful blue-green rainbow of color at the height of its struggle for life. Nature can be stunning, even in the throes of death.

The leader line showed above the water, indicating most of the fight was over—man and fish were spent. With engines in neutral, Stone took hold of the leader with one hand and pulled the fish close enough to the transom to wield the gaff hook with the other.

As the large bull mahi-mahi cleared the bulkhead, forty pounds of fish in Stone's estimation, it slid across the deck still flashing its array of colors, its mouth narrowly missing Lloyd's foot. He had moved out of the way of the sharp gaff hook as soon as Stone brandished it—gaff hooks could become extremely dangerous no matter how careful or competent the handler was. Lloyd, who'd quickly stood up when the gaff came out, sat back down and fell back against the cushioned backrest, his energy depleted. He let his weary arms fall like sticks to his side.

As he sat catching his breath, letting the pleasure of the catch wash through his spent muscles, he suddenly sat up, alert, his successful catch and weary muscles forgotten.

"Eh, Stone. Try look way back in the water." Lloyd stood and was pointing at something a fair distance behind them, hoping Stone could see the object being pointed at. "That looks like a *wahine* out there on a surfboard, and I think she's waving at us. Can you see her?" His energy suddenly revived. "What do you suppose someone would be doing this far out on a surfboard? Maybe she's *pupule* in the head perhaps." He exaggerated the word, making a circling motion at his temple as he kept staring at the woman—he didn't want to lose sight of her in the commotion that was being generated by the waves and motion of the rocking boat.

It took Stone a few seconds to spot what Lloyd was pointing at. Just as he caught sight of her, she disappeared into the trough of a wave, reappearing as the next wave moved under her. She was still waving and appeared to be yelling to catch their attention, but she was too far away to be heard. Her actions, though, were very clear: *I NEED HELP!*

"Hang on, Lloyd," Stone shouted as he quickly brought the yacht about and powered up, aiming the bow toward the girl, the mahi-mahi free sliding across the wet, now very bloody, surface of the deck.

"Eh, Lloyd, put the mahi in the cooler and stow the rods and reels. It may get a little chaotic in this surf trying to bring her aboard."

"Let's figure the surfboard is expendable if things get too dicey," ventured Lloyd. "Last thing we need is for something like that smacking into the side of your boat and cause big damage. Oh, so sorry," he hesitated, grinning ear to ear as he looked up at Stone, "I meant your yacht."

Stone could only smile at his friend's choice of words as he guided *Wailana* up and over the large, threatening swells. All Stone's friends had learned long before to accept his adamant insistence on calling *Wailana Sunrise* a yacht—never, never a boat.

It took longer than both men thought it would to reach the girl, the wind and waves uncooperative in where they wanted to go. Finally, coming in as close as he dared, Stone called out to her, "Can you swim?" His words lost some of their distinction amidst the thunder of the breaking surf and the wind.

As soon as he spoke, he realized his choice of a question to ask might have sounded somewhat stupid. *What in the world would she be doing out here if she couldn't swim?* he berated himself for not thinking first. He couldn't hear her reply but saw the quizzical look she flashed him in response. *She thinks it was a stupid question as well*—he didn't bother asking anything further, deciding their competency as rescuers had taken a direct hit.

"Lloyd," he directed, attempting to save some lost pride, "tie a line around a life jacket and get ready. We're going to be coming in hot. I need to maintain control in this surf. Get ready to throw the jacket at her when we get close enough." If there was a time he wished his yacht were bigger in order to accommodate a tender, this was the time. But it wasn't, and there was nothing he could do about it.

Working both throttles and helm, he brought *Wailana's* port side up as close to the girl as he dared, keeping the bow facing into the oncoming swells. He was very aware of the potential that a wave could suddenly propel them dangerously close or even over top of her. Anyone who knows anything about water from throwing sticks in a pond as a kid would know that a boat, with its motors idling, has no more control than that floating stick. The difficulty of a successful rescue at sea was mostly at the whim of the waves.

Directing his voice to her once again, Stone yelled, "We're going to toss you a life jacket. Take hold and wrap your arms around it. We'll drag you over and pull you aboard. You're going to have to let go of your surfboard." He immediately got another *look* from her—whatever she was thinking, he was starting to like whoever this girl was just from her facial reactions.

She managed a nod and let go of the board preparing to catch the jacket Lloyd was about to toss, but she immediately went under as a wave rose up and washed over her. The yacht was simultaneously nudged dangerously close to where she had been.

Lloyd's fast toss put the life jacket almost directly over the spot where she'd went under. As she surfaced, she grabbed onto it and brought it snuggly up under her chest, gasping for breath.

Working quickly, they hauled her to the swim platform that extended two feet out from the transom, and using her arms, both men brought her quickly on board.

As she stepped on the yacht, Stone and Lloyd still grasping her upper arms, her legs shook from exhaustion. She immediately pulled to a halt, put on the brakes, forcefully extricating her arms from their grasp. Her expression registered what could only be interpreted as a flashback to some action part of a *Friday the 13th* movie. She took in the huge amount of blood splattered over the entire deck as well as on the hands and arms of her rescuers with a considerable amount having found its way on her own skin from their manhandling. A visible chill coursed up her spine as she hesitantly took a step backward toward the edge of the swim platform.

The men exchanged an uncertain glance, before immediately breaking into grins at the obvious humor of the situation. They quickly realized what the girl saw and were certain they knew what she must be envisioning. Lloyd spoke up quickly to assuage her apparent revulsion to the carnage before it prompted her to jump back in the water. She may be thinking that the ocean offered a safer place to be than being in a vulnerable situation with these two.

"No worries, young lady. It may not appear so, but you're safe with us. We just brought in a very large fish a few minutes before we spotted you and decided you were more important than washing all the blood off the deck." Lloyd proceeded to open the fish box, partially holding up the mahi-mahi by its tail for her inspection but more so for her understanding.

"Now that you're safe on board, however," he continued, attempting to sway her thoughts in a different direction, "you can help us clean this mess while you explain what the dickens you're doing way out here, in this kind of weather, on a surfboard. My god, girl, that's not too smart," he admonished, exasperation quite evident in his voice. How people allowed themselves to get into such bizarre situations always astonished him. He was also thinking that whatever story she had to tell couldn't help but be an interesting one when they finally got around to hearing it.

Somewhat appeased, though still apprehensive, Annie stepped through the transom door onto the blood-soaked deck, her foot almost slipping out from under her in the process. Her legs were wobbly from her surfboard experience, and she needed to sit or she was going to fall onto the blood-covered deck.

All three had instinctively taken their eyes off all the blood and glanced toward the surfboard that had drifted a distance away. Annie, still not certain these two were fully aboveboard in their thinking, was wondering if she might still be better off by jumping back in before the board drifted beyond her reach—she could theoretically still escape. It was a matter of revulsion and the nauseous appearance of so much blood, but more than that, the sight of that beautiful creature, now very dead, was something totally foreign to her as well as quite repulsive. She wondered if she and Taylor could ever find enjoyment in killing a fish for their dinner—she didn't think she could. *Be interesting to hear his thoughts on that.* She was beginning to feel more secure, knowing she would see him very soon.

"Don't save the surfboard," she finally volunteered after several long moments, letting go of her apprehensions, giving more thought to the ordeal she'd just survived. She decided the men looked and acted quite harmless and was feeling safe aboard their boat. "I don't need a surfboard that badly," she finally conceded.

Stone was tempted to go after it himself. Good surfboards were expensive, and he knew Lloyd's son, Kawika, enjoyed working on them during his spare time. He hadn't noticed any damage beyond some scuff marks from bumping into something, but better judgment finally won out and he put the surfboard out of his thoughts. He instead turned his attention back to the situation at hand, swinging *Wailana* into a wide turn and putting them on a course for the harbor that was now two or three miles away—they had drifted a long way from where they had caught the fish.

As Lloyd began hosing the blood off the deck and, with Annie's help, wiping everything down, Annie began telling the story of how she and Taylor were so fortunate having been given a boat and how that gift brought her to the point of having to be rescued. She didn't need to mention it as it was obvious in her words that she was very anxious to see her boyfriend again.

Chapter Eight

"Instead of glass floats," Annie continued telling her story to her two rescuers as they headed toward the harbor, "I found that darned surfboard we just let drift away." The relief in her voice at having been rescued was evident and came through the telling of her story. She was also experiencing a feeling of foolishness at hearing her own telling of events, but she didn't bother to mention that. She was feeling enormously grateful the men had come along when they did, not at all sure she could have made it through too many more wave hits. At the mention of the surfboard, she inadvertently cast her eyes back in the direction she had last seen it, but the trade winds and ocean swells had taken it from sight— evidence of her ordeal was washed away.

"That great-looking surfboard," she continued, still gazing astern for any sign of it, "had washed up and gotten wedged in the boulders of the breakwater. It suffered a few dings from the impact, but nothing apparently too serious. It appeared to be in good enough condition, and the waves so enticing that I decided to grab a few rides on it. I wiggled it lose from the rocks, threw it in the water, and jumped on." She unconsciously shook her head remembering her unthinking actions.

"I paddled out figuring I would just go a short way beyond the breakwater, catch a couple rides, then come in, and meet up with my boyfriend. Before I knew it, though, I was out beyond the end of the breakwater and being swiftly pulled further. I had let myself get caught in the wind and current," she told them, amplifying the drift with exaggerated arm movements. "I know better and should have been paying attention, but I had been enjoying myself too much and simply got captured by the excitement."

Lloyd and Stone caught each other's eye with a look of understanding. Their actions on many past occasions while out fishing reflected in much the same fashion as their new friends' actions, much to their chagrin—getting caught up with something and overlooking better judgment. To know better is not necessarily a precondition to doing anything differently.

"The waves just kept increasing in size." She was obviously reliving her experience in living color, her arms raised up over her head as she balanced on tiptoes demonstrating the enormity of what she had experienced. "I quickly reached the point they became terrifying. By then, I was so scared all I could do was hang on to the board for dear life and hope the current would eventually bring me back to shore." Her story continued as they neared the harbor's entrance, and as much as he didn't want to, Stone had to interrupt her.

"I'm going to miss the rest of your story, Annie. I'm sorry. The next few minutes will require full attention." He briefly pointed at the channel in front of them and the rolling surf surging between the breakwaters on both sides. He assumed there was no need for further explanation.

The surf was surging into the harbor at such an angle and size the waves were breaking across the entrance and virtually closing it out, much like an avalanche tumbling over the only pathway available. It was definitely going to be a challenge, but one Stone knew he was up to—as long as nothing unforeseen occurred, like one of the engines deciding to stop, God forbid. Stone's broad experience with boats was a valuable asset; perfect timing and speed were needed to ride the flatter more stable water that existed between the swells and to maintain control. Stone knew if the girl wasn't on board, he and Lloyd would have turned back toward Oahu long before attempting to challenge this unwelcoming entrance. A miscalculation of speed or wrong turn of the wheel and one of those waves could easily pick up his yacht and surf it straight into the rocks like the surfboard Annie had found.

He was a skilled helmsman and kept a strong focus as they moved between the breakwaters, finally sliding into the harbor's calm, protected water. The others on board must have felt Stone's tension as all talking had ceased, and they had anxiously been clutching at the yacht's safety rails as the yacht made its way into the harbor.

Stone eased off his white-knuckle grip of the wheel. Looking around the almost-empty harbor, the only other boat he saw was a Boston Whaler riding at anchor off to his left. He assumed it was Annie and her boyfriend Taylor's, which Annie quickly confirmed. She became noticeably concerned, though, as she looked around at the empty harbor, seeing no sign of Taylor anywhere.

"He should be here," she exclaimed in alarmed disbelief that he wasn't. She called his name several times, casting her eyes about in hopes of spotting him, waiting for a reply to her calls that wasn't coming. Uncertainty was quite evident in her voice, anxiety obvious on her face. She'd mentioned being out on the surfboard for three, maybe four hours, and had been positive Taylor would have already returned from his hike by that time and would be somewhere close by and looking for her. She knew he would be frantic with concern by this time at not being able to find her.

Could he still be hiking? she wondered. As ridiculous as she thought that was, it was a real possibility. She knew he could lose track of time when he got involved with something he enjoyed, *kind of like my recent escapade,* she thought, but it was not his habit whenever she was a part of the adventure.

"This just isn't like him," she cautiously told the two men. "He's generally very aware of obligations he's made and people's expectations of him. He is the kind of guy who is forever trying to do what's right, if you know what I mean. He abhors criticism.

He said he'd be back within two hours, and I know he would have made sure he was."

As she was explaining all this, she was absently making motions with her arms and hands as if that would prompt Stone to speed up and get them to where he planned to tie-up. She was convinced something serious had happened to her boyfriend and desperately wanted to be on land and start hunting the surrounding bushes in case he was hurt. Stone was stepping up his pace as much as he dared—no matter what, he wasn't going to jeopardize his yacht by taking shortcuts.

He jockeyed *Wailana* into a wide space between two pylons as Lloyd ran lines around cleats on the bulkhead fore and aft. One of the old cement posts had a short wooden ramp connecting it to the main bulkhead—they would use it to make their way up and across the short distance to dry land.

Before he followed the others ashore, Stone hit the yacht's horn, sending out three short blasts, the sound magnifying as it echoed off the harbor's water and surrounding brush, obliterating the inherent solitude.

The sudden blaring caused Lloyd and Annie to jump almost a good foot up off the deck in startled response, their faces suddenly bleached white.

"A little warning next time would be helpful, Stone." Lloyd was busy bringing normal hearing back to his ears. Annie was doing the same.

"Sorry, people. I wasn't thinking. Woke you up, though, I bet." Stone looked at them with a huge grin. Looking at Annie, he was convinced the loud horn served the purpose and brought her focus back on point.

If Taylor was close enough to hear that sound, he would undoubtedly come to investigate, and Annie was carefully checking the surroundings for his appearance, but he didn't show. Everyone clambered up onto the ramp and cautiously, in single file, walked to the bulkhead and dry land.

With the lack of response to his yacht's horn blast, they decided to head out onto the trail leading to the camp. It was the trail both Lloyd and Stone figured Taylor had taken. Before joining the search that looked as if it would start whether he was a part of it or not, Stone took a moment and walked a short distance away from the others to use his cell phone. Teri picked up on the second ring.

Chapter Nine

$\mathcal{T}$eri White was Stone's wife. They had married ten months earlier in a quiet ceremony at the Diamond Head Unity Church east of Waikiki, a serene setting on the gentle slopes of Diamond Head crater. Lloyd had been Stone's best man and often kidded Stone about the *truth* of that status of best man whenever the opportunity arose.

Teri had been enjoying the quietness of her closet-sized office that the department had given her in the geology building. Space was at a premium in the decades-old building, but the smallness of the space didn't bother Teri in the least. When her cell phone rang, she smiled when she saw Stone's name pop up in her caller ID. As goofy as most of her friends thought it was, she'd had special graphics installed on her phone that caused Stone's name to squiggle like a tired hula dancer accompanied by the background beat of her favorite Hawaiian group, the Kahauanu Lake Trio. Along with the squiggling and singing was a firework display that fired off a salvo of color behind Stone's gyrating name. The whole display was a little overboard, and she knew that, but it never failed to lighten her heart and made her friends shake their heads in bewildered amusement, as well as an admiration of the love being displayed.

"Hi, honey, you and Lloyd back from fishing already?" Stone heard the *I hope not* undertone unspoken in her voice. He understood completely where that tone was coming from. She loved him dearly, and he knew that, but he also knew she needed and enjoyed her personal time and didn't want it to end just yet.

At that moment, she'd been deeply engrossed in reviewing a new research paper and wanted to finish it before heading home. Stone would understand if she didn't rush home, that was a given, but it was more the idea that she would feel so darn guilty that, had she stayed, her enjoyment would be lost knowing he was home and waiting to tell her about the day's big fishing news that he would surely have.

Teri worked in the geology department at the University of Hawaii. Besides putting in long days on her four-day workweek, she would usually gravitate to her office whenever free time allowed, which was pretty much any time the two men took the yacht out fishing—she could rely on it 90 percent of the time.

The Geology Department employed Teri as the sole liaison between the department and the individual geologists who were working in the field throughout the Pacific basin. Her work made her privy to everything the Rock Doctors, as she fondly called them, were doing and the discoveries they were making. She figured she was about the luckiest woman in the world in the daily efforts of her work.

Besides the enjoyment, she always relished her time spent around home—both homes. When they got married, each had brought a house with them into the relationship. Stone had his two-story A-frame beach house he'd named Kaikanani. In his mind, his house was truly beautiful so why not call it that. Kaikanani was in Kaneohe, centered in the backside of Kaneohe Bay, on the water's edge, enjoying an expansive view of the bay.

Teri had a home in Nuuanu, the historic section of Honolulu. She had also given her home a name, that of Halepuanani, a house of flowers as there were so many growing in every nook and cranny of her yard. They decided early on as their relationship grew serious that they would keep both homes until they knew in what direction their married lives would take them in.

Teri enjoyed raising flowers, and her home gave fair testimony to her green-thumb ability. Geology, though, remained her first passion, something she could never get enough of. She had been pleased to learn that living in Stone's beach-side home in Kaneohe was like a geology lesson all its own with the ever-changing shoreline often exposing lost treasures hidden beneath the sand—coral pieces and bits of lava rock showing the tiny green coloring of olivine. It would be a troubling and difficult task to rid their lives of one of their homes, which they both enjoyed. She knew Stone felt the same.

* * *

Stone, sensing his call was going to be lengthier than he anticipated, held the phone away from his ear. With awkward hand signals, which he wasn't certain Lloyd understood, he made a gesture he hoped signified that he and Annie should get started on their hike in search of Taylor. It was obvious that Annie may do that anyway with or without him as he caught the anxious look she aimed in his direction. Either Lloyd understood the signal or Annie had stood idle long enough and wasn't going to wait any longer, both began walking toward the trail faintly visible through the tangle of vegetation on the far side of the harbor. Stone would just have to catch up with them.

Speaking rapidly, he explained the situation the best he could to Teri, reassuring her that he and Lloyd were safely tied-up in the harbor. Teri knew Hale O Lono Harbor, having been there a few times, so she knew what he was experiencing. He never wanted her to worry about where he was or whether he was all right. He knew she would worry if he didn't call, but more importantly, he knew with absolute, unfailing certainty that she would make sure that he *did* become fully aware of her feelings when he finally reached home had he failed to call first. He wanted to avoid that particular discussion, if at all possible.

"It sounds to me like you boys have gotten yourselves right into the middle of things—once again. Why am I not more surprised?" Her voice was light. "You're doing the right thing, honey. I'm sure you'll find this Taylor guy, and everything will be fine."

"I have no idea, angel, what time Lloyd and I will get back to the yacht club. It depends on what we encounter looking for Taylor and what the weather does in the meantime."

"Call when you find him or when you know what the weather's going to do about your return. Please don't chance it if things don't look good."

Before ending the call, he suggested she whet her appetite for some fresh mahi-mahi—she *loved* fresh-caught mahi. Unfortunately, he realized his mistake as soon as he spoke the words. He shouldn't have mentioned their catch—it may not make the trip home with them if dinnertime arrived before they left.

"Don't worry about rushing back, honey," she volunteered. "If necessary, you and Lloyd should spend the night there if it gets too late. I'll be fine. We can enjoy the fish tomorrow just as well as tonight."

Stone knew without a doubt that if he and Lloyd spent the night, that fish was going to be their dinner. They would just have to do their best to catch another one on the way home.

Chapter Ten

$\mathcal{S}$tone felt apprehensive leaving his yacht unattended. Remote harbors, such as this, always brought that emotion to the surface. He'd never had any problems, but stories of break-ins and damage, whether there was any truth in them or not, were always circulating. The fact that no other boats were in the harbor, except for Annie and Taylor's, helped soften that uneasiness. He also felt certain the growing enormity of the ocean swells would keep most other yachtsmen land-bound. This wasn't the sort of weather for pleasure cruising. It was more for sitting in a nice, cozy coffee shop with a good book. He gave *Wailana* a silent blessing, locked the cabin door, and stepping off, headed to join the others. He figured they couldn't have gotten too far ahead in that short a time.

The only land routes in or out of the harbor were two: either a red-cinder road for vehicles or a footpath that led east for hikers and wanderers. The cinder road, a service road long abandoned, had a gate adorned with a firmly attached, corrosion-encrusted lock, a sure sign it hadn't been used for a very long time nor would it be any time soon.

Walking around the gate to follow the road meant a very long walk to the nearest highway. Looking west presented nothing but dense thickets of mingled kiawe bush, too thick and hostile to pass through; to the east, the road led to the small village of Maunaloa. A resort development had been built farther north of La'au Point on Papohaku Beach, but that was too far distant to have any effect on the harbor area.

The footpath leading away from the harbor led to and beyond the scout camp and eventually led to Maunaloa further beyond. It was the trail Annie and Lloyd were on and was hopefully the path Taylor had taken as well. She had mentioned his wanting to see the scout camp and what it encompassed. The trail hugged the coastline as close as the terrain and dense undergrowth would allow. Assessing the trail and its unkempt condition it was in, it was apparent that it had been a long time since it had seen a volume of foot traffic—much the same as the gate lock.

Stone pushed his pace and caught up with Lloyd and Annie very quickly. They were discussing the camp, wondering what it looked like and how far away it remained. The heat of the day had become intense making the hike difficult.

"I know the camp pretty well," offered Stone, adding to what they had been talking about when he joined them. "I camped there on a regular basis when I was a kid, a lot of years ago. He had to smile at the memory and the implication of his age. "It's at least another thirty minutes hike so let's not push it too quickly in this heat.

"There's a lot of small buildings and shelters scattered around the cleared area, or at least there was back then, and several wooden troughs built for collecting rainwater. Last time I was there, the place looked like everything would fall apart in the next stiff breeze. There are no plans in place to do anything about it as far as I know. It seems that the scouting higher-ups wanted to find a place that was easier to access and were turning their backs on this property. I'll be surprised if there's anything left standing."

"Maybe," Lloyd added, speaking to no one in particular, "the boyfriend got caught up in the nostalgia of the place and is still exploring. There must be a lot of history still lying around."

"That'd be great if that's the case, Lloyd."

Not wanting to voice anything negative and chance making Annie any more anxious than she obviously already was, Stone knew Lloyd was intentionally not mentioning the possibility that Taylor may have gotten injured, and Stone was going along with that. He would have been wandering around the old buildings just as anyone would be who was intent on exploring. Stone needn't have been concerned about volunteering his thinking, though, because Annie quickly voiced a similar thought.

"If those buildings are falling, Taylor may have gotten hurt if anything happened to fall on him. Hopefully, we're going to run into him coming back down the trail and hear some wild adventure stories." She turned and looked expectantly from Stone to Lloyd, hoping to see some positive confirmation from either of them.

She only saw blank stares looking back neither willing to voice the uncomfortable feelings they were experiencing.

Chapter Eleven

$\mathcal{T}$he trail to the scout camp was not easy to follow and difficult to navigate. The dried grass and weeds, their existence reliant on a minimal of moisture, had taken over the trail and camouflaged most hints of ever having been traveled, and other traces of an old rut were the only clue that remained of a myriad of young and eager feet that once trampled there.

If one didn't stare too intently at the ground and allowed their eyes to become unfocused a degree or two, a subtle outline of the old trail was still discernable. The ever-present and non-native kiawe trees, a relative of the mesquite, hard-wooded and somewhat scraggly, had done its best to diffuse what little of the path's existence remained. A recent hiker, probably Taylor, had left telltale indications of having recently been there—a few freshly broken tree limbs and faint footprints through the tall ground cover were evident.

Not being properly dressed for hiking added considerably to their difficulty. None of the three had any inkling when their day began that they would end the day tramping through such a harsh, prickly environment. Because of their lack of proper clothing, bathing suits not qualifying, their bare legs were being brutalized by the kiawe trees' sharp needles and the tall weeds that boasted finger-sized clumps of prickly kukus. Lloyd's standing habit of wearing long pants was saving his legs. Stone and Annie were seriously envious.

Kiawe trees had adopted well to the arid climate. Their presence had created a helter-skelter array of fallen branches that were host to long, sharp needles that easily penetrated the sole of a shoe and played havoc with a hiker's foot. The rubber slippers that all wore were being gradually shredded and was accompanied by a continuous chorus of *ouch, auwe,* and a dictionary of other words uttered under the breath as they slowly made progress. Periodically having to stop, they leaned against a tree or each other to extract a particularly harsh kuku. It became good reason for all to stop for a moment, kuku or not.

Stone led the way doing his best to divine the clearest path. Annie was trailing behind him, being very vocal about the constant pokes and scratches. She knew she was verbally overdoing, it but the grumbling was serving to take her mind off a deepening concern for Taylor. She couldn't help but think that if she had gone with him like he wanted her to, things would have been entirely different. She prayed she was wrong, and that all was well with him.

Thirst was a big concern. They had started out with individual bottles of water but had already consumed most of that. Stone desperately hoped and prayed that some of the old hand-cranked pumps in camp that accessed the artesian well were still operational. If they had been vandalized, removed or both, he wasn't sure what they would do to secure water. He couldn't stop thinking that if he and Lloyd had been fishing on the Kalaupapa side of Molokai, the opposite side, they would have had lush, green cliffs, deep valleys, clear streams, and bountiful waterfalls. He was also certain that had that been the case, Annie may not have survived. That realization made all the discomfort he was experiencing worthwhile.

The slow pace afforded the men a chance to get to know more about their hiking partner and vice versa. When Annie mentioned the large windfall her partner received, not mentioning the amount, the story struck Stone as being quite odd. As a successful financial consultant with his own company, he'd heard all kinds of stories of money showing up in people's hands unannounced and unprepared for. He would never deny the truth of her claims unless and until proven unfounded. The fact remained, though, that inheriting a sizable amount from an auntie that Taylor didn't know of just sounded off base. Maybe it was the way in which Annie described it as a *huge amount*. Normally if a family had an auntie worth any kind of serious money and she passed away, everyone would know her name and, most likely, how old she was before she made her transition and dumped her stack of dollars on one of them, and why just one of them when other siblings were involved? It was an odd story.

Trail talk moved on to people and family as Lloyd brought up his family and his son's, Kawika's, successful business. But when Stone mentioned Pops Koa and his daughter Viane, though, along with Leilani Davis and her daughter, who was also Pops' recently reunited daughter Lokomaikai, Loki as everyone called her, Annie came to a halt, exclaiming quite loudly, "No way," an incredulous look consuming her face.

"Are you telling me," Annie excitedly questioned, taking hold of one of Stone's arms, "that you know Loki Davis? Does she happen to live in Hawi on the Big Island? This is wild."

When Stone confirmed that indeed that was the Loki he was talking about and explained she was a calabash part of his family, Annie was visibly astonished and quite delighted.

"That's the most bizarre thing I've ever heard," she said. "Loki and I have been Facebook friends for over a year. We met online in a book readers' group discussing the novel *Deep Green* written by a local author, but I haven't met her yet. We've talked a lot about the way her father unexpectedly showed up in her life, and his name is also Pops. I remember that. Who could forget a nickname like that?"

As they continued hiking, the tangle of tree branches overhead began lessening and allowing more light to penetrate as they neared the scout camp.

Stone saw an old fire pit that he remembered along with some cut timbers once destined for the fire pit dug close to the trail—the camp was nearby.

Originally, the Boy Scout camp had consisted of several wooden buildings spread over two or three acres along the ocean. There was a pavilion in the middle where meals were taken and special gatherings took place. Various other buildings scattered around the property that served as troop shelters, storage facilities, and the all-too-necessary outhouses.

It gave Stone an eerie feeling to walk into the camp. The last time he had done so, the place had been bustling with activity— scouts milling about like ants doing the work their leader directed them to do. Now it was quiet, ghostlike, almost devoid of sound other than their own footfalls, a few birds, the distant sound of waves breaking on the nearby shore—along with the remnants of past thoughts, hopes, and fading desires everywhere he looked.

As they neared the center of the camp, they saw several of the buildings had been reduced to nothing more than piles of rubble. A few remained in various stages of collapse. Centrally located in the cleared area of the camp was the open-sided pavilion that was surprisingly still intact. It was an imposing structure appearing to be much too large for its surroundings. The pavilion looked much like it once had—weathered but still quite usable. The wood supports on most of the other structures had dried out and lost their strength to hold even themselves upright. Wild vegetation came to the rescue of a few, holding them braced against their trunk, not allowing the structure to fall. Some trees had inevitably found their way through the floor and resembled overly proportioned indoor plants.

Wood fence posts were still visible, many still in surprisingly decent shape with long fencing pieces attached or lying on the ground close by. Stone remembered setting up tents and raising the troop flag over a certain area they always tried to be assigned to because of the proximity to the mess pavilion and latrine—those fence pieces were gone.

Several of the old wooden troughs strategically place here and there around the camp were still in place though most no longer sat level to the ground nor had all their planking. Hand pumps, tall and gangly with their handles hanging by their sides, still stood sentinel, standing watch over their assigned troughs like long-obsolete statues bearing witness to an inactive solitude. Their job, when set in motion by the long handle and someone's strong arm, had been to fill the trough with water and provide a drinking source and supply for the scouts' needs.

Now the troughs were filled with dead leaves and debris; the pumps, long idle. Grass had sprouted in the damp humus inside them, and bees—the ever-present bees—were everywhere seeking whatever moisture they could find. Kiawe trees provided food and shelter to the bees, which accumulated by the thousands in each trough, drawn by the lingering scent of moisture. Stone suspected the bees were the main cause for the camp closing down. Too many scouts had returned home with too many stings.

Walking into the center of camp, each one caught up in the wonder of what they were looking at—a once thriving but too-infrequently used camp, built much too far from the island's main town of Kaunakakai. Each of them wandered off in different directions, pulled by what they saw, allowing their imaginations to run free.

Stone and Lloyd were walking back toward each other when they heard Annie cry out for help.

"Taylor." It was all she said in a frantic, urgent voice. "Help me," she yelled, "*hele mai*, come quick. Hurry, hurry, hurry."

The men were beside her in seconds.

Clearly in evidence among a thousand bees milling about the open trough was an arm, a leg, and part of a T-shirt sticking above the rim. The rest of Taylor—the bare skin of his arms, legs, his back and neck, everywhere not covered with clothing—was a mass of stings and a cloud of bees. Judging by the way his body hung in the trough, it looked like he may have tripped on an exposed tree root, landing headfirst in the trough. His sudden appearance probably startled every bee close by causing them to attack.

He looked to be semiconscious. His eyes were partially open, tracking aimlessly in a slow side-to-side movement, and he was mumbling, "Give . . . give all . . . give," repeated over and over. It didn't require a medical degree to see he was in desperate need of immediate professional help.

Annie leaned over straining to hear what he might be saying. She was hysterical, her hands and arms moving erratically above him, unsure of where or even if she should touch him but needing desperately to do something other than swat at the cloud of bees that were being freshly disturbed and landing on her exposed skin.

Acting as rapidly as they could but with needed care, the trio lifted Taylor free of the trough and awkwardly carried him a distance away, laying his back on the ground. Unavoidably they, too, suffered numerous stings during the brief rescue.

Hoping there was cell phone coverage, Stone opened his phone and found three bars waiting for him—a good sign, thank you, God.

He called a close friend hoping to find him in his office or at least within cell phone reach. Stone knew if anyone could help right then, it was his friend Mike Kalama.

Chapter Twelve

"*A*loha, this is Mike Kalama," the voice on the other end declared.

Stone had called Mike's personal cell number, hoping it would be the fastest way of reaching him, and he was right.

Sgt. Michael Kalama, besides being a tall, muscularly built Hawaiian, perpetually smiling if things were going smoothly, was sergeant-in-charge at HPD's downtown Honolulu substation on Maunakea Street. He and Stone had been friends for more than forty years since both met as members of Hui O'Kainalu, a group of twenty men who gathered monthly to enjoy one another's company, play horseshoes, and drink beer.

"Aloha, Mike. I'm glad to reach you. I have an emergency, and medical help is needed ASAP. You're the only one I know who can do all the necessary magic to help the situation."

"Eh, Stone, lucky me. You're giving me a tall order that sounds serious. Bring me up to speed on what's happening."

"It's critical, Mike." Stone spent a short two minutes briefly bringing his friend up to speed on what had happened and who was there with him. Mike already knew Lloyd. He relayed that Taylor had received what appeared to be several hundred bee stings and was semiconscious, repeating the word *give* over and over.

Mike knew that Stone was prone to exaggerating and mentally discounted the beestings down to a hundred. Still, no matter the actual number, that was more than anyone could sustain and remain happily healthy without professional intervention.

"The biggest problem, Mike, is that we're holed-up in that old abandoned scout camp east of Hale O Lono Harbor on Molokai."

"*Auwe*, that is a tough one. Never been there but know a lot about it. I didn't know it was still there. You're going to need a rescue team." He began to break it down out loud, mainly for his own benefit—Mike always thought more clearly if he said things out loud. "*K-kai*," he began, using the frequent local way of referring to the town of Kaunakakai, "has EMTs, but they'd have to drive to the harbor. That'd take them forty minutes, full burn, by the time they got going. Castle Medical here on Oahu has a chopper and a response team sitting at the ready. They could get there quicker. Your friend is going to have to be brought to Castle for treatment anyway, so using the chopper will save time. This is the way it needs to happen, Stone. You okay with that?"

"Yes, Mike. I'll leave all the details up to you."

"Let me ask you. Can you see a clearing anywhere around you that could accommodate a chopper landing?"

"No, unfortunately there's only old buildings and lots of kiawe trees."

"Okay, hold on a minute. I need to call Castle before we go any further."

Mike was away from the conversation for less than a minute before coming back on the line.

"We're good to go. So here's what you're going to have to do," he continued. "All of you, injured and otherwise, will need to start hiking back toward the harbor. That'll save us time. I'll mobilize the response team at Castle and have them in the air, hopefully within a few minutes. They'll meet up with you somewhere on the trail unless you're a lot faster at hiking than I suspect and reach the harbor first, but keep me posted on your progress."

"Okay, Mike. Have the chopper guys hit the ground at the harbor and start hiking east. We'll rig something to carry Taylor and begin hiking west back toward the harbor. It sounds like that's going to be the best we can hope for."

"It'll be a tough hike, Stone. You'll be carrying dead weight, pardon the unintended reference, but I know you're up for it. Fortunately, I've got a slow day going"—he sounded relieved—"so I may come over with the chopper and help where I can. I need to clear everything with the Molokai PD anyway, and I know they'd feel better if I'm on the ground overseeing things when the rescue happens. I'll call them from the chopper and clear the way. I'm only three minutes away from the hospital as we speak, just passing the old Waialae Drive-In and the dump road cutoff, so I'm very close."

"Mahalo, Mike. See you on the trail shortly."

"Okay, brudda. If you don't hear from me before, I'll see you in the bushes." He was chuckling as he hung up.

The *bushes* was certainly the right description for the area. Maybe *bone-dry with red dirt and scraggly tree bushes* would be a more apt description.

Stone looked around for Lloyd and Annie, spotting them crawling out from beneath one of the shelters and dragging what appeared to be an armful of well-used rat-nest material behind them.

Human nature was a wonderful thing, especially so were the kids like scouts are concerned and told to police the camp when it came time to leave. Sweeping unwanted objects under shelters and out of the line of sight of scout leaders and attending parents was the quickest and most efficient way to finish a cleanup job with the least amount of effort expended. A treasure trove of unwanted things could probably be found in the crawl spaces beneath buildings.

When Lloyd shook out their found treasure, he held it up in order to have a better look. It was an old sleeping bag left over from better days, originally red by the looks of it but was now a time-faded pink. He continued to hold it up in Stone's direction for him to see.

"This ought to work for putting together a travois sort of carrier." Lloyd apparently had the same idea in mind for how they would have to carry Taylor back to the harbor. It wasn't going to be over anyone's shoulder, and there was no question about Taylor being able to walk out under his own power. Lloyd had heard part of Stone's conversation with Mike and had gotten the jump on finding what was needed, and Annie had found two sturdy pieces of well-dried-out, and therefore lightweight split-wood fencing posts and enough rope to bind it all together.

"When and where does the helicoptered-in help arrive?"

"They should be on their way any minute, Lloyd. Mike says the responders will meet us along the return trail. We'll have to do our best to drag Taylor as far along the trail as we possibly can and hope we meet up with them relatively quickly. How are all your bee stings?" he asked each in turn. "Mine hurt like crazy," he volunteered, doing his best to resist the urge to scratch each one.

They both nodded, and claimed they were feeling much the same, trying their best to remain upbeat. No one was willing to dwell too long on themselves with Taylor hurting so close by.

He was still hanging on, still semiconscious but no longer trying to communicate. Annie rushed back and forth helping to rig the pole carrier while spending time hoovering over her boyfriend, busily repositioning some found material she had placed under his head to make him more comfortable. She couldn't help but wonder what he had been trying to tell them, *Give what and to who?* She decided he had been hallucinating and knew they would have fun giving it reason when he returned to normal and was able to listen to what they claimed he'd said. She worried, though. Taylor didn't appear to comprehend what was taking place around him—he no longer looked responsive, yet his eyelids remained partially open. She wasn't sure if that was good or bad.

Stone saw their three water bottles leaning against the trough Taylor had nose-dived into. They were filled to the brim with clear, sparkling water.

Lloyd saw Stone looking at them and, with a grin of satisfaction, said, "Annie tried the pump where Taylor was so she could bathe his arms and legs, and ta-da, water came." He emphasized his words with arms spread wide as if he was acting on stage. "Made the bees living there quite happy too."

All they had to do now was tie everything together, get Taylor comfortably lying astride the poles, and pray the sleeping bag and ropes held together long enough for the four of them to reach help or the harbor, whichever came first.

Preparations ready, they began the arduous task of dragging the ragtag travois holding Taylor as far as they could along the difficult trail, all the while praying that the responders would arrive quickly. Stone pictured them being physical fit and were, hopefully, fast hikers. Taylor desperately needed the help that was on its way.

* * *

It didn't take long to have things ready to roll once Mike finished his call to Castle Medical Center requesting that they make ready the helicopter and alert the responders. Pulling up beside the helipad, he was pleased to see four individuals, two men and two women, already seated in the chopper, its rotors slowly turning and the bay door wide open as they waited for him to arrive. It had been less than five minutes since he'd called. He made a mental note to thank the hospital administrator and lead responder for their efficiency.

As he climbed aboard, the door slid closed, and they were immediately airborne, heading out across the Kaiwi Channel toward Hale O Lono Harbor, thirty nautical miles distant. They'd be at their destination in under fifteen minutes.

The sky was a cloudless blue. The earlier storm winds had died away as afternoon slowly turned toward evening. The surface of the water below them was still roughened by rolling whitecaps. An ocean angered by the winds was unhurried in calming down, as the chopper lifted higher above Lanikai Beach and the Mokulua Islands. It was smooth flying—*a very good omen*, thought Mike.

He watched as the island of Molokai grew closer. He could see the rock breakwater in the distance jutting out into the Kalohi Channel from Hale O Lono harbor—now just minutes away.

Chapter Thirteen

Sweating profusely as the trio fought, jostled, and shoved their way through the brush. The day had heated up as they approached midday, making their task even more strenuous. Two tracks in the soil followed closely behind as the poles supporting Taylor dug deep into the ground under his weight gouging out smaller rocks and tufts of weeds. It was putting a lot of strain on Stone and Lloyd hiking side by side, each holding on to one of the poles as they moved in the direction of the harbor. Each were saying silent prayers that the rope bindings forming Taylor's makeshift carrier would continue to hold together until help arrived. Additional strain was being placed on the poles along with the two that were pulling them as they continually snagged on outstretched tree branches. The result was frequent and abrupt stops, more wearing on the hikers than the actual hiking.

The trek from the scout camp was much more difficult than they had imagined it would be under the circumstances. Taylor was not small nor was he lightweight—he was heavy, and the rig, bulky.

Before leaving the scout camp, they had rushed to put the travois together. The aged and flimsy sleeping bag was stretched between the wood poles and tied as tightly as possible with the found rope. They were doing all they could to hurry their efforts but only succeeded in losing valuable time when one of the ropes holding everything together got stressed beyond its worn-out capability and suddenly came apart, collapsing the entire rig and dumping Taylor unceremoniously to the ground. Even with the tumble, he remained silent and unresponsive. They would have all given one another a high five if he'd uttered nothing more than an ouch, but he remained silent. Fortunately, he hadn't been high off the ground at that moment, so his fall was relatively soft. They quickly went about rerigging the drag poles and resecuring the tattered sleeping bag before setting off once again.

They shared in the effort, taking turns dragging the makeshift sled. With two of them pulling the arrangement offered the third person an opportunity to take a break for needed water and a few much-needed deep breaths of air while also clearing a path forward for the others. They were discovering that sweating in the heat, although very uncomfortable, was a mild blessing and helped expel a portion of the bee toxin from their systems cooling their skin. The strain of their efforts was also serving to overcome a degree of lingering pain—the pokes and scratches from the kiawe thorns and the irritation from the kukus were overshadowing the rest of their discomforts. It became easy to forget they had other minor pains, like lingering bee stings, when a tree spike pushed through a shoe and punctured the tender soul of a foot.

Even with alternating turns at pulling Taylor, they were quickly reaching a point of exhaustion and dehydration. Stopping for a short rest or break, they finally and happily heard the distant sound of a chopper touching down somewhere not too far distant in front of them. They assumed the sound was coming from the harbor, and that indicated medical help was coming to the rescue. It was a beautiful sound to hear. They knew the responders would do what they could to reach them in the shortest time possible.

Taking a moment to stop and rest, it became very tempting to stay right where they stood, sit down, and wait for the help to come to them, but a quick glance at one another dispelled that thought like a puff of smoke—it would be at Taylor's detriment if they did, and each subconsciously knew that. Without words, they began moving again, albeit with a little less gusto.

Quickly, within minutes of the sound of the chopper's motor dying away, the quietness of the area returning as they heard footfalls rapidly approaching.

Soon after, four young, obviously in good shape, responders quickly came running into view visible through the tree branches and heading their way. All of them carried identical, small red backpacks, presumably filled with the necessary medical supplies. A woman, coming in behind the leader, also carried a collapsed gurney. Mike Kalama, discernable several yards behind the responders, had slowed his pace to a fast walk. His normally perfectly pressed and creased uniform was showing signs of the abuse from unforgiving tree spikes, thorny vegetation and the sweat of exertion.

The medics immediately took over, lifting Taylor free of his makeshift rig. They laid him on their now-expanded gurney and huddled around, speaking to one another too softly for anyone to distinguish words. It was quite apparent they all had their own well-rehearsed tasks to perform.

Mike picked up the haphazardly constructed travois and moved it out of the way so no one would accidentally trip over it. He stood back taking a better look at it as he wiped sweat from his brow and eyes with the back of his hand. His smile broadened as Stone and Lloyd came over to him.

"You put this thing together back at camp, huh? Looks like pretty good scout training to me," he observed. "You as well, young lady," looking approvingly toward Annie standing off to the side. "MacGyver himself would be proud." Stone figured Annie may be too young to understand that reference, but he let it go.

With Taylor flat on his back on the ground, the medics close around him, one of them brandished a large syringe filled with a clear-yellowish liquid and swabbed an area on Taylor's arm with alcohol. In quick fashion, Taylor had a large quantity of epinephrine flowing through his veins as they began to strap him tightly to the stretcher. The drug would hopefully sustain him until they could get him to the hospital.

Stone introduced Mike to Annie just as the medics hoisted the stretcher and headed off toward the harbor. They made the whole process appear much too easy—clearly well-trained for the task.

"*Hele mai.* Let's talk as we go," suggested Mike, as he led the trio off at a quick pace. "We'll need to hurry along if we are to keep up with them."

As the chopper lifted off, it swung around to the right in a tight turn and headed back toward Oahu and Castle Medical Center, its accompanying noise receding with it into the distance.

* * *

A peacefulness quickly settled over the harbor as Stone and Lloyd sat down on the bulkhead beside *Wailana Sunrise*. An outdated and corroded power box, evidently left behind from days gone by and plainly no longer usable, was perfectly positioned as a backrest.

They watched the chopper for as long as they could as it morphed into a small speck in the waning sunlight. Their thoughts and prayers were riding with the man they'd never met cruising high above the Kaiwi Channel accompanied by a young lady wrought with worry and fear. They hoped she and Taylor would be all right; they were already thinking of Annie as their friend. Mike went back with the chopper, claiming his need to return to Oahu as soon as possible. They would have enjoyed his company on the yacht for the evening, but he claimed duties that needed him. He promised, though, to catch up with them when they arrived back on Oahu the next day.

With Taylor and Annie gone, Stone and Lloyd were left with the task of shuttling both boats back to the yacht club on Oahu.

They talked of taking the small boat back to Maui and tying it up in the Lahaina harbor, but they both put the kibosh on that idea. They were sure Taylor would welcome the opportunity to drive his own boat back to Maui after he recovered. It would also give him something to look forward to while recuperating at the hospital.

The decision, then, was made. They would stay the night in the harbor and head out early in the morning. They sat back and relaxed knowing they had done a good deed today, and both felt good about the outcome. They also knew they had fresh mahi-mahi waiting in the cooler to become their dinner.

Chapter Fourteen

*S*tone valued his friend, Mike, and put a lot of belief in the sort of man he was. Not simply for his friendship, which was invaluable, but also for his undeniable dedication to his chosen profession. Mike had devoted his life to the safety and well-being of the island's people, and he took exceptional appreciation of his own abilities and the speed with which he could arrange things and events to move in the direction needed. The swiftness in getting help to Taylor's side had been vital if Taylor was to have had any chance of coming out of this ordeal.

* * *

By the time the helicopter carrying Taylor landed at Castle Hospital, his condition had not improved. He was pale, his skin a ghostlike hue. His lips were chalky, and his eye sockets appeared deeply sunken. As the technicians quickly wheeled him into the ICU, he was breathing with a steady albeit not with a very strong rhythm.

He had lapsed into a semicoma shortly after the helicopter had lifted off Molokai. Now he lay in the ICU surrounded by countless monitoring devices, rhythmic pulses, and nurses with harried and concerned looks. They all acknowledged their patient gave the impression that he was not doing well. They worked feverishly to change that, and at one point, it appeared the outcome was positive, raising their hopes.

Taylor suddenly came to life, seemingly talking, and a nurse brought her ear so close to his lips she could feel the warmth of his breath, her hopes escalating.

"Give back . . . gotta give all . . . Annie should—"

But that was all the nurse heard as Taylor once again began to fade and become unresponsive.

The attending medical personnel had performed all the necessary tests and life-saving tasks swiftly and instinctively, their professionalism unquestioned. A doctor and two nurses had immediately taken over when he initially arrived in the ICU, but now all his responses were quickly diminishing. It became questionable whether he could even make it back to awareness or not—and he didn't.

The heart monitor flatlined and held at a steady heart rendering, no-response tone. The doctor in charge, Dr. Krivoi Gorshenski, looked up at the somber faces of his nursing staff hovering over Taylor and gave the briefest of nods to Gayle, the head nurse, and she began to tenderly pull a white sheet over Taylor's face.

Later, during the required debriefing session, something that automatically takes place whenever patients die, the attending staff would all agree that there had been too much venom in his system when he was first brought in. There had been too much damage done to vital organs for too long a period before the needed medications had been administered. There was nothing else they could have done or would have done differently.

Annie was in the family waiting area nervously pacing from corner to corner when Dr. Gorshenski came through the door accompanied by his nurse Gayle, both their heads down in private whispered conference. As the doctor approached Annie, the nurse gently squeezed her arm and broke away from them and headed down the hall. The doctor had things he needed to impart to Annie. Mike was standing off to one side, phone to his ear speaking to one of his patrolmen.

Annie instantly came to attention when the doctor began to speak softly to her. Mike was partially listening but didn't need to hear the precise words to know the direction the conversation was taking. He watched helplessly as Annie collapse on the couch, sobbing uncontrollably. He'd been here too many times during his career and abhorred these moments and the feelings of uselessness that lingered.

One of the attending nurses came over and sat down next to her, resting a hand over hers, comforting her the best she could. She sat there in silence as Annie continued to sob, face buried in the nurse's shoulder.

Without delay, Mike moved farther away and called Stone to let him know what was happening. He also told Stone that he'd called Pops's house on the Big Island wanting to get Loki's phone number. He was going to let her know as well. Stone had told Mike when they were hiking back to the helicopter about the recent connection Annie had made with Loki on Facebook. Mike knew Pops and his family from several years prior and, as luck would have it, found that Loki was spending the night with her mom and Pops, so he was able to talk with her without having to put up with the questionable phone connections that were inherent with calls to Hawi, Loki's home.

On hearing the news about her FB friend, the friend she had yet to meet, and at Mike's suggestion, she began to make plans to fly to Oahu for a few days. She told Mike that she'd rent a car at the airport and drive to Stone's Kaneohe house and would wait for Annie there.

Saying aloha to Loki ending the call, he called Teri's cell phone to let her know what he had arranged without her prior approval. He was hoping, after-the-fact, to gain her blessing. Teri was at her own house in Nuuanu Valley feeding her fish at the time and was delighted with the prospect of having Loki and her friend, Annie, stay with her and Stone at Kaikanani for a few days.

"Besides," Teri exclaimed, looking down at Sunshine, the largest and oldest koi in her pond, "I'm delighted to have another opportunity to see Loki and to meet this surfer-girl and offer her some comfort. God knows she'll be needing plenty."

After the phone call ended, Mike gave his aloha to a still weeping Annie and headed back to his precinct.

Teri, disconnecting from Mike, went about feeding her fish while thinking of the enjoyment she would receive from having Loki and this new person, Annie, staying with them. Unaware that she was standing in thought, a hand full of fish food still hovering over the pond and waiting fish directly below, one of them turned quickly causing a splash of water that caught Teri on the arm bring her awareness back to present—Teri had to assume it coincidental, but she smiled nonetheless—who knew what fish thought.

She had twelve koi along with several mosquito fish living in her basement pond. She could probably claim the distinction of having the only pond in a semi-open-walled basement in Hawaii and perhaps even beyond these borders. Leaky water pipes a few years before had left two feet of water confined in her basement with no drain. She repaired the leak but left the water and immediately went out and bought fish, fish food and a water filter system. A few lily pads floated around as well as an occasional toad that had jumped over the short wall and made its home. Hawaii is dubiously blessed with an abundance of toads.

* * *

In a call to Stone as he headed for the precinct, Mike relayed everything that was taking place. He knew his friend would approve of the plan to have the two girls staying at Kaikanani, which he had set into motion—he did.

Chapter Fifteen

Sunset, Hale O Lono Harbor

$\mathcal{S}$tone and Lloyd were settled into the ease and calm of the late afternoon, having made the decision to wait for morning before taking both boats back to Oahu. It would be too problematic if they were to attempt it now with night quickly approaching.

They had hauled two deck chairs off the yacht and were reclining in the afternoon shade, talking quietly about the day's events: the improbable rescue, the hike, the fun it would be to take a helicopter ride—under much different circumstances, they both chimed in simultaneously. They also talked at length about Taylor, his condition, and the probable outcome of what he was going though. They were cautiously optimistic that all would be well and were looking forward to the back-yard barbeque Annie invited them to as soon as Taylor was back to health and able to return home to Maui. Their relaxation ended with the phone call from Mike.

The news was heart-wrenching.

Both men felt the immediate impact of sympathy for Annie and of what she must be going through right then. Even though they barely knew the woman and didn't know Taylor at all beyond what Annie had disclosed to them, it had been quite easy to see the depth of her love for him—the words she had expressed during their hike spoke volumes about how much she cared about him.

Stone couldn't help but wonder how Teri would feel given a similar situation. He had a too-frequent habit of putting himself into precarious situations; it was part of his nature to push things, sometimes to the extreme. Perhaps seeking some sort of adrenaline rush, he wasn't sure. He didn't want to think about all that right then, but instead resolved to be more vigilant of his surroundings and more aware of his activity choices, immediately berating himself, knowing he'd made similar resolutions in the past, usually after something unanticipated had happened, like now. He would continue to attempt to improve that behavior.

The late afternoon was making its way toward evening. The laughing and joking that would normally exist at the end of a day of fishing had morphed into quietness and contemplation after Mike's call.

The storm surge was easing off, and the winds were calming to little more than a gentle breeze. There would be a good tailing wind tomorrow for their journey back to Oahu.

"If the water's calm enough," ventured Lloyd, "let's run a towline and drag Taylor's boat instead of driving both back. It should be safe enough if we pay attention and don't try setting any speed records." It was a veiled reference to Stone's inclination toward speed.

"And if we're *really* careful," Stone's grin was wide, adding to Lloyd's suggestion, "we can rig up two handlines and run them short. We're bound to pick up a few more kawakawa along the way, especially with the calming seas."

It was a plan they would think about and decide in the morning. The events of the day remained heavy on both and they didn't feel it was the right time to build enthusiasm for tomorrow.

They talked of the uncertainty of life and the need to make the most of every available moment: squandering time was not an option. The brevity of life lent a need to do more fishing in the future. Maybe they could even talk their wives into tagging along occasionally.

That would take a lot more thinking.

A calmness settled over the harbor as the sun continued to set. They cleaned and cooked the three kawakawa, deciding to keep the mahi for Teri, and ate them along with some cold rice they'd brought as they watched and waited for the green flash as the sun disappeared below the horizon. Unfortunately, there were too many clouds in the way.

They planned to leave at daybreak before the normal trade winds had a chance to generate any appreciable waves.

Oahu, late the next morning

*E*asing into Kaneohe Yacht Club with *Kalia* riding in tow close behind, the two tired fishermen were relieved to find the small harbor empty of its normal midday activity.

The men had woken up and managed to get underway, leaving Hale O Lono Harbor before sunrise with the hope of catching a calm ocean before the trade winds had a chance to came up and bring the surf up with it.

Stone nudged Taylor's Whaler to the club's bulkhead and held it steady as Lloyd jumped to land and went about securing it. As Stone powered over to his assigned slip, he noticed a fellow clubmate standing aft on his impressive-sized sailing yacht waving at him in acknowledgment. Stone knew him only as Chuck and happily waved back as was their habit. The greeting had become almost a ritual whenever Stone came into or left the club's harbor and Chuck happened to be out on deck of his yacht, which he seemed to always be. He had yet to meet the old sailor face-to-face but promised himself that he would do so one day soon. To Stone's knowledge, Chuck never took his yacht out of the yacht club's basin but could always be seen standing on deck polishing this or sanding that as if the yacht was the most precious possession he owned, and maybe it was. He had heard that Chuck had a wife but could only wonder at the level of commitment that the two must share since he rarely left his boat and she was never around the club. He decided not to spend a lot of time pondering it—wasn't his business to do so anyway.

After both boats were secured, the men drove to Castle Hospital to check in on Annie. They needed to let her know they were available in case she was feeling lost, which they were certain she would be and wanted to find out what they could do to help her. They assumed it would all be totally overwhelming for her at this point in time.

In his phone call, Mike had mentioned that the hospital was in the process of setting up a bed, so Annie could spend the night, knowing she had no other place to go, but they also wanted to keep an eye on her growing depression. As it turned out, the hospital had empty beds—something that didn't happen often, which worked out well for Annie. Tonight would be different, and Stone would take her to his place where she could stay until ready to go back to Maui.

They found her in a waiting room sitting and staring off into space. Her eyes were puffy and wet, her face withdrawn, blank of emotion. It was obvious that the night of sleep had eluded her. She appeared not to be holding together at all well.

Hearing the events that transpired and not wanting to dig too deeply at this point of time, Lloyd stayed with her while Stone went to find the doctor or one of the nurses and hear more details and what had happened and what they suggested needed to be done next. It was obvious that any of the details that needed attending to would fall on his and Lloyd's shoulders until Annie was back to some form of normal and able to handle things for herself. Stone had no qualms about helping her in any way she needed and was equally certain that Lloyd felt the same.

Nurse Gayle, busily working on some paperwork, noticed Stone approaching her desk. Putting her pen down and looking up at him, she cleared her throat before speaking. From her experience, she was able to surmise the what-happens-now look on his face and the direction the conversation needed to take, and she was right.

With little hesitation, she told him the hospital would arrange for Taylor to be transported, probably the next day, to the city's morgue in Honolulu for an autopsy, a necessary formality in cases such as this, she explained. She suggested that arrangements could begin now for Taylor's internment or cremation.

This was going to be Annie's call and was probably going to be a very difficult decision for her to make. Stone figured that he and Lloyd were her current family by default, having stumbled into the situation, so they had little alternative but to see it through, which was all right with them both. On their hike to the scout camp, they'd learned that neither Annie nor Taylor had any other family they could call upon for help, so Stone and Lloyd were now her family by default.

Stone went over and sat down in the waiting room next to her and gently took hold of her hand. "Instead of you going back to your cabin"—he hesitated to add *alone* and chose not to—"I understand Mike mentioned or rather volunteered," he smiled approvingly at her, "the possibility of you coming to my home for a few days. I think that's a great idea if you're up to it. It'll give you time to get your head straight while being surrounded by people you can trust and rely on. It would help me as well having you close. There will be a lot of details that will need tending to.

"I also understand"—another soft smile, shaking his head slightly at the depth of his friend's display of friendship—"that Mike called Pops's house and suggested that Loki come over and stay at my place together with you for a few days. She may even be on her way already. You'll enjoy meeting my wife Teri, and I have a feeling Bert won't want to leave you alone. I hope you have no problems with cats—overly affectionate ones, that is."

"I love cats," she admitted weakly. "You don't really know me, Stone. You sure my staying in your home won't be a problem? I really do need some time to figure out what I need to do. I dread going back alone. There are so many things to think about. The cabin's filled with Taylor's things as well as my own, and he has no close family that I know of to send anything to. I'm not even sure I ever want to go back to that place. Taylor and I were so happy there." Her eyes were filling with tears as she looked up at Stone. "Our plans . . ." Emotions finally took control, and she was unable to finish the thought she'd been about to share. There would be time over the next few days to talk it all out.

Gently taking both of her hands, he volunteered, "Teri will love having another female around the house to talk with. Two when we include Loki. I'm sure there's girl talk she'd enjoy a lot more than my tired old tales and complaints. I'm not the best listener on that score." He smiled and patted her hand.

"On our hike, I think I mentioned," he continued, "that Loki is a relatively new entry into my family, much like you are now." He was trying to lighten her mood with more smiles. It wasn't working too well. Understandably, the hurting remained too deep inside. "This'll give us all an opportunity to get to know both of you. I suspect your friendship with her is going to transcend a fair bit of the future."

Lloyd was walking up to them; he'd been talking with the nursing staff who worked on Taylor.

"Eh, Lloyd, Loki is flying over to stay with Annie for a few days, and both have agreed to stay at Kaikanani until Annie knows what she wants to do. Why don't you and Pam come over and join us for dinner tonight? We can fillet our mahi-mahi and get the barbeque cranked up. I bet Loki will love seeing you and Pam again." Lloyd and his wife, Pam, had met Loki in Hilo when the whole family was first introduced to the daughter Pops wasn't aware that he had at that time.

With everything that could be done at the hospital done, they left. Talking with the nurses, Lloyd had learned that Taylor would be transported to the morgue within the hour.

It was obvious to both men that it was breaking Annie's heart to walk out the door knowing she was leaving Taylor behind forever. Stone dropped his friend off at his car, and then he and Annie headed over the Pali Highway to the airport to pick up Loki. She'd decided not to rent a car after all. Apparently, Teri had talked her out of it.

Chapter Seventeen

*A*nthony Gravello, Tony to those who knew him, or those who *cared* to know him that well, had the fortune of possessing an endless charisma. The few friends he had came to him for the pleasure of his company. Clients walked into his financial consulting firm for that same compelling reason but primarily because he knew finance well and how to create wealth, and clients sought that expertise in hopes of reaping the rewards.

He was, however, not an easy person to work for, as office employees and his house staff would readily agree. He was aware of that without the need of being reminded. For reasons quite clear to him, he had a chip resting on his shoulders that was the weight of a cement block.

He had been forced to migrate away from Sicily as a young man, away from his family, away from all those he cared about, and he bore a massive grudge as a result. He had loved his home in Palermo and would have been happy to stay there forever surrounded by his large family. Unfortunately, he inadvertently crossed the wrong way on a path with his oldest cousin, the cousin destined to become the head, the Godfather, of his crime-oriented *famiglia*. In Tony's view, it had been nothing but a simple misunderstanding, but it had been taken far beyond proportion.

His sensitive and extremely insecure cousin didn't consider anything to be a *simple misunderstanding*—the cousin saw it as a dangerous affront against his taking over the family. The whole dispute carried the markings of an experience that was destined to trigger future hardships for Tony, almost guaranteeing him a much shorter lifespan if he were to stay.

Anthony Gravello had been a young, energetic man at the time and made the decision to leave home and make his mark on the world elsewhere.

With a considerable financial blessing from his mother, powerless to intervene in family matters such as this, he had migrated to Hawaii. He favored the islands, though he'd never been there, because of the distance from Sicily, literally halfway around the world. It helped his decision knowing that no one in his family had ever thought of visiting the island paradise much less migrating to it, so he felt secure in the knowing their thinking was unlikely to change anytime soon.

At just over six-feet tall, still in his fifties, Anthony Gravello had rich olive skin and dark handsome features and an endless ability to charm that made young women's knees weak. His deep, clear voice carried an unmistakable accent pointing directly back to his heritage, which only served to make him all the more attractive.

He kept his thick coal-black hair slicked back and held in place by an oil slick so thick one would expect to see drippings roll off his forehead. It had been speculated by a few that this was probably the number 1 reason he was currently single with few prospects on the horizon.

His round face and thick neck were squarely buoyed by immense shoulders and complimented by immaculately tailored Italian-cut suits and expensive silk ties. His signature piece of clothing was a matching cravat. It was old style, but that never bothered him. He was never without one, even in the humidity of the tropics. Put together into one human package, he was a handsome, confident, large man with a commanding yet charismatic presence. He could draw people to him like free food at a luau.

The downside, or perhaps the better side of his Sicilian, crime-oriented upbringing was a soft spot in his heart the size of which was beyond measure. Growing up in his crime-oriented family, he'd learned to shield that soft nature and learned instead how to turn on a hard, tough exterior at will whenever needed—to instantly become the demanding SOB that was expected from a Hawaii-style godfather of a small, close-fitting group of employees. The woman he finally married and the daughter he subsequently adopted saw this softness in him and loved him for it—for a short time.

Tony Gravello had been fortunate when he first arrived in the islands having walked into an enormous home at Black Point, on the back slopes of Diamond Head. It came with a large piece of property bordered on three sides by the ocean. The area was perhaps the most sought-after in Honolulu because of the inherent natural beauty. His home and property were the iconic images of being beyond-wealth. At the suggestion of an employee, he named his new home Pohakau, the Anchor. It was precisely how he came to view his new home.

His office in this titanic-sized mansion was paneled in dark, high-gloss mahogany, giving off an awe-inspiring sense of wealth. Portions of each wall, other than where the floor-to-ceiling glass windows overlooked the infinity pool and the ocean beyond, were crowded with heavy wooden bookshelves housing more antique, leather-bound volumes than one could expect to read in a lifetime. Titles such as *The Cosa Nostra*, *The Battle of Benevento*, *Sicily's Rebellion*, *The Kingdom of Sicily* lined the shelves. As a visitor, it was not too difficult to imagine that the man sitting at the desk in front of you had probably read every one of them, including a set of leather-bound Louis L'Amour novels, Gravello's favorites for the rare times he relaxed.

Tony Gravello's office and the house in general were decorated mostly with objects from Sicily. In every room, there were several carved busts and small statues of great men from Italian, Roman, and Sicilian history. The likes of Aeneas, Cincinnatus, and Julius Caesar were placed throughout. Gravello himself showed an eerie resemblance to several of the ancient stone carvings—a likeness he enjoyed.

When Anthony Gravello first arrived in the islands, seventeen years prior, he founded the financial investment firm TGL & Company. There was no *company* per se. He had simply added the word to give an impression of being a larger firm than it actually was. Located in the AmPac Towers on Bishop Street in downtown Honolulu, his offices occupied the entire twenty-third floor of the modern twenty-five-floor building. His being two floors below the penthouse constantly gave him the conception of being two floors below the status he thought he deserved and was a constant irritant to him. Nothing he did, legal or otherwise, though, and he tried them all, could budge the existing penthouse tenant to vacate. He had hesitantly given up trying.

TGL & Company employed ten people, small for his industry, but it had become an enormously successful capital investment company. Anthony Gravello's clients, some of the wealthiest in the islands, generally gave him carte blanche to invest their money on the best path Gravello saw fit in order to increase their investment. He was quite intuitive in market strategy and succeeded in making the most of his abilities.

His firm was coming up on its sixteenth anniversary. It had made him a multimillionaire and had placed him in the social circles of the most elite in Honolulu. The Island Country Club had given him a free membership solely, so it appeared, for their own bragging rights.

Unfortunately, as successful as his company had been over the years and as rich as he had become because of it, the work was no longer exciting. He did extremely well at investing his client's money and making them wealthy, but he was becoming dissatisfied. He knew financial markets like he knew his name and enjoyed an innate ability to divine the direction financial markets would move on any day and took full advantage of that, but it was no longer enough.

The dark side of all his financial successes and of his less-than-contented life since his wife and daughter had both left, was that he was growing tired—tired of business and, yes, tired of making money. But more than any of that, he had become tired of America. He desperately wanted to return home to Sicily and live out his remaining years, relaxed and carefree, in a style he knew and loved so well. He could afford the very best, so why not enjoy it all? He had convinced himself that his family would welcome him back with open arms after such a long absence.

Perhaps it was the easy success or his growing weariness that led him into developing a plan, something with a familiar excitement to it. He initiated an elaborate Ponzi-type scheme ala Bernie-Madoff-with-a-twist, and his gambit quickly began to experience an overflow of cash. It raised his spirits. This would be his finest and final moment before leaving the islands.

Things got so involved juggling the company's legitimate record keeping independent and secretive from his personal and illegitimate records that he decided to hire a young man he'd heard of named Jason Baker. Baker, at the time, was working for a local CPA's office doing charity tax work and had been thrilled at the offer to work for TGL.

His job with TGL was to assist in keeping the books and the volumes of paperwork for all TGL's clients organized and current. He was intentionally and logically kept in the dark about the illicit cashflow being funneled into Anthony Gravello's secret account. Having Jason on board freed Gravello to concentrate more on this *other side* of his affairs and allowed him the luxury of daydreaming of an eventual return to Sicily.

Jason Baker proved himself to be a brilliant employee, excelling at financial dealings, much like his boss. He kept all the client accounts updated as well as the volumes of IRS records, keeping them straight and timely while Anthony Gravello dictated the overall investment avenues and strategies. Jason was highly qualified and very intuitive and had been of significant help to Gravello over the past six years he had worked for him.

It came as a thunderbolt shock, then, when he discovered that the employee he trusted most, Jason Baker, his right-hand man, had managed to uncover his private money flow and had the gonads to somehow set up a money drain of his own, filtering cash from Gravello's personal cash flow. How Jason managed to figure out Gravello's illicit system was a puzzle, but he had. On top of it all, the insult to cap off the injury, Jason had suddenly quit and moved to one of the other islands. Gravello suspected it was Maui after having overheard Jason mention the island a few too many times.

He needed to find Jason. Retrieving his money was not nearly as important as his desire to make Jason Baker pay for his crime, and Anthony Gravello happened to employ a man who, he sincerely hoped, would be able to do the job that was required.

He punched the number 7 on his cell phone. The number had a specific significance and triggered a knowing sound on another phone, a phone in the pocket of Milo Palma. Milo heard the sound, but it took him a few moments before action followed— that ringtone rarely sounded. He was immediately aware of the significance and quickly headed for his boss's office.

Chapter Eighteen

Milo Palma was the main enforcer for the Gravello family in Hawaii as well as a bodyguard for the man himself. The position of *enforcer*, though, was a vague cover-all term, often causing Milo to shake his head in humored wonder whenever there was a lull in enforcement-type matters needing doing. He considered himself more of a gofer than an enforcer of anything. When nothing else was happening that demanded his skillset, which was 99 percent of the time, he would be in one of the many gardens helping the gardener pull weeds or would be running an errand for the kitchen staff when no one else was available. When things were very slow, he took time to walk the beach fronting the Outrigger Canoe Club. It was his favorite. He loved that beach more than any of the many others he could have chosen from, deeming the women there much classier and more to his liking.

Born in Palermo, Sicily, he had begun his career working for the Gravello *famiglia,* the family that once controlled much of Sicily. He had worked with the family for ten years. At thirty-five, which was considered a tremendous accomplishment in a crime family, his career was pointed toward the top of the pile. Simple continual attrition helped that rise since his work lent itself to short lifespans and quick endings.

His current boss, Anthony Gravello, had been one of the up and coming major players in that family—past tense. Milo often questioned himself why he had chosen to follow Tony Gravello to Hawaii instead of staying in his homeland and a well-paid future to look forward to with others in the family, but that was the choice he made, and he didn't like revisiting past decisions knowing they could never be changed. Besides, he had to admit that he had a pretty good life here—he loved Hawaii.

Milo was the unofficial number 2 in this family next to the big man himself ever since Gravello had divorced his wife. He lived in relative comfort with his own studio cabin on the edge of the property next to the ocean. His kitchen consisted of a hotplate and bar-sized refrigerator, but he was always welcome in the main house's kitchen, which he made frequent use of. He knew the cook, Catena LaRosa, had taken a shine to him, and he knew she would open her kitchen to him at any hour. He was certain she would have opened a lot more to him if he'd let her, and the thought crossed his mind many times.

At night in his confined space, windows wide open to the ocean, Milo would be lulled to sleep by the magic sounds of the waves just a few feet away. The studio was small enough that the open window on the opposite side from his bed, away from the water's edge, allowed him to keep his ears attuned for any sounds coming from the grounds around the house. All part of his duties.

The housemaid and the cook were his favorites, and he always received special attention from them both. The butler simply put up with him since there was nothing to be done about it, and the gardener basically kept his distance—he kept his distance from everyone, not just Milo. Benny Vitali, the newest employee in the family, was his buddy and fellow *enforcer* and was pretty much Milo's shadow. He was also Milo's friend.

Talking with Catena one afternoon, they were comparing notes on their boss and the unusual behaviors they'd noticed lately.

They had both worked for Tony Gravello for about the same number of years and could sense when things were moving in a different direction. Tony Gravello, they agreed, was short tempered, much more so than usual. His normal alertness would fade without warning, and his eyes would grow dull as if his mind was on a journey somewhere else. But the main thing they could not explain was his ability to disappear. He could disappear somewhere in the house without warning only to appear hours later. Clandestine searching would never disclose where he'd been or how he got there.

Since there wasn't much happening around the house and Catena had gone on an errand, he was about to head out for a walk on the beach when he was summoned by phone.

Chapter Nineteen

Entering his boss's office, Milo became acutely aware of the silent hostility that surrounded the big man at his desk. He didn't think it was being directed at him, and for that, he was grateful and breathed easier as he went in.

Anthony Gravello was seething. After summoning his employee, he had gone into his office and settled into an overstuffed chair, his favorite. He had placed it specifically with a view of the ocean spreading out before him allowing the tranquil setting of the turquois water to wash some of his anger away. It usually worked, but this time it was not. He had allowed Baker's actions to get to him, and he wasn't sure exactly what he needed to do about it.

He realized it wasn't the money causing the anger; the amount the man took from him was minimal in comparison to the fortune he had accumulated. Maybe not minimal, he wasn't sure. Since Jason had been keeping the books, any amounts shown were not necessarily accurate—it could be over a million dollars, but Gravello had no way of knowing without spending hours adding up numbers. He didn't need that money in order to carry out his plans to return to Sicily—he had more than enough to live there in style for the rest of his life. He even had enough to give his daughter,

Loki, that same comfort. But Jason's actions and his audacity angered him beyond any anger he'd felt in a long while. He wasn't about to let him get away with it either. That sort of forgiveness was not part of the Gravello family DNA.

"Find him, Milo." It was a direct, uncloaked order.

"From things I've heard, he's probably somewhere on Maui living with that bartending floosy he met down in the Perch lounge. You and Benny fly over there and find him, and when you do, stick to him like tree sap. Where he goes, you go, and note down every place he shows the slightest interest in, and then I want him here in my office. Don't intercept him yet, though, call me first. I may have more instructions depending on where he goes and what he does when he gets there. And, Milo . . .," a lengthy pause followed as his boss swung his chair around to face him directly. Milo watched his boss's eyes bore into him. "I want no excuses, you hear me? None. Unless you and that buddy of yours want to be out in the water trying to keep a cement block tied to your legs floating." It was his favorite threat.

It was the best assignment Milo could have heard. He could finally make use of his talent of finding people. He'd been quite good at doing so back in Sicily for the old Gravello family; this would be a snap. And he had just what he would need—a few pieces of equipment he'd yet had a chance to put to use and had been anxious to see what they could do.

When he initially arrived in the islands, he'd met a fellow countryman who ran a specialty shop on Hotel Street in downtown Honolulu. He'd gone there and bought some listening bugs and a tracking gadget. There was a special app for his phone so he could hear what the bugs were picking up and follow a map showing where the tracking thing indicated it was going. He'd never read the instructions, though—something he'd have to do before chasing after this Jason guy. He'd read all that on the thirty-minute flight over to Kahului.

Upon landing, he and Benny rented a car and found a motel room for the night. They would begin their search early the next morning, but right now, they had research to do, like get road maps and mark the key spots on it they'd have to check out. With no idea where on Maui Jason had moved to, Milo had the feeling this search was going to be a long one. That thought made him a little nervous considering his boss's expectation of a quick resolution.

The only thing the two men had to go by was a company photo of Jason and a news clipping from the *Honolulu Advertiser* of an article published about the Perch when it first opened. It carried a photo of Paul Hender, the new owner, standing next to his waitress, Annie Gaines. It wasn't a lot to go by, but then Milo prided himself of his ability to track down people. He didn't look forward to having to make daily update calls to his boss, though, but he would survive those.

Early next morning, the duo was outside Kahului's main post office, the first planned stop, just as the mail delivery personnel were loading their vans for the day's delivery. It had been Benny who came up with the idea, which surprised Milo. Benny figured that postal delivery personnel knew or knew of almost everyone in a community and Milo had to agree.

With a cock-and-bull story about being hired to find a runaway girl and the pictures of both Jason and Annie, they approached the carriers, one after the other, asking if they knew the two people, explaining the two were recent arrivals on Maui.

On their fifth try, the woman carrier they approached, upon hearing the runaway story and pocketing the two one-hundred-dollar bills she'd been offered and said yes, she knew of the couple and said they recently moved into a cabin on her route. She went on to say she'd briefly talked with them three days ago. She said she liked the wahine very much, but the guy appeared to be very nervous and had quickly disappeared into their cabin.

"The name you just asked me about, though"—the woman hesitated as if having second thoughts on what she was about to say—"that wasn't the name the guy told me. It looked to me like he was holding back, but then he reluctantly said his name was Taylor Gordon. Maybe he's not this Jason person you're looking for. That photo sure looks like the guy I'm talking about though. Maybe he has a twin brother or something. Don't know if this helps or not."

The carrier didn't say anything further but turned and went back into the building. She wasn't about to give them a chance to ask for the money back. Besides, the last thing she needed was to be seen by other carrier's giving out that sort of information. She was a recent hire and was certain her new boss would frown upon that sort of thing, especially about the money part. Single moms had to make their way somehow, hadn't they?

Before Milo could express what he was thinking, Benny voiced his opinion that everyone around this place seemed to have a lot of secrets. Milo nodded in agreement—that was his thought precisely.

He was also thinking of the name switch. As far as he was concerned, it really didn't matter what the name was as long as it was the guy he was told to find and follow and since his boss gave him the photo he had to assume Mr. G. had looked at it and would have said something if this wasn't right. *Things can sure get confusing when crime is involved,* Milo thought to himself.

It was still early morning, so they drove up the Haleakalā Road to the route number the mail carrier had mentioned. A cabin rested at the end of a long red-cinder driveway. It appeared vacant at first glance until they noticed a light coming from one of the windows. Somebody was home or had forgotten to turn it off. They continued up the road a short distance before turning around and parking where they could watch for any activity without being too obvious. With no confirmation that this was where his quarry was, Milo waited before calling his boss. It was still early morning anyway and Mr. G. didn't like phone calls before eight, wanting instead to sit and enjoy some coffee. He also didn't like guesswork. He wanted only the hard facts.

The duo didn't have to wait very long before the man they were hunting, Jason Baker, emerged from the cabin.

They watched as he busied himself attaching a boat to an old Explorer and then watched as the wahine, Annie Gaines, came out carrying a cooler and bag that she lifted over the gunnel of the boat.

Milo made a quick call to his boss and informed him that they had their quarry in sight and would follow them. He would call later and keep him informed of what was happening.

They both sat and watched as Jason and the wahine pulled out of their driveway, boat trailing behind, and headed downhill. Milo followed them to the boat ramp at Kihei, their quarry obviously intent on putting his boat in the water for some ocean time.

Pulling into the parking area, Milo jumped out, leaving Benny sitting wondering what his friend was doing. All Milo appeared to do was walk past the boat, circled it, and came back to the car.

"What was that all about?" Benny could see no reason for Milo having done what he did.

"You'll see, Benny," he had a big grin. "I managed to stick that tracking thing onto the inside of their boat. You and I can sit back here in the shade, have something to eat from that lunch wagon across the road and watch where they go and when they're coming back. All very simple."

But such plans were rarely simple. Jason and Annie didn't return.

When Jason and his girlfriend first took off in their boat, Milo made Benny get out and sit under a tree while Milo went back up to the cabin to look around. Expert that he was, he easily found his way into the cabin. Searching it the best he could, he came away with nothing that would indicate where his boss's missing money had gotten to.

Back at the boat ramp, he sat with Benny watching as the afternoon turned to night. There was still no sign of Jason. They were parked next to Jason's boat trailer, so there was no possibility of missing him, and the tracker's blinking dot on his phone screen still showed the boat was on Molokai.

When Milo initially decided that he had to call his boss to tell him that Jason had managed to slip away in a boat, he'd thought seriously of fabricating a story that would put him and Benny in a better light. But he didn't do that. He had simply relayed the bare honest facts, along with his unavoidable culpability in it all as well.

Milo's uncle, Luca DiSalvo, who had once been a muscle with the Gravello family in Sicily, had advised Milo on the day Milo boarded a flight in Rome bound for Honolulu and a new job with Anthony Gravello. "Do your job, *paison*, and never, never, try to pull wool over that man's eyes. He will know this, mark my words, and you will pay dearly."

Milo had always heeded that advice.

When Gravello answered Milo's call, he didn't sound very concerned. He was obviously anxious about the money and getting hold of Jason, but since the boat trailer was there and Milo had the boat clearly positioned on his tracker, he was more relaxed. It was clear to Milo when he disconnected the call that he and Benny were expected to sit there even if it took all night—which it was, and they did. They talked about Gravello and his riches and jealously laughed.

Milo could understand his boss's desire to get hold of Jason. Stealing money, apparently a lot from what he could deduce, was something that was not easily ignored.

What Milo didn't know, and had he known, he would not have been so lighthearted about it, was that his boss was involved in pulling off the greatest scam in Hawaiian history, and if caught, Milo stood a good chance of being dragged down into it.

In reality, Anthony Gravello's was not the greatest scam Hawaii had witnessed. That honor went to the arrival of the missionaries a century and a half earlier. They came to the islands to do good and, as the saying goes, ended up doing quite well for themselves, walking away owning most of the Hawaiian kingdom.

Milo's shock hit home first thing the next morning. Checking his tracker, he watched in silence as the telltale blinking dot moved slowly toward Oahu. The man he was instructed to not let out of sight under any circumstances would soon be landing somewhere on Oahu and could then quickly disappear.

Thinking of the call to his boss, he had to make sweat broke out even in the cool morning air.

Chapter Twenty

"*W*here . . . is . . . he . . ., Milo?"

Milo nervously swallowed several times before enough saliva returned to his mouth to reply.

"We don't know where he is, Mr. G., but we'll catch up with him again. Don't you worry. When he and his lady friend took off in the boat yesterday, Benny and me had no way to follow him. The bug I planted in his boat showed them on Molokai on the southwest part of that island. We got bugs planted in his car also, Mr. G. We're doing everything we can."

Milo continued to sweat, and it was not from standing in the blazing sunshine. "We waited for him and his lady to return, but they didn't. His boat trailer's still at the Kihei ramp where they left it. Last night, I bugged the phone in his cabin since no one was there and had a look around but didn't find nothing about your money. We were keeping on top of him best we could, Mr. G. He and his old lady must'a stayed the night in Molokai, then took off for Oahu early this morning since my tracker shows his boat heading toward Kaneohe Bay.

"You want me and Benny to come back to Oahu and watch for him? I can get a guy that lives here on Maui, name's Blaise Domingo, to watch the cabin—I don't think he's busy doing nothing right now. He could be at their cabin in five minutes and sort'a keep an eye on things. He's a good man, Mr. G. You can count on him."

"Like I was counting on you?"

Milo swallowed hard; his throat had suddenly become very dry again.

"Sit tight before you mess up something else. Exactly where does your tracker show their boat right now?"

"It looks to be close to the east side of Kaneohe Bay. There's a yacht club there, and I'm thinking it'll be heading there."

The phone went dead. Apparently, Mr. G. was finished talking for now. Milo didn't know if that was a good thing or not, but at least, when he was talking on his phone, he knew his boss wasn't in the neighborhood behind a tree pointing a gun in his direction.

"I think he's going to call us back, Benny."

"Yeah, okay." Benny was always very agreeable. Nothing disturbed the emptiness of space that rested on his shoulders. Milo envied him for that calmness and naivety. Nothing would ever bother Benny sufficiently to raise his heart rate even a beat.

As expected, his phone rang. It had only been a few minutes.

"You and that hang nail lucked out." Gravello's voice had lost some of its edge. "Seems our boy had an accident on Molokai and was rushed to Castle Hospital. The guy at the yacht club said they flew him in by chopper, and someone else was towing his boat to the yacht club."

"Lucky you. You got a reprieve, Milo. Get your butts back to Oahu. Get the name and address of the guy who's dragging the boat back, then call me. Don't go to his place, you got that? Just call and give me the details. Then go to the hospital and check around about how sick our boy is and whatever else you can find out. And Milo . . .," the pause was excruciatingly long, the voice that came back was again threatening, again slow, and very deliberately spoken, "I'm going to tell you this just once. Don't mess up, or you'll both find yourselves dangling on the end of a short anchor rope, family member or not. You got me? Tell your friend Blaise to keep track of who comes and goes at the cabin—and tell him he'd better not screw up, or he'll be on the end of that rope with you."

Suddenly Milo was sorry he'd brought Blaise into this without apprising his friend of what he was getting into first. Milo had spoken with him just a few minutes before. Milo knew Blaise would be quickly hung out to dry if anything went wrong, and he wouldn't even know he had been in the game in the first place.

The phone was dead before Milo could muster a response. Good thing since he had nothing to respond with anyway.

No sooner did Milo's phone call with his boss end than another call came in.

"Eh, Milo, Blaise." Blaise was usually brief with words. "Okay, I'll watch this cabin up here but only for two days. You know how desolate that part on the mountain is? More than two days I'll be comatose from lack of circulation. You know, there's hardly any air up here? Two days, Milo, and I'm gone."

"Two days will be great, Blaise. Both people who live in that cabin are over here on Oahu, so there shouldn't be anyone coming around."

"Am I suddenly in hell or what? No people, no excitement, no air—I don't even own a dog. Maybe I gotta make that two hours 'stead of two days. Two minutes maybe."

"Two days, Blaise, will be perfect, and while you're being bored up there, remember you're getting well paid for your time."

"Yeah, well . . . I'll call you should anything happen. If you don't hear from me, all's well, and I'll be gone."

"Mahalo, Blaise. Tony G. appreciates you doing this for him."

"Tony G.? That's the guy you work for? We talking Anthony Gravello here? Make sure you tell him I'll be watching extra good."

* * *

Tony Gravello took a deep breath, sat back, and closed his eyes. It was exhausting to keep up the *mean guy* persona he had to use with men like Milo. He had no doubt that if he eased off in the least bit, they would walk all over him, and it wasn't in him to allow that to happen. He'd built his local family's reputation as a person to be anxious about to meet his needs. His blood family in Sicily had continually drummed that into his head. Deep inside, he wasn't that man—not even close. Early in life, he was taught the words to say and the necessary actions that needed to accompany those words. It worked for him both here and back home in Palermo when he was growing up—that was all that mattered.

When the stolen money was back in hand and Jason properly punished, he would leave here. Maybe Tuscany instead of Sicily. That would be nice. There, he could lose the tough guy and live the easy life he was always meant to live. He would enjoy good wine and make some close friendships, something he had never allowed, could never allow himself to do.

* * *

Milo and Benny pulled chairs over to a lawn table at Kaneohe Yacht Club and sat down. They had arrived back on Oahu and luckily found where they had parked their van. Even bright red vans could get lost in airport parking lots.

They had driven straight to Castle Hospital hoping to discover something good to relay to the boss. They feigned being close friends of Taylor Gordon's family, feeling good for remembering to use the name that Jason was probably admitted under. They were immediately informed of Taylor's passing.

After hearing that news, they were then told by an obviously overworked nurse that any additional information would have to come from the immediate family. The nurse refused to give, or just didn't know, any local contact information when they asked. Since they had lied about being close to the family, they couldn't very well press the issue too far. They were already being scrutinized by a nurse who appeared to be in charge, standing in the close background.

Milo called his boss and told him the news. The stillness that followed was louder than a bomb dropping. After a lengthy silence, Gravello finally spoke, demanding they find either Jason's girlfriend or the guy who brought the boat in from Molokai.

Milo knew they had no option; they had to find them. The yacht club office was no help to them and wouldn't divulge any information when Milo asked who towed it in. The woman they were talking with at the counter pointed out that they weren't members of the club and really shouldn't even be there, but Milo's smile had turned her head just enough. In a soft voice spoken for Milo's ears only, she said they could hang around and wait for the owner to show up if they wanted to, adding that she'd see to it that the bar, normally available for members only, would be open to them.

She mentioned that someone would show up for the boat before nightfall since it couldn't remain on the bulkhead overnight—it was club's policy. She did say that if no one showed up, the club would move it themselves, at a cost to the owner of course.

Waiting for someone to show an interest in the boat would be very pleasurable since there were chairs and tables in the shade of coconut trees resting close to the edge of the club's swimming pool. Several were empty. Besides, they both agreed; there was always something interesting to watch around swimming pools.

There were two cold Primo beers waiting for them at the bar.

"Complements of the office," noted the bartender as he appraised them both. Primo Beer was like an institution in the islands, brewed locally and easily available. Milo and Benny's waiting time was looking better all the time.

Chapter Twenty-one

$\mathcal{A}$s Stone and Annie drove up to Aloha Airlines baggage area, he saw Loki waiting at the curb. He found a spot six or seven car lengths away. It was a normal congested Sunday at the interisland passenger pickup area as locals and visitors alike traveled to or from one of the other islands.

"Since you've only seen Loki on Facebook," he said to Annie, "there she is." As he pointed, a tall auburn-haired young woman wearing a comfortable orange-red colored muumuu, a *kukui* nut lei casually draped around her neck came walking toward the car. Loki had been watching the faces of people in cars as they slowly passed by looking for a first glimpse of Annie. Meeting a person for the first time but already a dear friend was a thrilling experience. Stone and Annie had already gotten out of the car and were standing, waiting.

When Annie watched Loki walk toward them, dodging the airport foot traffic, Annie realized she could have recognized Loki anywhere from the Facebook picture she had looked at. With her short cut auburn hair, a large smile displaying perfect white teeth, Loki was a standout in any crowd. Her tall, full figure was a plus and would easily cause men to turn their head backward for a second look, and many on the airport walkway did just that.

"This is so exciting," she exclaimed, as she walked up to them. She gave Stone a hug, then quickly turning to embrace Annie. "You look just like the picture on your website." The two women stood holding each other's arms taking in first impressions of a new friend.

On their way to the terminal, Annie had insisted Stone stop at one of the lei-seller stands that lined the entrance roadway where she bought two beautiful plumeria leis. She placed the leis around Loki's neck as they embraced. Annie's somber mood that she experienced after driving away from the hospital leaving Taylor behind had lightened considerably even if just for these moments.

Not to be left out, Stone added his plumeria lei to the growing pile around Loki's neck, giving her cheek a soft kiss. He'd bought a lei at the lei sellers stand as well.

Annie and Loki had met by chance in a blog chat room sponsored by the author of a novel they had both read, *Deep Green*. They had both made similar comments about what they'd read and soon discovered many other similarities between them, not only in the book but also in their personal lives. They'd quickly became internet friends, and emails abounded. It had been a surprise to both to learn they each lived in Hawaii, albeit on different islands, which added appreciably to the fast pace their friendship took.

It had been their intention to meet each other someday, but neither could have foreseen the circumstances surrounding the actual occurrence. Loki had originally thought she would go to Maui and see the cabin Annie spoke of and meet her boyfriend, Taylor. Annie, in turn, was anxious to see Hawi, and the small rural community on the Big Island that Loki raved about.

There had also been a curiosity on Annie's part to discover some answers. She was puzzled about what made her new friend tick—what was making her ask certain questions, seek information that would ordinarily be reserved for established friendships. She had a premonition that Loki was shielding herself from someone or something, and it was her hope she could be of help or at the least gain a clearer understanding.

Early in their friendship, as they went about acquiring knowledge of who each of them was, Loki had made huge assumptions, not too well disguised, that made Annie nervous. She had mentioned Annie's boyfriend several times, but to Annie's recollection, Annie had only briefly mentioned Taylor, simply in passing. Taylor had asked her specifically early in Annie's and Loki's communications not to say anything about him, and she had honored that. Then there was Loki's almost obsessive questioning about her and Taylor's finances. As tempting as it was, she'd decided not to mention the inheritance Taylor received or was going to receive, again at Taylor's insistence.

Now seeing her new friend face to face, Annie was beginning to think she had been making too much mystery out of nothing—being critical where there was no substantial reason to be so. Maybe it was just Loki's way, and Annie had accepted that.

* * *

The drive to Kaneohe over the Likelike Highway went quickly. Loki was talkative with an ongoing stream of questions and comments. Stone remembered that quality of hers from the time he first met her in Hilo at Pops's house. Stone had not been able to spend much time getting to know her as he and Teri had been rushing to get to the airport, so he found it refreshing to hear her chatter and gain some understanding of who she was.

She was part of his extended family, and he owed it to her as well as to the entire family to get to know what he could about her. Stone prided himself on being a good listener and had no doubts about getting to know her well. He looked forward to time spent in doing so.

Loki sat in the middle of the back seat for the entire drive, all the while leaning over the center console virtually becoming the third person in the front seat. Studying her reflection in the rearview mirror, Stone could see both Leilani and Pops in her features as well as some undefined character, all her own, which only enhanced her beauty.

The drive to Kaneohe went quickly, and they soon pulled into the carport in front of Kaikanani. Not surprising, Bert, was sitting on top of the rock wall enclosing three sides of the carport waiting for them; it was her favorite spot out of the sun. As was the cat's habit, she laid down and hung her head low over the open gate with a closed paw stoking the air as Annie and Loki walked through beneath her. Stone picked her up off the wall, placing her on his shoulder for the walk into the house. A gentle breeze and a recognizable fragrance of the ocean wafting in off the bay greeted them.

Stone and Teri lay awake talking late into the night after the girls had gone to bed. The girls' two rooms were also on the lower level of the two-story A-frame toward the front of house, just a few feet away from the sea wall and the soothing sounds of the bay. Normally, sleep came quickly when they weren't playing around and getting each other aroused, but that was not the case tonight—Stone wanted to talk.

"One odd thing I noticed during the drive from the airport," confided Stone, "was the frequency that Loki's conversation drifted into finances when she thought she and Annie had a private conversation going. A lot of their conversation too was about how Annie was going to make out in the future without Taylor there financing the way. It seemed forced, as if digging for some specific information. I have a strong feeling there's some ulterior motive going on there."

"Why are you bringing up these suspicions of her? It sounds like you're trying to be a detective looking for a crime to solve. I'm betting Loki is thinking of asking Annie to go back to the Big Island with her to stay in Hawi for a while and wants to justify it on a financial basis. They seem so compatible. Going to Hawi might be the best thing for Annie. It'd also give us more reasons to visit Hawi ourselves." She moved in tight against Stone. "I hear there's a great restaurant and gift store there called the Bamboo Garden and a very quaint boutique B and B."

"As always, *kuuipo*, you make good reasoning. Must be why I love you." The words spoken as he rolled onto his side, facing her. "Now that we have that dilemma solved, you want to play around a little? It's still early. Or is this closeness I feel coming from you just teasing?" He moved so their arms and legs made contact.

"Exactly what sort of playing around did you have in mind?" her voice melodic as she moved closer yet, consuming any air space left between them.

Chapter Twenty-two

Kaneohe Yacht Club's lawn

*M*ilo and Benny had walked down to the water's edge for a short break. Relaxing was good, but some stretching of their legs was needed. While they looked over the harbor, choosing which boat they would like to own if money was no object, they failed to notice the influx of people to the club's pool area—it was apparently that time of the day. As they walked back to the grassy area looking for a place to sit, they saw an elderly couple, perhaps in their eighties making motions of vacating their chairs skirting the edge of the swimming pool. Milo and Benny moved quickly and were seated and pushing the recline button before the departing couple were ten feet away.

Settling in once again to the waiting game, becoming totally relaxed as they took in the activity of several kids horsing around in the water, movement on the waterfront twenty feet away caught Benny's attention. He poked Milo's arm, directing his friend's awareness. They both watched, bewildered by the activity of a young teenaged girl wearing a yacht club T-shirt, as she untied the line holding *Kalia,* the boat they'd been watching, and began dragging it away—an unexpected move with the potential to cause

Milo a severe case of heartburn if he should have to call his boss again.

They both quickly relinquished their comfort and moved to the waterfront so rapidly one would suspect they'd been suddenly goosed. Their abrupt action drew curious stares from several people half asleep around the pool. Benny's beer fell to the ground as his elbow glanced off the bottle, which was sitting much too close to the table's edge in the first place. Not quite in panic but also not sure what they needed to do about this new circumstance, they came to a halt and stood watching as the girl awkwardly dragged the boat toward an adjacent pier. They guessed the club wasn't expecting the owner to show up, so they were moving it for them as the office woman said they would.

Maneuvering with the one rope attached to the bow of *Kalia*, the young girl walked a short distance out onto a pier at the left side of the harbor and began fastening the rope to one of the cleats. She added a second line to the boat's stern, rechecked both lines and, apparently satisfied they would hold, headed back toward the clubhouse waving cheerfully to a young couple lounging on the grass close by.

"This don't look so good, Benny. It looks like they're making a permanent home for it. This might complicate things if nobody's planning on showing up."

"Why do you think they're doing that, Milo?"

"If I could tell you that, I would own my own villa in Palermo." Milo gave his sidekick a quick frowning glance, not sure Benny picked up on his subtle humor. By the questioning look on Benny's face, the comment totally baffled him. Milo let it go.

They had been assuming that since Jason was no more, someone would come and pull the boat out of the water and take it somewhere that would hopefully then lead them closer to the girl and Mr. G.'s money. It wasn't a well-thought-out plan, but that was all they had. They had still been hoping it would happen in that fashion, but this unexpected new twist was creating a big wrinkle.

Milo's hopes still rested on the same guy that towed it from Molokai showing up to haul it out. At least that would give them a lead to follow. So far, though, they'd had little success finding out who that person was. They were at a standstill. Milo figured he should call Mr. G., but he really didn't want to. Besides, what would he say to his boss? *Guess what, someone moved the boat?* He put off the call until he thought up something else.

They walked out on the pier, and as they were standing looking at the boat, puzzling over their next move, a heavily built elderly man, in tank top and bathing suit, came out of a cabin on the enormous yacht tied to the adjacent pier. He clutched a beer can in his beefy hand as he crossed the deck and leaned over on the railing next to them, almost in their face. The odor of beer followed him like a cloud of smoke.

The tank top and tufts of gray hair found daylight around the armpits. The neckline looked clean. An attempt had been made to tuck it into his bathing trunks, but his enormous belly wasn't allowing that. The shirt claimed the man to be a supporter of breast cancer. It was somewhat at odds, though, with the baseball cap he had on that proclaimed to be Built *Ford* Tough. He had the hat Trump-style, hanging low over his eyes.

"How-z-it going?" he said in a localized cheerful voice. "Nice Whaler you got there. Wouldn't mind a ride in it someday. You fellas going to be my new neighbors?" A loud belch followed his words. He brought his closed fist up to cover it. A polite gesture but far too late as the stale odor of beer drifted their way. Both Milo and Benny enjoyed beer, but the secondhand whiff was never a pleasant one. They backed away a step.

Before Milo could respond, the man tilted the can, swallowed whatever was left, then proceeded to squash it with the apparent ease of a TV wrestler. His strength was a paradox to his general appearance. The man made his way back below deck, returning quickly holding three beer cans dripping with pieces of ice.

Without words, he handed one over the railing to Milo and another to Benny, then turned and began walking back toward the stern. Talking over his shoulder as he went, he indicated with his free hand that they should follow. "Come aboard and let me show you around my yacht. My name's Chuck, by the way. Is your friend coming back to join us?"

Milo didn't want to go aboard and end up wasting time even if the beer in his hand was encouraging him to do so, but with that out-of-the-blue question thrown at him, he couldn't help but climb aboard, Benny was right behind him. "What friend are you asking about?" His curiosity had been piqued, and he wasted no time asking.

"That fella who towed your boat into the harbor this morning. I see him around a lot and keep planning on meeting him." Pointing at a sleek and quite impressive-looking powerboat on the pier across the narrow harbor, he stated, "That's his yacht over there, right?" It wasn't a question but more a statement. "The guy always waves when I see him. Seems nice enough. Got him a real looker for a wife. What's his name by the way and how long you known him?"

Avoiding the question Milo instead asked his own, "What did you say your name was?" Milo could feel the imagined pressure from his boss easing off a bit with this new channel of information.

"As I said before, the name's Chuck. Chuck Norris, but not that famous one." He gave a short laugh while patting an overly sized stomach not very well concealed by the tank top. It was probably what he said and did every time he gave his name to emphasize that there was only one difference between him and his famous namesake. "What'd you fella's say your names were?"

"I'm George," lied Milo, "and my quiet friend here is Charlie."

Milo hoped Benny wouldn't say anything and question why Milo had given those names. Sure enough, he could tell Benny was about to say something but luckily at the last second noticed the look on Milo's face, a look Benny knew that preceded comment, so he remained quiet. Milo didn't think it was a good idea spreading their real names around—he'd have to remind Benny of that, again. The less anyone knew, the better off everyone was.

"So, Chuck, do you happen to know where the owner of that boat lives and what his name is?" He pointed at Stone's yacht across the harbor.

Chuck turned to look at him with an odd questioning expression. Milo thought maybe he didn't hear and was about to repeat the question when he realized his mistake. Apparently, Chuck was sober enough to catch it as well. *How could he not know the person who towed what Chuck assumed to be Milo's boat into the harbor?*

Milo did a quick tap dance and covered his words as best he could. "A friend made all the arrangements, so I never got to personally meet him. I'd like to go by his house and thank him, maybe pay for the fuel he used."

Chuck's features softened into his former smile as he pointed across the bay. "I know his house is right over there by that pier that's falling apart. Don't know for sure which of those three houses is his, but I've seen his yacht anchored there a couple times. I do know he drives a Ford Explorer, a red one I believe, if that helps. Don't know his name, like I told you earlier. The office girl will know. Offering to pay for the gas is a good thing."

With the slip number of Stone's boat and a cover-up lie ready to tell, Milo made a quick stop in the club's office. That was all it took, and he had the information he wanted. That cover-up lie and maybe the fact that the woman behind the counter in the office seemed to cozy up to him helped her to open up and answer Milo's question. He and Benny walked back toward their van with Kensington Stone's name and address in hand. Now they had something to report to Mr. G.

Chapter Twenty-three

*M*ilo knew from previous encounters that before confronting his boss in person, he had better use the phone to alert him about what they had discovered; for some reason, it went across much better over the phone. Later, he'd see him and report everything in person. He had found from experience that a little forewarning went a long way in making his own life flow a lot easier and made his boss's life much less volatile. Something about face-to-face surprises that invariably gave way to his boss's temperature increasing.

All that knowledge was well and good, but he still didn't relish the thought of making the call. *Any* conversation he had with his boss involving information departing from Mr. G.'s expectations caused a chill to run down Milo's spine. He would often disconnect from a call never being certain he had done the right thing or had simply dug a future grave a little deeper.

He finally bolstered his nerves and made the call.

"The guy's name is Kensington Stone, and he lives right here in Kaneohe," he explained, hoping the news would be received as a positive step forward. He was pleasantly surprised at the reaction and thought the boss was in a good mood since he was speaking softly. That was very encouraging.

It didn't last. "I have his address, Mr. G., and I can see his house from right where I'm standing." Milo went on to explain his chance meeting with Chuck Norris and how the information had been freely offered. He didn't mention his chance meeting with the club's office clerk, an encounter that was still causing him a sense of expectation.

"Stay put, both of you, and stay away from that Norris character. Sounds like the typical *niele* sort—nosy, always sticking his meat in somebody else's oven." The analogy his boss used gave Milo a mild jolt—the office woman again.

Mr. G.'s soft-spoken voice had apparently been put back on a shelf. It was back to the tone Milo had first anticipated—unpleasant, demanding, and very much condescending. "You've screwed up enough letting Jason slip past you. You and that scab that slinks around with you better keep a watch behind you." Milo wasn't sure what that meant, and he didn't want to ask for clarification. It was a different kind of veiled threat than most Milo had experienced. The boss continued, interrupting Milo's drifting nervousness, "I'll let you know if and when things change. Don't get far away from your phone. I'll call when I need you to go into action." With that, Mr. G. was gone.

As Milo pocketed his phone, he couldn't help but wonder about the ongoing antagonism his boss showed toward Benny. He finally figured that Benny must look like or act like someone Gravello had once known. He wasn't going to worry about that right then.

* * *

As Tony Gravello disconnected from Milo's call, he sat back and wondered, as he often did lately, about the reasons for acting as he did and why he couldn't just show his true self to those who worked for him. Why did he have to be a hard-ass all the time? Unfortunately, he knew he had to. It was the card he'd drawn from the deck of life; it was the way he was taught. He appreciated that Milo would call and appraise him of things. Of course, if he didn't, Milo would quickly learn what hell on earth was all about. The overriding issue at this time was that he be kept up to date regarding everything surrounding the late Jason Baker if he ever expected to see his money again.

Tony Gravello liked Milo. Milo was Sicilian and was his blood family, the only son of his first cousin's oldest daughter. Hopefully, Milo was smart enough to see the *whys* of his boss's actions—*after all, it's a cultural thing, isn't it? I've been away from Sicily too long,* he again thought with regret.

He put the phone down and moved to his favorite, overstuffed old brown leather chair facing the window that gave him an unobstructed view across his infinity swimming pool to the ocean beyond. There was little he could do right now about softening his stance with his men; the metal shape was cut. He had no choice but to continually show his hard side if he was to retain control of his small tribe. *At least until I can leave with all the money and return home. I may even take all those buffoons with me.* That surprising thought made him smile.

He took a deep breath to relax, needing to refocus his thoughts. It was time to do what he must do. He reached and retrieved one of the throwaway cell phones he kept on a lower shelf of the side table. He kept several within reach; he was never sure who might be tracking his phone calls, even to family.

He made his call.

It rang several times before a woman's voice finally answered and said, "Aloha." Tony could feel the hesitation coming from her. It was palpable even though she should have been expecting his call.

* * *

Annie and Loki were enjoying some quiet time together sitting on the seawall at Stone's house sipping a glass of chardonnay. A small plate of *shoyu poke* rested between them; two pairs of chopsticks balanced on the side of the dish. It was a picture-perfect afternoon as the water in the bay showed hardly a ripple, and the warm breeze blowing off its surface caressed them like soft silk against their skin. The wine was just right for the midafternoon, creating a lightheaded, mellow mood. They were relaxed and gently probing each other's past as they continued building their unfolding friendship.

For Annie, having Loki there was helping her relieve an extreme emptiness she was currently experiencing at the loss of Taylor. She was about to retrieve the bottle for a refill when Loki's phone rang. Loki hastily excused herself and walked quickly to the back of the yard among the banana trees next to the carport before answering. It wasn't a familiar phone number, but she was sure she knew who it was. She'd been expecting the call but, at the same time, hoping it wouldn't arrive.

"I was going to call you soon and report in," she said into the phone when she heard the familiar voice. "I just got to Stone's and Teri's home in Kaneohe a couple hours ago and haven't had a chance to find out anything. I'm going to need a day or two to get the information without raising her suspicions. Should I call you back at this number when I have something to report?"

It was a reply that didn't sit too well with the person on the other end of the line. Her posture stiffened and her facial features hardened as she responded to what he said next. "Let's face it, Father. You've gone this long without it. In fact, you weren't even sure it was missing until recently, so I'm sure you can wait another few days. In fact, I'd be willing to bet you're still not even sure of the exact amount involved." Loki wasn't the sort to allow anyone to gain an upper hand—the independent way she was raised had succeeded in producing a survivalist. Tony Gravello knew that of his daughter all too well; it was how he had raised her, but at times such as now, he wished he'd done differently.

There was a muffled response Loki didn't quite hear, but her father was already gone before she could ask him to repeat it.

She walked back to the seawall where Annie sat waiting and sat down again. She noticed her glass had been refilled while she'd been on the phone. That was a good thing; she certainly needed more. Hopefully, a little intoxication would help them both relax a bit more and enable Annie to talk more freely. Loki wasn't sure what Annie would do when she discovered what her new friend was being coerced into finding out from her. *A bridge yet to be crossed, but hopefully much farther down the road.*

Ruminating about her new friend while she had been off talking on the phone, Annie was aware that something felt forced in Loki's friendship. It didn't feel like they had connected all too well. There were still the odd questions about finances and money issues that didn't jive with Annie's perception of where they were in this friendship. At this point of time, she rationalized; she was willing to chalk that up to the unsettling series of events that had suddenly brought them face to face. Annie knew that her own outlook on how she felt was being filtered by all the emotions that had bubbled up and covered the surface of her thoughts, so nothing, she reasoned, would appear in its true light. Her world had become abruptly different from what it had been when she and Loki first begun their friendship on Facebook. She knew that and wanted to make the necessary adjustments.

Loki was quiet after the phone call, sitting back down beside Annie on the seawall, sipping her wine. She had nothing to say right then; the phone call was still burning her attention. The more she and Annie had talked, the closer they had become. It was a natural flow of a beginning friendship. Sadly, Loki realized she was beginning to really value Annie as a friend, something she'd had much too little of in her life, and she wasn't feeling good about the role of Judas she was having to play to satisfy her father but could see no way out. The unfortunate thing about it all was she had absolutely no one she could talk with to find any clarity *other* than Annie—the very person she was being asked to deceive.

After a lengthy silence and soul-searching, Loki decided it was time, she had to tell it all.

Chapter Twenty-four

Looking toward the front yard and the bay, Stone could see the girls sitting together by the seawall deeply involved in a conversation. The look on each face was very serious, intense. There was none of the happy laughter that two friends would normally share but more like two opposing poles of a magnet.

He decided he'd best let them work through whatever it was that was going on between them. To facilitate things and give them absolute privacy, he made up an excuse that he and Teri were leaving for a short time and promised dinner would come home with them when they returned. It was important the girls have more time alone to talk and get to know a little more about each other and hopefully resolve whatever it was that was so important right then. He was certain that Annie had a laundry list of matters she could use help with, and maybe that was what they were discussing. Since Taylor was no longer in her life, the next best thing for her well-being would be to have a dear friend she could rely on.

As he and Teri drove away, heading toward Honolulu, he fully expected Teri to object to leaving the girls alone this soon after they arrived, but she didn't.

They drove a distance up the Pali Highway, through the tunnels to the leeward side, the Honolulu side of the Koolau's, and pulled into a wide spot off the highway not far beyond the tunnel opening. It was a cleared and cindered area designed just for that purpose. It was also an area frequented by sightseeing tour buses in their quest to provide the tourist passengers with a good view of the Upside-Down Falls. It was an unusual sight to watch a waterfall pour through an open area in the Koolau Mountain only to have it fall halfway down the cliff and disappear into a bloom of mist. Nuuanu Valley and downtown Honolulu were majestically spread out in front of them.

Since the airport run that brought Loki and Annie to his house, Stone hadn't had a private moment to talk with Teri, and he really needed this time away from the girls' possible interruptions. He was experiencing thoughts and judgments about Loki he couldn't figure out, but he knew Teri's strength of intuition could help sort everything into neat bundles. He trusted Teri's perspective and suspected she had already picked up on similar vibes.

"It's her questions and the intent with which she asks them," he explained, speaking of Loki. "Wouldn't two women coming face to face for the first time be more inquisitive about what makes the other tick and what likes and dislikes they have versus how much money one of them has and how bills were going to get paid? If I didn't know better, listening to the two of them talking in the car on the way home, it appeared like Loki was playing detective hunting for specific responses instead of getting to know a friend. Did you pick up on any of that?"

"We have very little knowledge to go by, honey," Teri laid her hand on Stone's arm in a connective way. "Loki came into our family with little warning from, in her words, a very disciplined upbringing. We really don't know much about her yet nor does Pops. Even Leilani, her mother, doesn't know all that much about her daughter's life. They're just getting to know her themselves. I talked with Pops a few days ago before I knew Loki would be coming over, and he said as much. Apparently, Leilani wasn't involved with her daughter's life at all before Pops came into the picture.

"Annie, on the other hand, is a complete unknown to all of us. I've spent all of an hour with her whereas you and your buddy Lloyd, although having been in her company for half a day, the circumstances from what you've told me couldn't have afforded much chance to learn anything about her either other than how physically fit she was for hiking. So we have two young women that we know relatively little about, attempting to forage a friendship in our front yard, and they're running across speed bumps, and you and I just have to sit on the sideline and wait for the outcome."

"You're forgetting, *kuuipo*. I know you. Even if you've only known Annie for an hour, you've formed an image of who she is and what makes her motor run. The same applies to Loki only more so since you've talked with Pops and Leilani and spent hours talking with Pops's daughter, Viane. Loki had to have been a part of a lot of conversations since she first showed up. I know you, and I also know how women gossip about things."

"Oh, you do, do you?"

Stone didn't like the look or the response he'd received. He knew all too well how easily he could stick his foot into his open mouth with little effort and when least expected. This was looking like one of those times although he was darned if he knew why.

Quickly backtracking, he added, "Hey, before you jump too high and come down all over me, I'm just trying to honor women's superior ability to arrive at conclusions and form opinions of those they meet. Men are a little slower at that sort of comprehension. We take our time."

"Oh, is that a fact?"

Apparently, that second generalization didn't do anything to improve his position.

"I'm happy to learn that bit of wisdom. And nice attempt at buttering me up, buddy, but I'll take it." Her words were stiff, but Stone could see the telltale crack breaking through her feigned injury to women in general as her lips creased toward a faint smile.

And here he had thought he was giving women a compliment—*one just never knew.*

He often entertained the notion that she did these quick bites for no other reason than to keep him off balance. He'd decided a long time ago that if that's what it took, he was fully in the game and loved it.

"Actually, you're partially right," she acquiesced a step or two in accepting his generalized appraisal. "I did notice there was something forced in her openness with Annie, which disappeared when I briefly talked with her. She appears uncomfortable, like she'd rather be anywhere else but there, which is really a surprise since she and Annie became computer friends so rapidly. From what Pops has said, she doesn't have much going for herself at her home in Hawi and is still being influenced quite profoundly by her adopted father here in Oahu.

"Annie also appears somewhat stiff and unable to relax, but in her case, that's somewhat understandable what with Taylor's sudden death and all."

"Are you ready to head back?" he asked, already turning the key before hearing her reply. "Let's stop at L&L Drive-Inn in Kaneohe for some bentos for dinner, then go home, and spend time with our two guests and see where they arrived in their friendship quest.

"Sounds like a good plan, *kuuipo.* Our best shot is to simply be supportive of both girls and give them a clear path for arriving at their own accord. There is a lot of planning that Annie needs to make, and we can all be a big help to her in prioritizing it all. What each girl has going independently will smooth out in time as they get more comfortable with each other. What do you think?"

"You're such a smart man," teased Teri. "Must be why I married you."

"Must be," he agreed and gave her a cheesy smile. "Do you remember the awkward time you and I had when we first came face to face?" Stone was willing to go there in order to change the subject.

"It was only awkward because you couldn't get your eyes off my chest." She gave him a playful punch on his arm to accentuate her words.

"Oh?" he responded, dodging her feeble yet quite accurate reply. "And I remember you eyeing me like I was a Hawaiian shave ice on a hot day."

"Ah, *li hing mui* syrup all over the ice with vanilla ice cream at the bottom. What more could one ask for?"

They were good memories, and both were smiling as Stone pulled into the first turnaround and headed back through the tunnels toward Kailua.

"Let's not forget to get poi when we're at L&L," she reminded him. It was Stone's *must have*, and Teri was also beginning to find its enjoyment.

Chapter Twenty-five

$\mathcal{I}$t was later than they thought it would be by the time they pulled into their carport. The lineup at L&L waiting for food orders had been much longer than anticipated. It was a popular dine-in or take-out diner and getting more so each day. The sun was close to setting, and the gentle offshore breeze was still working its magic at sweeping away the day's blistering heat as they walked through the gate. The air would soon change to onshore and bring with it the night's coolness in time for sleep. They were greeted by an expected meow from up on top of the rock wall.

They noticed the girls had gravitated to lawn chairs set up on the small beach. Their bare feet buried under the cooling sand and being washed by the small, almost nonexistent ripples.

In unison, both girls looked back over their shoulders when they heard the gate close.

There was a look on their faces that confronted Stone and Teri, which conveyed their discussion of deep importance had yet to be exhausted. Both smiles at seeing their hosts were clearly forced. Whether that subject had been along the lines of what Stone and Teri had been discussing, neither were able to determine, but whatever they had been talking about certainly appeared disquieting and obviously unsettled.

"Are you ladies okay with Hawaiian food tonight?" Teri asked as she walked toward the beach and the girls. She wanted desperately to intervene as a mediator and help them overcome whatever their difficulty was, but she was not invited to do so. "Stone decided that's what he'd like tonight, and I willingly went along." She gave them a *shaka* sign and a grin to convey camaraderie as well as to let them know she was pleased with their decision. She loved Hawaiian food right along with Stone and hoped the girls did as well.

"The menu," she continued hoping to gain interest as well as encourage some change in the girls' energy, "includes kalua pig, *lomi* salmon, squid luau, *lau lau*, and poi." She was checking faces for reactions to the food choice for the night. If either of them objected, Teri was ready with a *hauoli* substitute, like mac and cheese, but both girls simultaneously expressed delight, albeit moderated by their current stress levels, at the chosen meal.

"I'll skip the poi," proclaimed Annie. "It's not my favorite food."

Teri began to laugh as she turned and headed toward the house. "Stone will be happy, Annie," still laughing over her shoulder. "He was hoping one of you would turn it down."

"There's some serious discussion still going on back by the water, and I'm more than a little concerned, honey," Teri quietly confided as they moved into the house. "The tension between them is so thick you couldn't cut through it with a sharp knife."

"Just what we were talking about this afternoon, I'll bet. There's something major and apparently not easily solvable going on between those two. They'll need to work that out themselves if they choose not to bring you or me into their discussion. For both their sakes, I hope they can find the way to work past it."

* * *

Annie had sensed the change in her new friend that began right after Loki received that phone call. She was formulating questions to begin asking, seeking the cause of the sudden change in attitude just as Teri walked up behind them and announced the evening meal.

The girls sat in silence for a few minutes after Teri walked back to the house. The interruption disrupted Annie's line of thought, and she was unsure again of what to say or how to proceed. Just before Teri's disruption, Loki had admitted that she was caught in a very tight spot—a spot she claimed could quickly end any chance of their becoming friends. She had been on the verge of explaining. Now they were facing the difficult task of getting back into the subject.

"So who was the phone call from?" Annie decided to press the issue full-on. "You were about to explain the immovable rock you were up against. By your brief words, I get the impression that I'm somehow the wall the proverbial rock is leaning against, and I don't even know what it is I'm supposed to be involved in. Keep talking, girlfriend. Dinner can wait."

"It's a very long and involved story, Annie. One that I wish I could wave a magic stick over and make go away." She went quiet after that. Annie decided to say nothing and simply wait. The silence was excruciating. Loki would need to say something, or their evening and their friendship would quickly drizzle to its end in silence.

Just as Annie was about to get up and head for the house, Loki finally shifted in the beach chair, turned toward her, and leaned closer, conspirator-style.

"My biological mother gave me up for adoption right after I was born. A Sicilian man and his wife became the only father and mother I knew. Life with them was not a dream as both were strict disciplinarians. Father is rich, and I had everything I ever wanted. Every girl's dream, right? I spent my days going to school at Punahou and coming home to a huge house on Black Point Road. I had the best of everything—a life of luxury as far as material things were concerned, but life remained difficult and not at all enjoyable. Friends were generally not allowed over, and boyfriends were nonexistent. My father and mother loved me, though. I know this. Mother was much better at showing it than Father, who held tight to his old Sicilian ways. I couldn't have known that that life of luxury came with strings attached.

"They began having problems that eventually ended in their divorce. I had just turned eighteen.

"About that same time, a woman came to the door claiming to be my biological mother. She was a sweet *hapa-Hawaiian* woman, and I loved her immediately. I had been told I was adopted when I was very young, so this was like a dream come true to finally meet her. She explained to me and to both my father and mother that my biological father had come back into her life, and even though I was already eighteen, she wanted me back as part of her new, reunited family. She told me what the past eighteen years had been like for her and what she'd had to go through since giving birth to me.

"Since my adopted mother and father were splitting up, that left me at home with a father who was ill-equipped to have an eighteen-year-old around the house. He readily agreed I should go with my real mom. My biological father lived on the Big Island. As a parting gift, my adopted father set me up in a house in Hawi, all paid for, along with a car and a small lifetime trust fund. So off I went to live on the Big Island, where I currently live."

Annie sat absorbed in the story. She was seeing what she hoped was the real Loki for the first time since they met at the airport and recognized what she thought was a genuine caring in her eyes. Loki's story explained a few things, but Annie knew there must be much more to prompt the phone call, and the abrupt attitude change and the odd questions she'd been asking. She sat and waited for more.

"My father is a good man, and I love him dearly, although I admit he can often be extremely harsh and demanding.

"Now for the difficult part of my story, Annie, and I won't blame you if you ask Stone to throw me out."

Annie was startled by that pronouncement, praying Teri wouldn't come out right then and call them in for dinner. This was a conversation that needed to be fully aired. She didn't know what to do or say in response other than to sit in silence and wait.

Apparently, Loki didn't expect or need anything to prompt her to continue. She'd gone this far and needed to finish her story.

"Okay, here's the situation, Annie. Please don't respond until I have finished. Otherwise, I won't have the guts to continue. Our meeting on Facebook was not by accident."

Annie's eyes immediately opened wide in astonishment. She was about to say something, but Loki held up both hands and gently shook her head to stop her, then continued.

"My adopted father's name is Anthony Gravello. He had told me to find a way to befriend you. That book review club we were a part of became the perfect venue. Your boyfriend, Taylor, his real name is Jason Baker by the way, embezzled a lot of money from my father, so my father demanded that I become your friend. I am to report on where his money went to. Jason, your Taylor, worked for my father's firm for a few years and was siphoning cash. My father suspects Jason told you where it is or where he hid it."

"Wait a *minute!*" exclaimed a shocked Annie, trying to recover from the bomb blast. "Your father is *the* Anthony Gravello, who owns the company Taylor worked at? And you're telling me that Taylor wasn't Taylor at all, but someone else called Jason Baker?"

"Yes. Please, Annie, let me finish while I have the guts to go on.

"My father wants his money returned. He had some men watching your boyfriend in order to discover where the money went. When your Taylor died, that left me and our beginning friendship as my father's only link."

The shock persisted but, by now Annie was boiling. If she'd had any tendencies toward violence, she would have grabbed a piece of coral off the beach and threw it at anything that was moving or do something even more dramatic. But violence wasn't a part of her, so she just sat there stunned and angry, silent, hoping the steam boiling in her brain would go away and allow her thoughts to clear. She had no clue what to do now and was about to get up and walk off when Loki placed a restraining hand on her arm.

"Annie, please stay. I need to ask for a very big and difficult favor. Can you possibly forgive me? I've never had a really good friend, and from just our few short hours talking, I see in you someone I want as that friend. Father asked me to do something that I didn't want to do in the first place, but his requests are hard to refuse, and I owe him so very much that I convinced myself there was no real harm in helping him—that was before I got to know you."

Right then, Teri called them from the second-floor lanai railing. It was time to come in and eat.

Everything to be said was said. Now it was time to let the incriminating dust settle and find out where their friendship was going to go.

Teri reminded them that Hawaiian food was not very appetizing when it got cold, so without further words, they both walked indoors.

Chapter Twenty-six

*D*inner was unusually subdued, bordering on silent. The girls sat at the dining table staring at the plates in front of them, stabbing at their salad and pushing the kalua pig around with their fork but eating very little. The food was perfect as far as Teri and Stone were concerned, but the girls showed no interest in eating. They were both apparently rehashing what they had talked about through the filters in their minds. It was obvious to both Teri and Stone, judging by the girls' unresponsive behavior, that something dramatic had occurred while they had sat talking by the water.

The mood at the table was affecting Stone, and after several minutes of it, decided he wasn't going to allow whatever had taken place to dampen his or Teri's evening and spoil what was to have been a fun evening getting to know one another.

Looking from one to the other, he finally said, "Something's going on between you two that's dulling the atmosphere of my house, and I won't accept it. Teri and I are both willing to listen and help mediate whatever's troubling both of you, but we need to know what it is if we're to help.

"When we left, you were both smiling, happy and seemed to be having an enjoyable time getting to know each other. We get back home an hour later, and you're both acting like someone purposefully threw a handful of sand in your faces. I think we deserve to know what's going on." Taking in the apathetic expressions he saw on both faces, he forced a grin in hopes of softening their mood and encouraging one of them to open up. "Who wants to volunteer to go first?" It didn't work, and neither spoke but continued to stare at the table.

Abruptly sliding her chair back from the table and standing up, a sad look crowding the features of her face, Annie declared, "I think you need to talk to Ms. Judas here. I'm going to gather my stuff and head back to Maui. I'll call Ballard Family Mortuary in Kahului and make arrangements for Taylor, if that's even his name." She glanced at Loki with an expressionless face for a brief second before stepping away from the table. "I'll call for a taxi if one of you will let me know when it gets here."

It was the furthest thing away from what either Stone or Teri had anticipated. He looked quickly at Teri, expecting or perhaps hoping she had something appropriate to say—he had nothing and apparently neither did Teri. They sat stunned.

Annie walked down the stairs to the bedroom and began pulling together the few things she'd brought. She didn't feel good about what she was doing but knew she had no other choice but to get out of there, get home to her cabin where she'd feel somewhat safer, and then figure out what needed to happen next. Stone and Teri had been more than kind, bending over backward to be helpful. She had held a hope they would all eventually become dear friends, but with Loki being a part of their family, Annie knew that wasn't going to be possible now.

* * *

The name bombshell hung in the air around the dining room table like a foul odor after Annie left. The three left in the dining room sat in silence until Teri finally spoke.

"Loki, I think we deserve a response from you. Those were angry words spoken and accusations made against Taylor and against you. Care to shed some light for us?"

Clearing her throat, looking at her hands resting in her lap, Loki said, "You're right. I'm very sorry. I guess it's now up to me to explain the deception I am a big part of. I sincerely hope I can change the direction things have suddenly started to move in. If you're to fully understand what took place, then it means telling you the long version, so I'll start at the beginning."

Stone and Teri unconsciously slid their chairs a little closer in an unconscious display of support as if teaming up against some unknown challenge that was about to slam into them all.

For ten minutes Loki repeated the story she'd told Annie, leaving out some of the details that weren't important for Teri or Stone to hear right then.

With a sigh, perhaps of relief having opened her whole story to the two people she respected most, she finished by saying, "I like Annie and really want to be her friend. You both walked through the gate a little while ago right after I had explained that story to her. I'm not exactly sure what she thinks of me, but by her words, I can certainly guess, and I really don't blame her for whatever her impression of me is. Looks like I have pretty much pulled the rug out from under the relationship she shared with Taylor. I have to add," she continued, "that the name thing only came up when my father couldn't find his former employee because the name Taylor Gordon kept showing up along with Jason's."

Stone and Teri had sat as still as a quiet morning listening to Loki tell her story. She was softly crying as she finished. It was with difficulty that she was able to finish the story at all.

Before either could say anything, Loki spoke up again in an imploring voice, "I feel shamed by all this. I like Annie, and since coming back into my mom's life, I have fallen in love with my new family, your family," she gestured to include Teri and Stone. "I cherish Pops and his renewed relationship with my mom. Having stepbrothers and a stepsister is incredible, something I never thought would happen to me. And having both of you as part of that family is incredible. I want to remain being a part of all that more than anything I can think of, but now I'm not sure that can still happen. My maneuvering and reasoning for getting close to

Annie, even at my adopted father's insistence may be too much for all to accept."

Momentarily overwhelmed by events, Stone mumbled something about understanding and the complexities as Loki slid her chair back and quickly headed downstairs in the direction Annie had gone, her audience left staring at one another, sitting at the dining room table, not sure where things would go from there.

Stone cleared his throat to say something, but nothing came out.

Chapter Twenty-seven

*I*nstead of packing the few things she had, along with the small bundle of Taylor's things that the hospital had given her—shoes and a few pieces of clothing—Annie, succumbing to tears, let herself fall on top of the pile in the middle of the bed and simply laid there. She was depressed as well as angry—angry at Loki for pretending to be someone she wasn't, and angry at Taylor, or whoever he was, for coming into her life and having her fall in love while lying the whole time and then dying before he could explain himself. Mostly, though, she was angry at herself for being so damn gullible and so trusting in letting people get into her heart so completely. She vowed it would not happen again.

She didn't really want to go back to Maui and the cabin. Not now, maybe not ever. The memories there were too strong and too recent, and all she had here on Oahu was her old life at the Perch. She had few friendships.

Before Taylor entered the picture, she'd spent most of her waking hours either working in the Lounge or swimming and working out at the health center in the basement of the office building—a very singular, directed life. She knew she had to stay close and make sure Taylor's burial was taken care of. She owed him that much and more, regardless of the name he went by. She wished, though, that she could simply walk away, disappear, move to Kauai, and let someone else deal with his body and the money he had hidden somewhere, if all that was true, but that wasn't who she was. She was certain Stone would handle the details if she asked him to, but she wasn't going to do that. She would never feel good about herself if she allowed someone else to assume her obligations.

She remained lying on the bed, mulling over thoughts of where her life would head from here. Her anger was dissipating, her tears drying. Now she simply felt sorry for herself, but she would get over that as well.

She realized she was questioning everything that had to do with Taylor. All the happiness they shared in their wonderful cabin, their new boat, and the talk about a life together they would share into the future—if what Loki said was true, then it had all been a fabricated illusion. He was neither her Taylor nor Jason of Loki's father. And now he was gone, and no further explanation would be forthcoming and who cared! She was moving past caring very quickly.

A soft knocking on her door brought her back into the present.

"Can I come in?" the voice asking the question was unexpected.

"What do you want, Loki?" her response was abrupt and unwelcoming. She was already overwhelmed and wasn't sure she ever wanted to see Loki again much less talk to her.

Loki came in anyway and sat on the foot of the bed at the opposite end from where Annie was stretched out, arms still wrapped around a few pieces of clothing.

"I hadn't really thought much about the impact of what my father was asking of me until you and I sat talking by the water a little while ago, and it all hit home, and I feel ashamed by my actions. I don't know what the result will be, but I'm going to call him shortly and tell him I can't do this any longer. I can't betray the friendship you and I have started."

"What will he say if you tell him that?" Loki's words had piqued Annie's natural curiosity.

"I don't know. I've never gone against his wishes to know what he'll do or how he'll react. His anger with other people going against him is unfathomable. I've witnessed it. Inside, though, he's a gentle, almost sweet, person who wants to be liked. He just has no clue how to go about opening himself up to receive any of that. Ingrained reactions to people, I assume, left over from an old-country upbringing."

Annie's nose was still running from all the recent crying. She pulled a bright-red-flowered hanky from somewhere under the pile and wiped the moisture away. She tucked it loosely into her jeans pocket before asking a question she really needed an answer to.

"You mentioned being my friend just now. Did you really mean that?" She had enjoyed getting to know Loki and had begun to think of her as a friend long before all this was put on the table. Most of her tears having to do with Loki had been because she suddenly realized that all the friendliness she'd felt may just have been a pretense in order to gain information, having no deeper meaning than that.

"Living on Black Point and all the money and prestige that goes with that, I had a lot of classmates I thought of as friends but discovered they were there only for the luxurious swim parties my father occasionally allowed and the distinction of knowing someone who lived on Black Point. Since moving to Hawi, not one of those pseudo friends has tried to call me, and only a few ever returned my calls.

"I'm going to tell him that you don't have any idea where all that money is, so he needs to take me off the hook and do his own thing and let you and I make a restart on our friendship. He still wants the money, Annie, and knows your Taylor took it. I'm afraid he is going to deploy other methods of finding it. I have no way of mitigating any of that."

"I don't have any idea where Taylor put it, Loki. If I knew, I'd give it all back to your father since it was really his to begin with, but I don't."

"Mahalo, Annie. That's exactly what I'll tell him."

"And about our friendship, I really want to be your friend. If you must move out of your cabin, I'd love it if you come to Hawi and stay at my place until you know what you want to do.

"Annie, I'm going to step out on the back lanai and call my father right now. Be right back. Wish me good luck."

Annie could hear Loki talking but couldn't make out any of the words. By the look on her face through the sliding glass doors, it was a heated and unpleasant discussion, and there were tears softly falling on her cheeks when the call ended, and she came back in.

"Are you all right?"

"I'm okay, mahalo for asking. At first, he didn't buy what I told him, but then he softened and said I did a good job and not to worry anymore about it, which came as a big surprise all in its own. I wish I could tell you what he might do.

"About coming to Hawi to stay until you sort out things, my offer stands, and I hope you will. I'd love to show you around my small town. There's a good restaurant called the Bamboo Garden close by my house that has a great art gallery and terrific food. I'll introduce you to a couple people I know there. Maybe you could bartend for them and make Hawi your new home." Loki was excited at her own ideas.

"That sounds really great, Loki. There's no question about my being able to afford that cabin on Maui. I can't even pay to have someone come and wash the windows on the place much less pay the high rent.

The girls embraced and walked back up to the dining room arm in arm, both displaying tear-soaked faces and happy smiles.

Stone and Teri were still sitting at the uncleared table, talking quietly. Both of them looked somewhat sullen as if they'd explored every idea in the universe and ran out of any further thoughts. Their expressions changed at seeing the girls come back into the room together.

"It would seem that you two came to some sort of understanding." Teri, now all smiles, walked over and put arms around them both. "Whatever you two decided, you can tell Stone and I, or you can keep it a secret between you. We won't press for details."

With that, Annie and Loki left Teri standing and sat down at the table. They started to eat since the food plates were still in place. The meal was cold, but a little microwaving did wonders for their returned appetites.

Part way through her meal, Annie informed her hosts that as soon as she could make the necessary final arrangements for Taylor, she and Loki intended to fly back to Maui, close the cabin, then go to Hawi together.

"You're both welcome to come to Maui and see the cabin," she offered. "I'd really like it if you would. I recall Taylor saying he'd paid six months' rent in advance so that cabin is mine for a few more months."

"Are you going to be okay now with Taylor gone?"

"Not really. I can't turn off the love he and I had or the wonderful memories that will linger even if I didn't really know who he was. I still love him and miss him, deceit and all," she smiled softly at her own words. "A lot of what we had was real. The things we enjoyed together were real. There are parts of being alive and full of life you can't fake. But life must go on, and I'm not the kind of woman who holds on to something that's no longer there just because some psychologist says a person needs to mourn for a given length of time. Taylor's gone. I'm still here, and having Loki's friendship and both of yours will help me smoothen a lot of that over. Loki has invited me to stay with her awhile in Hawi, and that's where I'm heading as soon as I can clean out the cabin. Either of you know anybody who wants a nice boat?" The girls shared a knowing look.

It was obvious that neither Stone nor Teri were going to be privy to the conversation that took place below in the bedrooms, but whatever its content, the girls had evidently agreed and had worked out their differences. Stone was okay with that. Teri was also but would *love* to know what was said that had turned their wheels back in this direction.

"We're going to take a walk around the neighborhood if that's okay," announced Annie. She had not appeared so happy or at ease since arriving. "We won't be long."

From Bayside Place and Stone's house, the girls walked past other waterfront homes on Mahalani Circle, extravagant waterfront homes that shared the shoreline of Kaneohe Bay. They then walked up a slight rise to an old cemetery, Greenhaven Memorial Park. It was a quiet, peaceful place to stroll, and there was a vine of wood roses next to the cemetery that had caught their eyes. With eager intent, they began picking several to take back to Kaikanani for Teri. Wood roses would last a year or more. They knew Teri would love them.

Chapter Twenty-eight

They knew they shouldn't go, but against their better judgment, Milo and Benny decided to go anyway. Taking their van from the parking lot in front of the yacht club's office, they drove the short distance into Kaneohe town, then down toward the area where the yacht owner's house was situated. Annie and Loki were still busy eating their warmed-up lunch.

Milo was quite familiar with the area. A year before, he had dated a woman named Julia, who lived in the neighborhood close by. Julia had decided she didn't want to hang around with him after only the second date. He was praying they wouldn't see her.

He drove into Bayside Place. It was a short cul-de-sac situated very close to Julia's house; he could see the front of her house a short way down the road to his left. Directly in front of them was the boat owner's house where Loki and the girl were staying, but there was nothing to see as there was a tall, moss-rock wall blocking their view of the entire yard all the way to the water's edge. Two cars were parked in the carport, so Milo figured everyone must be home. They turned around, and Milo, breathing a sigh of relief, drove back to the yacht club. The chairs they'd left beside the pool remained unoccupied. Benny was quite happy about that. He'd found it a quiet and pleasant place to sit and take in the view.

They sat down and got comfortable again, then waited. What they were waiting for neither was too certain—Mr. G. hadn't been too specific on that part. They thought there was a chance, well, Milo thought there was a chance, a slim chance, the girl would come for her boat, and they'd be able to corner her, and in so doing, be able to report some positive progress to Mr. G.

As far as Benny was concerned, he wasn't thinking—he was gawking at two young girls swimming backstroke past them. Other than that, there was nothing of importance happening. Neither were complaining though. There was shade. The bar was within a short walking distance, and the bartender wasn't bothering to check if they were members or not, thanks to the office girl having cleared that hurdle for them. The pool, as tempting as it was in the heat, was filled with young kids whose parents, in all probability, used the club for after-school babysitting while they were at work or elsewhere. Even the kids' noisy voices didn't bother them as they nursed cold Primos and leaned farther back in the lounge chairs and relaxed.

Beer bottles empty, Milo volunteered to do the honors and walked to the bar for two more. He failed to hear his phone ringing, which he'd left on the table. Benny, fearing it was their boss and not wanting to anger him by making him wait, hesitantly reached for it.

"*Buena sera.*"

"Who's this? Is this Benny? Where's Milo? He's supposed to be answering this phone." It was Mr. G.

Instantly coming upright in the chair, his nerves beginning to shake, and not wanting to get Milo in trouble, Benny said the first thing that popped into his head, "Milo's in the head but should be back in just a couple minutes. You want for me to go find him for you?"

"Don't bother. I haven't got time to wait. Tell him I want him to go get my daughter. He knows where she is." With that, Gravello was gone just as Benny saw Milo walking across the lawn two brown bottles held tight in his hands, both dripping with cold frost. Benny thought Milo had been gone a lot longer than it took to order two beers.

Before Milo could sit down, Benny, flabbergasted by his collision with the boss and having to wait for Milo to return to tell about the phone call, jumped up and confronted him.

"Milo, the boss just called you, and I picked up the phone. I figured it was him and didn't want him to get angry at you 'cause you weren't here. Did I do the right thing, Milo?"

Milo felt a tinge of dread float through his chest. "What did he want, Benny?"

"He wants you to go get Loki and bring her to him. He says you know where she is."

"We both know where she is, Benny. Tell you what, I'm going to stay here and watch the boat. It's important we don't miss the girl if she shows up." What he really wanted to do was go back to the club's office and spend more time with the office girl. They were getting on well, and Milo could see a lot of future possibilities.

"Benny, you go get Loki, then call me. We'll go from there."

* * *

As Benny rounded the corner heading down hill toward Bayside Place, he saw two girls in the grassy area between the road and the old cemetery. They were busy picking those weird flowers hanging off the telephone post, the ones that Benny liked so well. They were his favorite flower because he knew they lasted forever—he liked things that last forever. He recognized Loki being one of the two girls. He'd seen her a few times around Mr. G.'s house. He didn't recognize the girl standing beside her, though. He figured it might be the one from the boat; the one they'd been keeping their eye out for. He drove past them slowly in order to have a better look. Luckily, they didn't look up as he passed. One was Loki; he was positive of that. The other one looked a lot like the one in a picture he'd been shown. Thinking about it, he remembered seeing her get into the boat over on Maui. If that was her, then she was the girl Mr. G. wanted to get a hold of. At the end of the block, he turned around and drove back, slowly stopping the van close behind them.

The girls were so engrossed in girl talk while they picked flowers they failed to notice the white van stopped and the large, brute of a man stepped out. When they finally saw him, they dropped all the flowers they'd been holding on to but stood frozen in place, unsure of what to do. Loki thought she recognized him as one of the men who worked for her father, but she couldn't be certain. This man didn't look at all friendly.

Besides grabbing the girls, the unfortunate thing running through Benny's thoughts was having to leave all those nice flowers lying on the grass, but he didn't know what else he could do. He was mad at the girls for being so heedless to throw them all away like that.

Chapter Twenty-nine

*B*enny may not have much going on up the ladder in his head, but his muscle-developed body was something one of those Captain Marvel comic book characters would aspire to look like. It was one of the attributes Milo liked best about his friend—he was strong and could be fast when he had to be.

He figured he may have roughed the girls up a bit more than necessary when he corralled them both. But within minutes, they were tied up in the back of the van, the ropes probably tighter than was necessary. Benny didn't know the difference between *tight* and something being *too tight*—there was only tied or not tied. Since the girls looked like they were friends, Benny decided to tie them both together so they couldn't help each other and end up getting away. Anyway, he was still upset with them over their carelessness with the flowers. *Do them some good being tied together for a while.*

Benny figured the boss would be real happy about him finding this money girl. Now he and Milo wouldn't have to sit and watch the boat. Other than the beer and nice-looking women in the pool, he had been getting real bored.

His call to Milo was short. "Benny? I thought it was our boss calling. Listen, Benny, don't bother me right now. I'm sort of tied up. I'll call you as soon as I'm finished."

Not knowing what else to do, Benny called Mr. G.

"Benny? Why are you calling me? Where's Milo?"

He did his best to explain that Milo was busy in the yacht club office, and more importantly, he wanted Mr. G. to know about both girls but wasn't sure what he should do next.

"Listen, Benny, I'm involved right now, so I don't want you bothering me. Wait, you said *both girls*? You know where my daughter and the girl from the boat are? That's great, Benny, but this is not a good time. Ice all that for a day or two. Tell Milo to call. I'll give him instructions on when to move in."

Benny had not made it clear that he already had both girls and wasn't aware of his failed message. Had Tony Gravello thought more about how his words would be translated in Benny's mind, he would have been very nervous, but it was quickly gone from thought. He hadn't meant to *literally* put the girls on ice; he really meant for Milo and Benny to just leave the whole thing alone for a couple more days. Milo would have known that right away.

It wasn't what Gravello had wanted to do, but some serious trouble had developed with one of the investors he'd been milking money from. If the situation wasn't smoothed over quickly and completely, he knew he'd be in jail within a week. He'd think about the girl later; at least, Milo and Benny knew where the girl was.

Before this spurt of trouble cropped up, he had been planning to tell Milo to bring Loki home to Pohakau. He needed to find out what she knew since she wasn't going to act as his spy any longer.

What he needed to do about Jason's partner, he wasn't too sure yet. All he knew was that she was now his only key to where his money had gotten to. Within two days, he'd have everything at work settled down and smoothed over and could then get back to the missing money and what to do about the girl.

* * *

Benny wasn't as dumb as most people thought he was, especially when it involved sex. He knew exactly what his friend Milo was up to with the office woman. He had seen her and had felt aroused himself, so he didn't blame Milo. He just didn't like Milo thinking he was pulling wool over his eyes. He figured he had an hour before Milo began to look around for him. That gave him time to put the girls *on ice* as Mr. G. was expecting him to do.

He knew someone who worked for the City of Honolulu Board of Water Supply. It was his only other friend besides Milo. Kimo York, this other friend, wasn't the kind to ask a lot of questions, so Benny called him, and together they devised a plan. *Kimo was good with plans,* thought Benny.

"Bring 'em over, Benny. I can always find a place to stash a couple young wahines. I take it there's a paycheck in all this, right?"

Benny wasn't too sure about that part, so he kept quiet.

"I gotta make a routine check of the aquifer pretty quick now, so hurry up and bring them here. They'll be comfortable down there for a day or two. You can call me when you want to pick them up, but you'll have to give me lots of warning. I got other things I gotta be doing. You understand right, Benny?"

* * *

The entrance to the aquifer is on the leeward slope of the Koolau Mountains, looking down on Pearl City and the navy's harbor further beyond.

The aquifer was simply a huge lake seven hundred feet below ground and one of the main aquifers that fed water to a thirsty Honolulu and surrounding communities. The access was via a forty-five-degree tunnel bored down to the water table below the mountain. A rail car was the only access and ran on a pulley system that enabled people to travel up or down the steep slope. It was usually just Kimo who went down unless his boss was showing the area to someone she was trying to impress, in which case they would accompany him down.

The ride down to the aquifer was slow and the air progressively cooler as Kimo took the girls, still bound at their wrists, deeper into the bowels of the island. At the lower landing, Kimo went about his brief work, checking necessary gauges before untying them and letting them out onto the iron catwalk two feet above the surface of the water.

"Don't know what this is all about, but there you go. This stainless steel walkway platform you're standing on goes a couple miles back." He pointed into the dark. He showed them the light switch for the small confined area and where an enclosed porta-potty sat waiting.

The rail car and Kimo were already beginning the assent back up the rails as he handed them a cooler. It was his lunch and a few sodas, he told them. Kimo was having a difficult time getting beyond, wondering if he was doing the right thing; he didn't like doing this. Benny was a friend, but this was going a bit beyond what a friend would ask of him even with a hopefully big paycheck involved, which he badly needed. He felt very conflicted. The girls didn't even seem the type to be involved with Benny, which meant it was Benny's boss calling the shots, and that made him seriously question why he ever volunteered to get involved. It was the money, and he knew it.

He was somewhat surprised the girls hadn't tried to overpower him and try to escape, which added to his confusion. If they had, he'd been ready to use force if he had to, but they just seemed stunned and did nothing.

* * *

Milo was walking along the edge of the yacht club harbor looking out at the distant outline of the mountains. He was wondering where Benny had gotten to. Milo was bored now that his lady friend had to go back to work and shooed him out. She'd told him she didn't want him hanging around her office causing a distraction. A large yacht entering the club's basin caught his attention just as his phone rang. He already knew it was his boss. No one else had this number.

Reaching into his pocket to retrieve the ringing phone, he absently took a step backward away from the edge but failed to notice a boat cleat sticking up next to his left foot. The cleat snagged one of his shoelaces and held on for a second, just long enough to allow his momentum to propel him down into the water—clothes, shoes, phone and all.

Somewhat embarrassed, hoping no one saw his swan dive, he used the bulkhead ladder close by to climb up and out of the water. Dismayed to realize his phone was gone, he headed for the office hoping his lady-friend had a lost-and-found towel and maybe a dry bathing suit that might fit. While there, he could use the office phone to call his boss back.

"Sorry, Mr. G., my phone fell into the water as I was answering it."

"Milo, that phone has numbers in it that no one else should see. Now you should make like a goldfish and go retrieve it. First, though, leave Loki alone for a day or two, and you and Benny come back to Pohakau. Now go take a swim."

Chapter Thirty

"It would appear the girls are getting along all right since they've been out walking for such a long time."

Stone and Teri were relaxing on their new rattan sofa that sat outside on the covered lanai overlooking the water. They were distractedly watching four yachts slowly cruising around the KMCAS base on the far side of the bay as they waited for the girls to come back.

"I sure hope they found a way to put their emotions aside. It'd be so ideal if both were able to form a close bond. Each of them is so fresh out of the water regarding any other friendships, Annie losing her partner and Loki making that big move away from her father and friends to the Big Island."

"After their struggles to find some common footing only to get laid out by Loki's bombshell, I didn't think it was going to happen." Looking at her watch for some sort of confirmation, she stated more than asked, "Didn't they say they were just going for a short walk? Look at the time. They've been gone for almost two hours." Teri sat, staring at her watch, the beginnings of concern etching into her features. "You don't think anything has happened to them, do you, honey? Maybe they got lost."

Stone absently looked at his watch but didn't really notice the time. At this point, he wasn't too concerned about the girls' delayed arrival home. "Let's give them another thirty minutes before we start worrying, *kuuipo*. All that *pilikia* they went through at dinner has probably given them a lot of things to talk about. There's lots of places around here where they could sit down in the grass to talk. Besides, they won't get lost. This isn't the kind of neighborhood anyone can get lost in, unless they try. No matter where they are, they can look and see the water on one side or the mountains on the other and get themselves reorientated."

"I'd feel better if we went for a short drive around Mahalani Circle and up the hill toward town and see if we can spot them anywhere. It'll be a lot more comforting than sitting here waiting for them to show up. Let's go," she said as she stood up. "I'll leave a note on the door letting them know where we went, just in case we miss each other."

As they drove Mahalani Circle along the water's edge, they found no sign of the girls. They turned up the hill toward Kamehameha Avenue and town.

As they reached the knoll of the hill skirting Greenhaven Memorial Park, Teri pointed to a small mound of wood roses carelessly scattered on the cemetery lawn not far off the roadway. "Someone picked all those beautiful wood roses, then carelessly left them there. How strange," she said. But as her words came out, she saw a bright flowery red handkerchief dropped in the weeds a foot or two away from the flowers. She had earlier noticed something that was eerily similar sticking up out of Annie's pocket when the two girls mentioned going for a walk. She had been about to comment on it at the time, but the opportunity didn't avail itself.

"Stop." Her voice was urgent, uncontrolled.

Thinking Teri was being overly exuberant in her desire to acquire a few discarded flowers, he nonetheless pulled to a stop several feet beyond.

"That's Annie's hanky back there in the ditch. I saw her with it before they left for their walk. Oh, Stone . . . I'm so afraid something bad has happened to them."

"Are you certain it's hers? Could be an old red rag that just looks like the one she had. A mourner at one of the grave sites close by may have dropped it as they were leaving."

A not-so-agreeable glare spread across Teri's face. It edged on a look of pity for some reason he couldn't figure out.

"It's hers. I'm certain. Women observe this sort of thing. We're not like you men, poor oblivious souls that you are. What should we do?"

Letting the dig go by and not being one to jump to quick conclusions, Stone got out to take a better look. He also wanted a few moments to collect some thoughts. Teri, being quicker on the start than he was, had jumped out even before he'd come to a stop and was already bent over the hanky for a closer look.

As he walked over to join his wife, something else caught his eye. Lying mostly buried in tall weeds was a cell phone, and he immediately recognized the brightly colored, almost iridescent, cover identical to one Annie always carried. He recalled making a comment about the color when he and Lloyd were hiking the trail with her on Molokai.

Holding the hanky up for Stone to see, "It's hers, Stone. I'm certain. What should we do now?"

Holding the cell phone out so she could see what he'd found, without words or thought, they embraced each other in their best effort to release their building fears.

In a soft voice, he answered her question, "Best leave it right where it is, *kuuipo*." Stone's intuition had already jumped into gear as a silent warning went off in his head like a distant church bell. He'd noticed on other rare occasions that his police training would react in various situations, much like an involuntary reflex. That training had been long ago, yet it seemed to remain with him.

Teri tilted her head back to look up at her partner. "What's wrong with you, Sherlock? Why shouldn't we take it and her phone with us? She'll want them back." A second of thought passed and she turned back to look at where the hanky had been.

"What could have happened to them?" The concerned, apprehensive look of a parent came over her face. "The girls must have picked those flowers. But then what? You don't just drop everything, especially your phone, and then walk away, particularly two girls unless something dramatic happened that caused them to. You don't suppose they started to fight with each other, and one of them, or both for that matter, ended up being taken into the clinic down the road beside the police station?" She looked up at Stone but saw only his back as he turned and started to walk away from her. He put Annie's cell phone back where he'd found it and continued to his car.

"Now what are you up to?" she questioned, seeing Stone nearing the driver's door of their car.

"To get my phone, sweetie. I want to take pictures of where both things are, then I'm going to call Mike Kalama and have him do a fast check of the local clinics around Kaneohe and Kailua— you might be onto something. I think it's best we check that out."

She smiled in response to the offhand recognition she'd received.

"Mike can do that kind of search a lot faster and easier than we ever could. If you're okay, let's stay here until either the girls show up or the police, and we know something more."

Mike was the right person to do the initial checking around— clinic staff would be more inclined to give the police an answer than they would an everyday citizen off the street, especially to someone who couldn't claim any relationship to either of them.

"What did he say?" Teri queried as Stone got out of the car having made the call to Mike and was walking back to stand beside her. She was anxious to hear any news, hopefully positive. Stone noticed that her posture and positioning as she stood there gave the appearance of someone holding vigil over a hanky and some flowers.

"Not a lot. He said he was in a short meeting but would call around and get back to us as quickly as he could. He agreed we should remain here until he knows more. He said he'd be quick. Chances are, he said, the girls simply went somewhere else and planned to return, and he may be right. The hanky may have fallen out of Annie's pocket, and she hadn't noticed its absence. But the phone! It would take an odd situation to leave your phone behind. Instead of standing here like two pieces of coral, let's at least sit in the car, listen to Cecilio and Kapono's music, and relax while we wait."

Mike called ten minutes later.

"None of the clinics have seen an injured girl or girls within the past few hours. Matter of fact, none all day. I suggest you grab the hanky and the phone, then go home, and wait to see if they show up. They could be sitting on one of the beaches close by talking and be unaware of the time. It's already getting dark, so I suspect that if they're all right, they'll turn up very soon." It was good to know he was taking Stone seriously, and Stone also knew Mike was intentionally leaving the found phone out of his discussion. That would remain in Mike's thinking until the answer became clearer. "If you haven't heard anything by midnight, call the station desk, I'll leave instructions, and someone will put out an APB on them. Do you have pictures of them just in case? I have to assume that one of the girls is Annie, the one I met on Molokai and again at Castle Hospital having just lost her husband."

"I don't have pictures of either of them, Mike, and yeah, she's one of them. She's the owner of the phone and hanky. The other girl is Loki Gravello from Hawi on the Big Island."

"Gravello is her last name? Any connection to Anthony Gravello, lives on Black Point off Diamond Head Road?"

"The same. Loki's his adopted daughter. It's a long story, Mike. You may want to hold off getting details until we talk in the morning. As far as pictures, we will need to get in touch with Loki's mother, who is also on the Big Island, but I don't want to startle her tonight. We'll call her in the morning if the girls fail to show up tonight."

"I hope it all turns out to be nothing, Stone, but know I'm here if anything comes up. I can't wait to hear how you're tangled up with the Anthony Gravello. You seem to have a knack for coming up with all sorts of *pilikia*? Call me tomorrow and give me the highlights."

"Instead of calling, why don't we have a beer at Smith's Union Bar in Chinatown? It's close to your precinct, and I'll give you the unabbreviated and uncensored version?"

"I'm on duty tomorrow, so a coffee here in the station would be better."

"Tell you what, I'll bring the coffee. I've had that stuff you guys call coffee, and it needs a lot of help. I think your people probably use it to torture bad guys into confessions."

Chapter Thirty-one

$\mathcal{T}$he cable car hauling Kimo back to the surface had barely had time to climb halfway when, far below, the girls began feeling the onset of the bone-chilling air that permeated everything. Surrounded by the crystal-clear, cold water, this distance below ground created a damp invisible and inescapable blanket that had already enveloped them.

The lucidity of their situation had been unusually slow to arrive, but their understanding of what had just taken place, of being rudely abducted off the street, was beginning to sink in—the reality of their situation becoming quite real.

The part they were struggling most with was why it had happened at all. Loki had a notion of *who* might be behind it, but the *why* was a big puzzle, but she decided to keep those thoughts to herself. To place blame on her adopted father without knowing any of the facts was not being fair to him. Besides, it was just a gut feeling, but one that was not easily dismissed.

Neither of them could understand why their abductor had pointed out the pile of blankets to them unless he wasn't in full support or understanding of the situation and was feeling sorry for them; he had appeared to be almost apologetic in his attitude. It was an openly kind gesture. The look on his face as he began his ascent, a look that both girls noticed, portrayed a man doing something he didn't think was right. Her father again, she was certain.

Each of them grabbed two blankets off the pile and wrapped themselves snuggly before sitting down and easing themselves back to rest against a cement abutment close by. Feeling somewhat warmer, thanks to the blankets, they put their minds to the task of analyzing their seemingly dire surroundings.

"Why didn't we fight him? What was wrong with us? I bet we could have overpowered that guy by the graveyard and gotten back to Stone's house."

"Don't know about you," offered Loki, deciding to divulge her initial view of what happened, "but I thought Benny was handing us off to another of my father's workers and that we'd find ourselves back at my old house confronted by an angry father. It was the only thing that made sense to me at the time, and that's why I didn't bother putting up a fuss."

"Didn't the ropes bother you?"

"Of course, they did, but Benny's not the sharpest pencil in the box, so I discounted that and began anticipating all the trouble the poor guy was going to be in when my father saw me hog-tied with bruised arms. Maybe it was my way of coping, but I was entertaining a lot of different thoughts and imagining my father putting Benny and this other guy in one of the old freezers we've been saving out in the garage, maybe dumping them out in the ocean."

"That's great, Loki," Annie was visibly angry with her friend. "What sort of daydream are you contemplating now? If it was your father, it appears he saved himself the trouble of wasting a couple old freezers and decided instead to keep them for use some other day and simply put us in this wet grave. He comes out a freezer or two ahead on this deal and saves big on not having to dig holes to bury us."

"Please don't be so sarcastic, Annie. I know my father has his faults but I also know he wouldn't cause me any harm. We're both in this together facing the same outcome. I've told you my initial reaction so tell me, why didn't you attempt to overpower the guy? You're strong and fiery. I may have taken the cue from you and jumped in to help if you had."

"Sorry for the sarcasm, Loki. I didn't mean it. I think I'm on overload right now. That's a good question. For some reason, I just accepted everything and went along for the ride. This whole episode has given the depression I was experiencing a jolt and brought me out of a very deep funk I'd sunken into. I think I was enjoying the experience of not being depressed. It was the first time since finding Taylor covered in bees and bugs that he didn't completely consume my thoughts. Not sure exactly what I was feeling. Numb, I guess, just going along for the ride.

"I sure miss my phone right now, not that it'd work from down in this hole."

"We're quite a pair, aren't we? What's that old saying, 'This could be the start of a great friendship.' I think Bogart said something like that." They both chuckled and let a reluctant smile spread across their lips.

"Yeah, that was Bogart in *Casablanca*. That was a good movie." They both began feeling more relaxed.

"Look, all that stuff is behind us for the moment. Let's see if we can get out of here. It's a long, steep climb up those rail tracks, but there's a tiny chance what's-his-name may have forgotten to lock the door up there. Maybe it's the kind that can be opened from the inside. I think the fire code would require that. Did you notice as he was leaving that he looked like he didn't really accept the idea of leaving us down here like this?"

"What I saw was a puzzled expression, like 'why am I doing this?'"

"Maybe he was hoping we'd climb the rails and check the door, so there might be a good chance of getting out. You game, or do I start climbing these stairs myself?" Having said it, Annie pulled the blankets off her shoulders, but immediately had to give her idea a second thought as a wave of cold damp air hit her and drove directly into her bones. She took in a reflexive gasp but stood up, letting the last of the blanket fall away.

"Are you kidding? We're in this together." Loki was quickly up on her feet as the blankets that had been keeping her warm also fell to the floor. An involuntary shudder shook her body.

"Man, that's cold," she exclaimed. "We're in this together, Annie. You want to go first?"

With the idea already taking on life, they tested the rail in the dim light of the control consul to see how best to climb. Looking up the rails, the absence of light consumed the world beyond a mere five feet away. They figured the darkness was going to be their biggest challenge; the end far above was hidden in the darkness.

"Wait a minute!" exclaimed Annie. "If the guys who come down here do whatever they do to leave blankets for themselves in case it's too cold, what would keep them from stashing a flashlight or two somewhere in case the lights go out?"

"Hey, Annie, that's good thinking. You're coming out of that slump with your head on. I'll look over here on this side. Why don't you search that control consul over there?" Loki pointed off to the left as she turned to the right and began looking through a series of stainless steel shelves next to the tracks.

They did a thorough job searching every possible place a flashlight could be stored, but they came up empty—there was none to be found.

"They probably have them stored on the rail car. That way, they'd have one wherever the car is. Maybe it's part of their belt equipment, you know, like a police officer with a suitcase full of leather stuff hanging around their waists."

They both laughed at the image, exaggerated in their minds, and immediately recognized how relaxed laughing could make them feel. With the laughter came relief, and they knew they were going to be all right. They just had to figure out how to go about climbing the massive number of stairs to reach the top.

Annie was looking all around the control panel. There was a huge supply of gauges and lights, three full rows of them, in fact, and each one dancing to its own unheard rhythm. To the left of all the gauges, a foot apart from the big panel, was a smaller stand-alone panel. At the center of this was a single toggle switch, apparently important enough to have its own panel and was within easy reach for someone already on board the rail car. The word inscribed over the switch gave her some hope. It simply said CAR, and on either side of it, a single letter was stenciled—*U* on one side and *D* on the other.

Feeling a tinge of exhilaration, Annie reached over and flicked the switch from what she figured was neutral to the *D* side. Nothing happened—no distant sound or swirling red light. She had been hoping the rail car far above them would spring to life and begin its long descent. Obviously, something else had to be done before it could be activated.

"Rats." The word came out louder than she meant and echoed off the cavern walls, making their world infinitely larger. Loki had been watching what Annie did and was praying for the same results, but her heart emotionally sank right along with Annie's and the echo.

"I was so sure that was going to be our way out."

Annie took a last look at the small panel and finally saw the keyhole farther down. "Rats," she said again, but this time so softly it was mostly to herself as she turned away from the panel to face Loki.

"The thing needs an ignition key."

Unfortunately, they both failed to see the small drawer partially hidden on the side of the CAR panel. In it were stored several small flashlights and a set of two keys—one that fit the keyhole directly beneath the switch that would have activated the car and the other for the door far above.

"Looks like we climb, Annie. Remember, one step at a time. Every journey requires a first step. We'll get there before we know it. Let's count stairs as we go and try to stay together. That way, when it becomes pitch-black we'll know where the other is by the sound of the voice."

"If we need to take a break for some reason, let's hold hands so neither gets lost."

Loki was standing facing up the long, steep, hidden incline. "You ready?"

"Ready as can be."

They began their count in unison as they climbed. "One . . . two . . . three . . . four . . ."

The way the rail track was constructed was that the narrow-gauge tracks were centered between steel stairways on both sides. A handrail ran up on the outside of both flanks. The engineer who designed the track probably knew there was a possibility that someone someday would need to either walk up or walk down if faced with equipment failure and didn't want them to step off the staircase. Little did he or she suspect that two captive women would one day require their use.

"Fifty-two . . . fifty-three . . ."

"Let's sit for a few minutes." Loki wasn't into fitness, and her thigh muscles were starting to burn like crazy. She sat and changed hands reaching across to hold Annie who was ready to sit as well.

"This is the pits," injected Annie. "We're probably not even a tenth of the way up, and it's a total blackout."

"I really thought my body was in a lot better shape than it feels right now. I think I need to exercise more," admitted Loki. "I've let myself go soft."

With that, as they began climbing again, both girls broke out laughing at Loki's admission. Laughter again helped to ease their mood. They couldn't know at the time, but the laughter they were sharing would set a tone that would remain with them as dear friends throughout the rest of their lives—the length of which was questionable at that moment.

First, though, they would find themselves having to search deeply for a reason to laugh much sooner than either could have anticipated.

Chapter Thirty-two

Kaneohe Yacht Club

*B*enny walked out of the yacht club office and headed toward the water. He'd intentionally parked the van in the club's main lot out of sight from passing motorists on Kaneohe Bay Drive. Walking through the office, he'd thought he would see Milo still there with the office gal, but she was busily keying in something on her computer. Milo wasn't there.

He walked out onto the grassy area and immediately saw Milo standing by the edge of the harbor's bulkhead holding a long swimming pool pole with a green net attached to its end. He appeared to be in the process of raking his hand through the soupy-looking mud that overflowed the edges of the net. There was a decent-sized pile of the muck on the grass close to where he stood. The yacht club people weren't going to be so happy about the mess on their nicely kept lawn.

"Eh, Milo!" Benny shouted when his friend looked up. "What are you playing in the mud for, and how come your clothes are all wet? Didja fall in? You're not likely to find too many treasures down there."

Milo knew his friend was trying to make a joke of what he saw and lighten the miserable look of disgust that was probably apparent on his face.

Milo gave his friend a long, hard stare trying to decide whether to force his friend over the edge into the water or just let him be. He figured he could make Benny go diving for the phone and save himself all the aggravation of net fishing for it. His phone by now, after this long in the water, would be little more than a useless lump of mud. He was also very tempted to leave the phone and accept whatever the boss was going to say and do about its absence.

Benny unconsciously took a step backward. There was a hostility coming from his friend he didn't understand or like.

"Seriously, Milo, what are you looking for? Maybe I can help you find whatever it is. I'm good at finding stuff."

He was, Milo had to agree. Benny possessed an uncanny ability for discovering objects that others had misplaced or lost and given up looking for. More than once, Milo witnessed his friend walk right up to the spot where the lost item was. It made Milo suspicious in a way because he could never explain it.

Not saying anything more, Milo stuck his hand into one of his front pockets and held the contents out for Benny to look at, knowing his friend would be impressed. In it, he held three quarters, a nickel, and a large encrusted and unidentifiable object about as big and round as a silver dollar; Benny was indeed impressed.

Finally relaxing a bit, Milo backed his anger off, after all, this had nothing to do with Benny. It was all his own lack of awareness of his surroundings. He told Benny what had happened.

"But you don't swim so good, Milo. Why would you jump in? Did you get to the bottom?"

"Yeah, Benny, I got down to the bottom. Where do you think I got this stuff from, thin air?" He was looking at the objects held in his hand. "I can manage okay in the water, you know." Relating his story for Benny's amusement, he continued, "When I came back up to the surface, I heard that guy Chuck standing on the back deck of his boat making all kinds of comments about why I'd be in the water with all my clothes on, so I got out and sat on the edge until he went away. The pool lifeguard saw me and brought this fish net thing over for me to use. Smart kid, he'd figured out that I'd lost something."

As he talked, Milo dumped the net full of mud on the grass on top of the existing pile and proceeded to plunge the net back in to scrape up another net full off the harbor floor. As the net broke the water's surface, the shiny black edge of his phone, barely visible, showed above the rim of muck.

"Ah, there it is, Benny," he exclaimed. "Finally. Good." Milo held the dripping phone at arm's length pinched between his thumb and forefinger as if it were a dead fish. He handed the pole and net out for Benny to grab ostensibly to do something with, but Benny was no longer paying attention. He was down on his knees, more interested in what else there might be in the muck pile.

"Hey, Milo, you think that phone still works?"

"Of course not, you large excuse for a guava. The saltwater would have already shorted out all the circuitry, so it's no good, but that doesn't matter. I still need to give it to the boss so he can see we still have it, and all his phone numbers remain secure.

"I gotta call him and let him know I found it. I'm going to have to use yours, Benny, until we get back to the boss's house where I can get another one. I also need to talk to him about what he wants us to do. That girl's boat is obviously going to stay where it is for now, so there's no sense for us hanging around here doing nothing.

"What have you been up to all this time? You've been gone for over an hour. Why'd it take you so long? And where's Loki? We gotta take her back to the boat guy's house and leave her there until we hear differently."

"That's not what Mr. G. told me."

Milo abruptly stopped walking and turned around. "What do you mean? You talked to the boss? When did you talk to the boss, Benny?" Milo's anger was building again.

"Just after I got the girls. I couldn't get a hold of you to find out what I should do, so I called him. He said for me to ice them for a couple days, so that's what I did."

"Them? What are you talking about *them*, and what do you mean you iced them? Where are they, Benny? God help me you had better not have hurt either of them, 'specially Loki."

"I got a friend to come helped me 'cause I had to hurry and get back here. You remember Kimo Balazar, right? The guy I was talking to last week in Honey's Tavern while I waited for you. Told me to call him if I needed some help. He's the guy works for the water supply for the island. You remember?"

"Yeah, I remember him. So what, Benny? You called Kimo, and he came and took both girls? Where'd he taken them? Tell me you know where he took them. We need to go get them and deliver them back to the boat guy's house. Mr. G. didn't mean for you to hide them, Benny. He meant to just leave them be for a couple days. You been around long enough to understand what he means. In other words, Benny, we were to leave them alone." Milo wasn't sure whether his anger at Benny or his fear of Gravello was greater; both were near the top of the list.

Milo dropped the net and began pacing before turning and coming nose to nose with Benny.

"Are you totally deranged? What kind of story did you tell Kimo? *Mio Dio onnipotente!*" It was not a good sign when Milo began referencing God.

He knew he was ranting mindlessly, but he couldn't stop. This could spell disaster for both of them along with their rapid demise if the boss's daughter was hurt in any way.

The swimming pool net was forgotten and left on the bulkhead as Milo moved in closer to Benny, waving his arms. He was somewhat aware spittle was flying with each word; it happened when he got too excited and tried to talk. Benny knew that as well and kept stepping backward, keeping pace with Milo's advance and accompanying spray. For anyone not knowing what was happening, it may have looked like a very awkward new dance step.

"He said something about a water reservoir—an underground lake sort of thing," Benny tried to explain. "You and me can go find it and get the girls back. Let's go, Milo." Benny half turned on the pretense of heading for the van. Unfortunately, he had no idea where this lake was and had no clue what direction to head the van in to begin looking even if Milo agreed.

With Benny's limited understanding, it took a moment before it dawned on him what may be happening. An abrupt chill brought him to a halt. Suddenly the full realization of what Kimo had told him when he had taken the girls became clear—it was an underground lake. How the heck were they supposed to find an underground lake that they couldn't even see? They had to get ahold of Kimo quickly.

Chapter Thirty-three

*M*ike Kalama's call came in early the next morning. Teri and Stone were sitting on the lanai nursing their first cup of coffee after a night of very little sleep. "We haven't had any hits as a result of the APB we issued early this morning, Stone, and nothing from the clinics or hospitals on the island either."

Mike had just finished talking with his patrol officers and the rookie he'd assigned to call the various medical clinics around Kaneohe and Kailua. He was hoping Stone would have something additional to report.

"The area canvas late last night of the people living in houses along that side of the graveyard didn't turn up anything useful. Someone reported a white van stopped across from their house about the time the girls would have been there, but they saw nothing that prompted a reaction. They claimed the graveyard draws a lot of visitors at all hours who park along the road closest to a particular grave, so they thought nothing of it. The witness didn't notice how long the van stayed around. Have you heard anything on your side of things?"

"I appreciate your getting involved so quickly, Mike. No, we've heard nothing additional on this end. I'm certain one of the girls would have called if they had planned on not coming back last night, and since they didn't, I'm assuming the worst. Neither one knows anyone around this area, so they wouldn't have walked into some stranger's house. I guess those people who saw the van didn't get a license number by any chance, did they?" Stone wasn't even hopeful.

"No such luck, sorry, Stone. Keep this under your hat since it's a real long shot, but records show that Anthony Gravello owns a white van along with five other cars, so we've sent a patrol car over to check on the van and to talk with him and see what he might know. It's a long shot. We always look at immediate family first, and I already know you don't own a van. The girls may be there and just didn't or couldn't call you. I'll let you know after they report in. They should be there soon."

"Mahalo, brother. In the meantime, I guess all Teri and I can do is sit tight and wait for something to happen, right? Maybe the girls will walk in the door any second with a wild tale to tell and take us all off the hook, but I'm not holding on to that possibility too tightly."

"I'll call you when we have anything more to go on, Stone. Sit tight, stay by the phone and maybe say a couple of prayers for them."

Chapter Thirty-four

$\mathcal{I}$t was about the last thing he had been expecting when he responded to the ringing of his doorbell and opening it to be confronted by two HPD officers standing directly in front of him. He knew he should have let Smythe answer the door chime instead of doing so himself. He still would have had to talk with them, just to see what they wanted so here he was.

The officers' badges were prominently displayed directly below the uniform's embossed names. They both appeared to be Hawaiian, and both seemed to be extraordinarily big men. Maybe that was simply his mind magnifying things. He figured that both could have been candidates for HPD's Metro Squad if they weren't already. Gravello felt comfortable in their company until they asked about the van he owned and where it was.

"My staff use it for grocery pickups, running miscellaneous errands for the household, hauling garden supplies, new plants— things of that sort. I believe its currently in use. Why do you ask?" They didn't immediately answer.

He hadn't asked the officers to come inside into the foyer to talk, nor did they request to do so. They seemed at ease with the conversation taking place on the oversized lanai fronting the main doorway. "May I ask you gentlemen again why my van has become so important to you?"

He still didn't receive an answer, nor did he really expect one. Instead, the officer in charge went on and to explain that although they didn't have a search warrant, they would appreciate being allowed to look at it when it returned.

To tell them no was not an option; Gravello knew this all too well. He had a strong notion of what this was all about and didn't want to display any emotions. His poker-faced action, even if unintentional, was well-practiced. Deadpan, emotionless facial features and body language were elemental training in his Sicilian family from the time he was old enough to be taught. *Let no one see your emotions, either good or bad.* Sicilians made excellent poker players.

Ever since hearing what that idiot employee of his, and Milo's sidekick, Benny had done, he had been hoping no one caught the license number of the van. Benny had sworn up and down and sideways to him that there hadn't been anyone in sight, but Gravello knew there were always *niele* neighbors somewhere, peeking out, watching all the comings and goings for anything worth building into gossip. He was also coming to know Benny and his lack of awareness, even the most basic.

He took a seat in a thick leather recliner on his lanai to wait for the officers to complete their inspection of his garage facilities and the several cars it enclosed. They had asked to see where the van was garaged when it was at home. All vehicles underwent weekly detailing, and had the van been there, it too would have been spotless. Gravello felt comfortable there was nothing lying about that would capture their interest.

Less than five minutes had elapsed when the officers came back to the front lanai.

"All your cars in that facility appear to have been recently detailed. Is that a normal procedure?"

"Officers, in my profession and in my position here in Black Point, I carry a great deal of pride in myself, my home, my business, and in all my possessions. Look around my gardens and tell me if you see so much as a single weed showing. Inspect my home, and you'll not see a speck of dust. Look at every one of my vehicles, and you will find no telltale sign of ever having been driven on a road. I hope this answers your thoughtless question." He knew he'd gone a bit overboard in answering a simple question, but his pride spoke up before his thoughts told him to hold back.

"Mr. Gravello, when do you expect the van to return?"

"I'm sure it will be back by late afternoon. If you'd care to return to look it over, I suggest you call to verify its availability. It gets frequent use."

Standing for a few seconds not knowing how to proceed, again the officer in charge nodded at his partner, said their goodbyes, and left.

* * *

At HPD headquarters on Maunakea Street, the two officers explained to their boss, Mike Kalama, that Gravello's van could not be implicated in anything because of the detailing it underwent. As far as they were concerned, it was a dead-end, but they would go back and check it out if he insisted. He told them he'd let them know.

Chapter Thirty-five

"One thousand nine hundred fifty-eight . . . one thousand nine hundred fifty-nine . . ."

"Let's take another break," volunteered Loki, "before we get to two thousand. My legs are about to fall off." Without waiting for a response, she turned facing back down where they just came from and eased herself down onto a step.

"Mine too," admitted Annie, quite willing to sit down. I don't want to count another step for at least a month."

They had been trudging up the metal stairway for the past hour and a half, maybe much longer, but neither could see their watches in order to judge the time elapsed. They had found it necessary to take many breaks along the way, and the breaks were becoming more frequent as they went. Still climbing in darkness, it was impossible to know how much farther they had yet to climb; they could see nothing in front of them except the dark void. Considering the chill of the air, and the lack of water, discounting their many aches and muscle pains, they figured they were doing quite well.

The climb had been done in silence except for the continuous counting. They had agreed early on that only one of them need to count, which would let the other save unnecessary exertion. Each counted to the next even hundred, then they would stop and rest before resuming the climb, and the other took up the count. All they had to do was keep in step with the one that was counting and call out if they needed an unscheduled rest stop. It was necessarily a slow climb because of the darkness and uncertainty of what lay directly in front where they would place their foot next. They had to hold one hand out in front, much like a blind person, feeling their way ahead.

As they resumed their climb, Loki took up the stair count, but immediately became aware of a subtle change; the status quo had altered in some unexpected way. The air felt warmer. The moisture that had enveloped them was now noticeably less. She was about to make a comment to that effect when Annie spoke.

"Loki, when you're counting, do you hear the slight echo coming back at us? That wasn't there just a few minutes ago."

They stopped climbing, holding the other's hand tighter across the track.

"Yes, I do," she exclaimed, amazement evident in her voice at this awareness. "I was going to say something about the air feeling a bit warmer. I sure hope that means we're getting close to the top."

"I hadn't noticed the air, but now that you mention it, it *does* feel different. It is a little warmer. I'm so excited!"

The discovery gave them a renewed feeling of energy and enthusiasm to climb a little faster even as their leg muscles set up renewed protests at the change. Each was feeling the slight warmth in the air and sensing the echo becoming more pronounced. The speed of their steps increased ever-so-slightly, but the top of the staircase eluded them until once again, they felt the need to sit and find their strength. It felt a little depressing to both girls.

"I'm hungry," volunteered Annie, breaking the silence. "When this is over, I'm going to need to find a luau happening somewhere, so I can stuff my stomach full of good old Hawaiian food."

"I wish you hadn't mentioned that. I have been successfully ignoring all my hunger pains right up until now, *mahalo* very much, Annie." They both laughed and stood, ready to resume their climb.

As they stood to continue, they'd taken all of two steps, hands waved in front to feel the way when Loki's hand hit upon something solid that was sitting on the track between them.

"Annie, feel this." So excited as she reached for Annie's free hand that she came very close to losing her balance. Had Annie's hand not connected with hers in time, Loki knew she would probably have tumbled down to God only knows where.

"Man, that was close. I'm glad your hand found mine so quickly." Guiding Annie's hand, they reached forward and together felt the hard, cold metal of the rail car resting on the track.

They both simultaneously let out a squeal; they were, or at least, very close to the top.

Not taking a rest, they continued climbing, one hand running along the upper edge of the rail car, the other blind caning the air in front.

A few minutes of climbing elapsed before they felt a wall and simultaneously failed to find another step as their foot took that imaginary next step but didn't find one there. They were on a level, hard-cement platform. The rail car was between them, and a solid wall rose up each side. It didn't take long running her hands slowly over the wall before Annie's hand found an exit door bar, and as soon as she touched it, an electronic switch made the red exit light come to life; they had reached the top at last.

Loki climbed over the rail car, and they both pushed on the door bar and eased the heavy metal door open. Sunlight flooded their enclosure, blinding them in its intensity as they stepped out to freedom.

Where they were became immediately known to them both.

A short distance away and below them to their right was Pearl Harbor with its numerous large gray battleships floating at anchor or tied-up on the wharf, the Arizona Memorial rested in the foreground. The water of the harbor sparkled in the sunlight. They were on the west side of Pearl City up on the leeward slope of the Koolau Mountains. They had a long walk ahead of them before they could find transportation but compared with what they had just endured they figured it would be easy.

Without their cell phones, they had no way to contact anyone to let them know they were all right.

Chapter Thirty-six

$\mathcal{I}$t turned out to be a much longer walk than either of them had first anticipated. Along the way, they stopped to ask several people for directions to the police station and received many wide-eyed looks and shakes of heads. All but the last person they asked had no idea whatsoever where it might be. Was that a good sign? They didn't know. A few became belligerent, perhaps at the possibility of becoming involved in something, but most were apologetic for not knowing.

With tired legs protesting the entire distance, they at last found what they sought—the Pearl City police substation. They swore that after this ordeal was behind them, they would sit with legs elevated on a soft cushion for a minimum of a week. One of the positive things to come out of their experience and, they were both delighted, was the symbolic act of putting additional glue on the bond between them. It was already strengthening, and they both felt it.

The desk sergeant at the substation quickly put two and two together having just read the APB when his shift started and knew immediately that these were the girls in question. He called the Maunakea station and spoke briefly with Sgt. Mike Kalama. He was told to let the girls use the phone so they could notify

Kensington Stone that they were all right. Mike gave him Stone's number since he was sure the girls didn't know it from memory.

Within thirty minutes, a patrol car arrived to give them a ride; first to the Maunakea station so Mike could talk with them and then home to Kaneohe.

* * *

The bizarre story the girls told surprised as well as puzzled Mike. It was a shock to find out that the city's water supply may have been jeopardized by the three people—something he'd always considered to be secure. He knew that anyone going down that tunnel was required to wear a sterile containment suit to keep outside contamination from getting into the water before they entered the tunnel for the railcar ride down. The girls mentioned that their captor hadn't worn any special uniform.

Mike didn't know what he needed to do about that infraction other than notify the Board of Water of what had taken place; they'd know what needs to be done. He figured they probably had some written procedure in place for just such occurrences.

He was also puzzled by the girls' inaction at resisting their captor. He thought he understood their reasoning for the inaction, but he still questioned it. Two healthy women should have been able to inflict some serious damage unless their captor was exceptionally big or very strong or held a weapon. On thinking further, though, he was glad they used their heads and saved themselves from any possible injury.

He understood most of their story, especially Annie's part of it. She was probably still feeling stunned from her boyfriend's bizarre death and still somewhat blasé in her attitude. A few of the things she'd said made him realize her mental frame of mind was still not fully up to speed.

The part he didn't get was Loki's thinking that it may have been one of her father's goons who initially abducted them. Why would she think her father would want her imprisoned, unless it was Annie he wanted, and since the two were virtually inseparable, it may have been a two-or-nothing toss-up. Her story certainly tied in with Gravello owning a white van. He made a note to go look at it himself.

Even in Loki's thinking, he knew he was missing an important element of her father's involvement. *What would make her think her dad was involved in the first place?* Something additional he now needed to investigate to find answers.

Since the girls were hesitant in filing a formal complaint against their abductor, the only crime Mike could discern that had taken place, other than their kidnapping, which was serious all of its own, was the blatant disregard for water supply restrictions, but that was beyond his jurisdiction and really had nothing to do with the girls. If they later changed their minds about signing a formal complaint, he'd take the needed action at that time.

With the girls safely on their way to Stone's house, he decided to find out who that employee was. He picked up his phone and made a call.

Without giving out too many details, a secretary at the Board of Water Supply provided him with a list of all their workers on duty the other day and asked if pictures of each would be of any benefit to the investigation. They were emailed within minutes. Mike left the precinct for the drive to Kaneohe so he could show them the pictures and see if they could pinpoint who their abductor was. They may change their mind about signing a complaint once they know more about who their gatekeeper was and see his face.

It was a good day for a drive over the Koolau Mountains. No matter what the reason, he always enjoyed a chance to go for a visit. It gave him an often-needed opportunity to relax on Stone's lanai, gazing out over the incomparable view of the bay. Maybe he could pick a few bananas to take back to the station—the dwarf apple bananas from Stone's yard were the best.

* * *

The identification was quick. The girls immediately pointed to the man named Kimo Balazar, but they also repeated their earlier stance of not wanting to sign a complaint. They explained that because of his perceived conscientiousness and obvious concern for their well-being, there had been no harm done other than a muscle ache or two. They explained again, more for Stone's benefit, that they figured he'd left the blankets for them and the tunnel door intentionally unlocked knowing they would find their way to the top and get out. They were simply reciprocating that kindness. There was always time to change their minds if facts proved otherwise. Besides, because of the events that had transpired, they were brought much closer together as friends, so it was all good.

After confirming that this was one of Kimo's days off, Mike made a quick call, and a two-man blue-and-white patrol car was on its way out to the Aiea Heights neighborhood and to Kimo Balazar's house with instructions to bring him into the Maunakea station. Mike would meet them there. Whether the girls signed a complaint or not, he still had to confront the man about his actions.

Chapter Thirty-seven

$\mathcal{K}$imo Balazar was not a happy man, although in the back of his mind, he'd been expecting someone to knock on his door. He prayed it was the last time any of Gravello's men would call on him for a favor.

Even with an element of expectation, he was still being embarrassed in front of his wife, his kids, and his neighbors as the HPD cruiser pulled in front of his house. He was also upset because this was his day off, and it had now been trashed.

He'd been looking forward to this day all week. There was nothing of great importance going on, an unusual occurrence with three young kids in the house, but he'd planned to sit in his front yard with a cooler full of ice-cold Primo close at hand and watch his kids playing with their neighborhood friends; he loved his kids and thoroughly enjoyed simply watching them play. His NFL team was in the playoffs, and that game was scheduled to start within an hour, and he had some serious dollars riding on the outcome. Apparently, none of that was going to happen.

An officer had a hold of his arm as if he were going to take off running down the road. That was what his dog would have done, not him. He had no intention of adding injury to this insult by trying to ditch the cops. *That would sure be a great example for my kids.*

As he was being crammed into the back seat of the cruiser, he became aware of the *niele* old bat of a neighbor who was standing on her front lanai watching the proceedings instead of her usual open-the-curtain-a-crack-and-peer-out approach. He waved to her, nonetheless.

The ride to the station gave Kimo lots of time to think. He knew at the time he shouldn't be doing what he was doing, but he owed a lot to the Gravello family for his job and for several scrapes Benny had been instrumental in getting the family involved in helping to eliminate. Besides, he had hoped Benny had Gravello's clearance in the first place, that the way had already been smoothed for him taking the girls—apparently not, or he wouldn't be in the patrol car.

He knew he had a rough side and could get into brawls quickly in bars whenever he was rubbed the wrong way. He hoped Gravello would come to his aid again and get him out of this mess, but for some reason, he didn't have a good feeling about that happening.

* * *

Mike knew of Balazar from bar fights he'd gotten wind of; he read the reports that crossed his desk. Balazar also had minor notoriety from playing sports at Roosevelt High School, so his name was not unfamiliar among old-timers around Honolulu. Hawaii was a very small community when all the visitors and military personnel were left out of the mix. Names and events circulated rapidly, especially so in Mike's line of work.

The formality at Maunakea Street station went quickly, much to Kimo's relief as well as surprise. He *knew* he'd end the day behind bars but was told there were no complaints filed against him. He sat and gave the officer a statement of the facts as he knew them and signed his name. Since he wasn't being charged with anything, no fingerprints were taken, although his were already on file from previous altercations he'd been involved in. He was quickly on his way home. At least he'd be there in time to catch the last part of the game.

Chapter Thirty-eight

*E*arly the next morning, two bedroom doors opened almost simultaneously in the short, lower-level hallway of Stone's house as Annie and Loki, stretching and yawning, smiled at seeing the other and the unexpected synchronicity of the moment. Without need of mentioning anything from the day before, both appeared relaxed, relieved to have the ordeal of the past two days behind them and emerging unscathed by the experience, except for very sore leg muscles.

They hadn't yet talked about it because neither was very clear on what was to happen next or what was expected of them regarding the other man, besides Kimo, who was involved in their abduction.

Loki was certain he was an employee of her father—one named Benny—but she didn't want to say anything more about that to Annie right then.

As for Kimo Balazar, they had no doubt they would hear something from Stone's policeman friend if anything further was needed. For now, they chose to let that unfold in its own fashion. They were happy it all ended so well, sore muscles and all.

Loki felt that she needed to call her father. It had been several days since she talked with him, and despite all his rough edges, she loved him. Right now, though, she needed to find out what the heck one of his flunkies was doing mixed up in this. Had the man been acting on her father's authority? He could have been acting on instructions from his sidekick Milo, or more likely, knowing Benny's propensity to get wires crossed at times, perhaps he had his own concept of what was supposed to happen. Knowing her father as she did, she suspected it was one of the latter two. She planned to call him in a few minutes after they'd had a chance to talk with Teri and Stone and exchange morning hugs.

When they finally arrived back at Stone's house last night, it had been quite late. They had felt too exhausted to question anything or call anyone, and apparently, Stone had chosen not to begin that discussion as well. There would be ample time for that as more facts became known, hopefully today. They had fallen asleep the moment their heads hit their pillows.

They climbed the stairs to the main level of the house, arm in arm as if already being the old dear friends they were destined to become. On the main level, they surprised Stone and Teri in what looked to be the tender, early-morning moments of a morning hug and kiss. Taking it in stride, not breaking the apparent cheery mood, both girls were quickly brought into their hug—group hugs were especially comforting in the early morning hours, especially after a trying day.

"Enough of this fluff." Stone's words were betrayed by his smile. There was little meaning in his voice as the hug remained, and no one moved to break it off.

"I think some coffee sounds good," volunteered Teri, and they all agreed. "Cups are on the counter. Get what you need, then I suggest we all move to the lawn chairs by the water and enjoy a few moments as the family we are. The sun is calling, and the heat of the day hasn't yet arrived." The idea of it all and the mention of coffee was the hug-breaker.

Once outside and everyone was settled comfortably, Stone brought up a subject different from what Loki had expected, but one she knew was at the back of all their minds.

"Something that requires attention and needs to be taken care of soon is the planning of Taylor's burial. Annie, I hope you're okay with my bringing this up right now and with all of us being involved. I don't think we can put it off any longer."

Annie knew exactly that Stone was going to bring it up. It had been weighing heavily on her thoughts even while she and Loki had been climbing unending numbers of steps from the water reservoir. She had been almost in fear of not getting out and of what would then happen to Taylor's remains.

"Annie," he said, pulling his chair around, so he could face her. "Do you have any plans or thoughts on what you want or what Taylor might have wanted?"

"As a matter of fact, Stone, I do, and I'd be so grateful if all of you were involved in this. I'm not too sure I could do this on my own. Taylor and I happened to talk about this very thing one day while we played tourists and drove around the island to visit Hana. We drove that narrow back road on our way back and came through Kīpahulu on the southeastern side of Haleakalā. There's a small and apparently quite old stone church a few miles past Hana. It looked like it hadn't seen life, pardon the sad pun, for a very long time. The amazing part of this place is the setting. It overlooks the ocean and has a wonderful old graveyard surrounding it, the kind of graveyard that people used to have pictures of the deceased encased in the rock grave markers.

"As Taylor and I walked the grounds looking at hundred-year-old gravestones, he mentioned that when his time came, that was exactly where he wanted to be." Trying to stifle a sob, she said, "Neither of us knew how soon that was going to be." Her last few words were spoken softly, almost as if whispering to herself. She held her hands to her face clearly needing a few moments as tears welled in her eyes and began cascading down her cheeks. She struggled to keep from openly crying until finally, unable to hold things in any longer, she bent over her lap, hands covering her face, and openly cried. Loki was quick to add the comfort of her arms across her shoulders, pulling her into her breast. After a few moments, somewhat composed Annie faced them again and continued, "Taylor said he planned to write that place into his will if he ever got around to making one. I guess that would be the best place to put him to rest."

"I know a guy working at Hawaiian Memorial Park Mortuary where Taylor was taken," volunteered Stone. "If you're okay with me asking, I'll call him and see what he can do to help facilitate that."

While the three women remained by the water, softly comforting Annie while enjoying their coffee, Stone went into the lower room off the lanai and made the call. It took more time than he expected, as he waited on hold while his friend went and sought answers. It was still early in the morning, and the man had just gotten to work. Finishing the call and satisfied with the response, he started back outside but came face to face with the three women coming in the door.

"We're hungry, sweetheart," volunteered Teri. "Let's finish this conversation and hear what you discovered up in the dining area over some eggs benedict."

Knowing he had little choice in the matter, he followed them up and went to work in the kitchen—breakfasts were his specialty: eggs benedict Hawaiian-style with SPAM replacing the ham.

With everyone's approval, the menu changed. Hollandaise took too long, and there wasn't any SPAM in the food pantry. So over platters of scrambled eggs, mushrooms, onions, garlic, Havarti cheese, Portuguese sausage, and brown rice, with some Hawaiian sweetbread toasted and smeared with poha berry jam on the side, they managed to hold off any serious talk until their hunger subsided a few notches and the food demolished.

"What did you find out, honey? asked Teri. "Is there a way for Taylor to be buried at Kīpahulu?"

"Yes and no." He put his fork down and cleared his throat. "The yes part is that Taylor can be turned over to Ballard Family Mortuary in Kahului, and they will take him out to Palapala Ho'omau Church at Kīpahulu. That's the easy part.

"The no part in all this is that he can't be buried there. The state is prohibiting any further burials at that church unless you're grandfathered in and already have a plot designated."

The look on their faces was a collective disappointment as each began to search thoughts for an alternative.

"Because of where it sits on the slope of Haleakalā," Stone continued, wanting to defray the obvious letdown and explain further, "the state has a moratorium on future burials there because of where it is and what it represents. The state is experiencing too many nonresidents wanting to bring loved ones to the islands for burial, and there's a real fear that all available land designated for gravesite use will be filled, leaving no place for our local people to go. Personally, I'd be willing to bet they also don't want the responsibility of too many people heading out to Kīpahulu because the road beyond Hana is unimproved and somewhat dangerous, but that's just my disapproval of many of the things the State of Hawaii regulates. Car rental companies probably helped push that idea as they don't want their cars traveling on that road, but that's again just my thinking. There are already a number of Hawaiian families who have first rights there along with plots already assigned."

This was something none of them had considered when they had earlier relaxed at the easiness of resolving Stone's question of where Taylor would end up. It had seemed the perfect solution.

Not wanting to accept that as an answer, Loki jumped in hoping to help ease things as Annie was suddenly looking very uncomfortable at this uncertainty.

"Why would your friend have even mentioned there being a yes part to all that? What's that part of all this?"

"The right question, Loki. I was about to come to that before I sidetracked myself. I have to ask Annie something first." Turning to Annie, he asked her, "Did Taylor have any problem with being cremated?"

This question caught Annie totally by surprise. It was not the question she would have expected to be asked, but one she should have anticipated.

"He never said anything about cremation, neither for nor against it. I honestly don't think he ever thought much about that part of dying. Why are you asking?"

"Because, as I mentioned, the state has put restrictions on burials there, but it seems in their infinite wisdom, they realize people are still going to want that area for a gravesite, so they have magnanimously offered that they have no objections to anyone scattering ashes around there. They'd have no control over that anyway. If you say it's okay, then Hawaiian Memorial will take care of the cremation, and we can either carry the ashes over to Maui when we go, or my friend at the Memorial Park offered to have the ashes out on the first flight, and the urn would be in Kahului waiting for us to arrive. Probably be simpler if we let them do that for us."

"Can Hawaiian Memorial do things that quickly? I want all this behind me as quickly as possible, so I can move on."

"If you give it your blessing, I can call Hawaiian Memorial right now, and it'll all be done overnight, and his ashes will be in Kahului by the time we get there in the morning. Do you want to go to the mortuary once more to see Taylor before this takes place?"

"No, but mahalo for asking, Stone. I see nothing to be accomplished by seeing his body again, except more unhappiness. What do you think? Should we do this tomorrow then?"

Chapter Thirty-nine

*O*nce the decision was made on how Taylor's remains should best be handled and Annie was finally able to come to terms with her emotions and with the way everything would be, the rest went smoothly and quickly.

At Stone's request, Hawaiian Memorial Park Mortuary provided an inexpensive urn to carry Taylor. No doubt Annie would be charged a nominal fee for it when she received the entire invoice for their services. Stone agreed to help her with the expenses if they were more than she could manage.

The mortuary cremated Taylor's remains overnight, and following Stone's arrangements with Aloha Airlines, the airline's air cargo division picked up Taylor's urn and delivered it to the airport for an overnight cargo flight to Kahului, Maui. A representative from Ballard Family Mortuary in Kahului was contracted and would be at the air terminal to meet the flight.

By midmorning, following their early flight to Maui, a car rental hassle because of where they were going, and a brief stop at the mortuary to retrieve Taylor's urn, Stone, Teri, Loki, and Annie were driving the fifty-two-bridge highway to Hana town. They continued beyond Hana to the Kīpahulu area a short distance past the Ohe'o Gulch and the Seven Sacred Pools.

They had decided not to make a stop at the beautiful Sacred Pools since there would have been little enjoyment to be found with everyone in such a somber mood. They were aware of the strain the experience was having on Annie, and none of them wanted to prolong the ordeal any more than was necessary. Annie sat in the rear seat beside Loki and had said very little since starting out earlier that morning. She sat quietly holding on to the urn resting in her lap, her knuckles white with tension as she clutched it tightly as if a strong wind might come from somewhere and rip it from her hands.

Passing through Hana, they traveled the short distance along the Piilani Highway, a wide jeep trail at best, toward the Palapala Ho'omau Congregational Church. With some difficulty, veiled by a profusion of wild vegetation, they finally discovered the narrow cinder drive leading to a small parking area beside the old carved-stone church. The graveyard itself, famous as the resting place of Charles Lindbergh, spread out a short distance beside and behind the church that skirted the short *pali* that led down to the water. Annie and Taylor had both fallen in love with this old church after they'd stumbled upon it during a weekend drive. The stone church dating to 1864, as the chiseled cornerstone read, was not easily overlooked but instead was something to be admired.

The day was perfect; their mood, including that of Annie's, was elevated by the serenity of the ocean-side setting. Everyone was feeling good about being involved in the process of helping bring this part of her journey to a close.

They might not have felt that way nor been so relaxed about the events of the day had they noticed the car parked farther along Piilani Highway, sheltered from view by several coconut trees and naupaka bushes. The two men inside the car were slouched down so they couldn't be seen but not so low they couldn't maintain their line of sight on the four people in the graveyard. They were there intentionally, not by chance, with only one thing of interest to them: Taylor's ashes and what was going to be done with them; but in particular, if there was something else going to be buried with him in an attempt to hide it.

Milo and Benny had specific instructions to not only watch the girl but to watch for anything being buried with the ashes like a key to a safe deposit box or even a bag that might contain money or something else that might lead the way to it.

They had arrived on the same flight as the other four, having taken great pains not to be seen or recognized.

No one in Annie's solemn group was aware of the watching eyes.

With Annie leading the way, the group slowly walked the grounds of the church, taking in the beauty and quietness that existed until Annie paused and looked around. Pleased by what she saw and how she felt about the very spot where she stood, she told the others she had found Taylor's perfect resting place.

The place she chose was beautiful. The small area beside the old church was surrounded by bougainvillea, bird of paradise, and a tall *hapu* tree fern blessed with brilliant red-and-white anthuriums growing beneath it. From where they all stood, they were aware of the faint trembling of the ground as wave upon wave rolled in and shattered itself against the outcropping of an ancient lava flow not far below where they were. Each crashing wave sent a cascade of water showering into the air gleaming in the sunlight. Without a doubt, it was the perfect setting.

It was a time for silence as each stood relaxed, taking in the special beauty of the place and offering up their own silent prayers. Annie removed the top of the urn, turned upwind, and let Taylor's ashes sail out over the cliff toward the water.

When she was ready and had regained most of her equanimity, everyone pitched in to help dig a small depression among the flowering hibiscus. They had agreed with Annie to bury the now empty urn here, the place she had chosen. They figured the state couldn't say anything or do anything about this kind of *burial*. In Annie's mind, burying the urn was second best to burying Taylor himself, but at least, this would give her a place to come back to whenever she chose to do so. It would serve to be a reminder of what was and what might have been. Loki carried over a two hand-sized lava rock, the largest she could manage, to mark the spot—a grave marker even the state wouldn't be able to complain about.

From the bushes, Milo made a mental note of the rock marker. He and Benny would have to come back and check the urn for notes or keys.

The group was back in the car, ready to drive away when Annie asked, "Stone, would you mind driving past the boat ramp in Kihei? I have to retrieve our car—my car," she hesitantly corrected herself, "and boat trailer. I'd rather not leave them there unattended. Besides, I'll probably need the car. After that, why don't all of you follow me up Haleakalā Crater Road and check out my cabin before I clean it out and leave it behind? You'll like it. The area's really beautiful."

"By all means, Annie. Let's go and have a look around. I'd love to see it, and I know Teri would as well." Teri nodded in agreement. Eyeing the rearview mirror, he noticed Loki vigorously nodding at the idea as well. Smiling at this, he said, "It appears Teri and Loki would like to do that as well, unless their nodding heads are signs of a loose bolt somewhere." Everyone appreciated the humor and the lighter mood it brought about, especially considering the circumstances of the day.

"I have to ask you both, though, if you're settled on not flying back to Oahu with Teri and me afterward?" Annie had decided to stay in Maui and clean the cabin before moving out of it, and Loki was planning to stay and help her. Stone continued, "You can stay at Kaikanani for as long as you want. Then we could all come back next week to help clear out your cabin. You said the rent is paid for the rest of the year, right, Annie? So you have lots of time. I'd look forward to being a part of that if you wanted some extra help."

"Mahalo, Stone, but I need to do this now without waiting longer. I need to clear out the cabin and begin taking Taylor out of my present life and putting him into memory. I won't be settled in my mind until I do so and leave the cabin behind.

"After that, I'll go with Loki to the Big Island and stay with her for a while and reload. I will need that time in Hawi, in a brand-new setting, to get my head on straight, and then I can figure out what my future is going to look like. I hope you and Teri understand."

It went without saying.

Twenty-minutes later, they pulled into the parking lot for the Kihei boat ramp and stopped behind a well-used Ford Explorer Annie pointed at before. The magnet key holder was still attached to the underside of the front bumper, and with a sigh of relief, she pulled it out. She'd been quite concerned wondering what she would do if it was not there. That old car was going to be an essential part of her life for the next few days.

The old Explorer gave Annie a fit as she attempted to get it started. Stone had just stepped out of his car to see what he could do to help her when the old machine came to life with abundant noises and several mechanical complaints. She pulled out dragging the trailer behind and headed for the Haleakalā Highway.

The scenery on the drive up was impressive in every direction one could look. Stone and Teri both agreed that it was quite easy to understand Annie's and Taylor's love of the area, particularly the location of the cabin as they turned off the highway onto the long cinder driveway. They could easily see what a magnificent view the cabin enjoyed. It gave one the impression of being able to see virtually forever.

As they were climbing out of the rental beside the cabin, Loki's phone rang. She moved away from the others to talk.

"That was Pops on the phone," she said as she disconnected the call and joined the others at the edge of a cleared area of the yard. "Apparently, my mother fell while the two of them were wandering around Kolekole Beach Park. Of all things, she was climbing on the breakwater trying to act young, looking for some *opihi* to take home. She broke her right ankle, and now Pops needs me there to help take care of her. He claims he's unable to do so himself."

"Where are your half siblings? None of them at home to help?"

"I wish, Teri. Viane is on sight at a geological dig somewhere in the Gobi Desert looking for some type of rare crystal formation and who knows where Sonny and John disappeared to. I'm the one that's available. Besides, it's my mom, not theirs."

Looking over at her friend, she said, "I'm so sorry, Annie. I have to do this. Do what you can here at the cabin but leave the big stuff for now. I'll fly back for a day or two as soon as I can and lend a hand finishing, and then together, we can go to Hawi. Maybe Stone and Teri can come back over at the same time, and we can all celebrate." She looked expectantly at them, heads nodding as she did. Loki was feeling quite sad as well as disappointed that she had to leave right then but also knew she had very little option.

Having admired the cabin and the view for a little longer, Annie stood in the driveway watching as Stone pulled out and began heading downhill.

Loki went to the airport with them planning to take the first available flight over to Hilo.

Satisfied they'd done everything they could to bring this phase of their new friend's life to closure, Stone and Teri flew back to Oahu and home.

It was an odd but beautiful ending to a day. The four of them, like a starburst sending out its rays, each taking a path in their desired or duty-bound direction, each aiming toward their individual outcomes yet all part of a new friendship.

The mountain was again peaceful and secure, all with the exception of two pair of eyes that watched from a distance as the girl's friends got in their car and drove away. Their target was now alone. Milo checked the app on his phone to see if the tracker was still functioning. It was. He'd have to remove it soon and recharge its battery in case the girl suddenly left.

Milo and Benny's being on Maui as well as being in Kīpahulu for the scattering of Jason's ashes was a result of Gravello's detailed planning and with the apparent help from an informant. He had been advised of the whole plan for Jason's ashes as well as the flights that had been booked. Milo knew his boss had strings attached to many people throughout Honolulu. *How nice it must be,* he thought, *to have the means to garner this kind of knowledge. It is like having access to a magical crystal ball.*

After the fiasco with the girls and Benny putting them underground without Mr. G.'s blessing, Milo chose not to do anything until he'd talked with the boss. When he tried to make the call, he realized the battery in the new phone had died, and situated where they were, he had no way to charge it. He told Benny to get out and find a place to hide where he had full view of the cabin while he drove down to the closest spot he could find to plug his phone in and make his call to his boss.

He didn't feel comfortable driving off and leaving Benny there, and he berated himself for such an oversight as an uncharged battery. He prayed Benny would stay vigilant and not find some comfortable spot to fall asleep. That was a lot to pray for.

Chapter Forty

$\mathcal{T}$he summit of Haleakalā was silent, standing stoic, like a giant sentinel in the middle of the ocean with its shoulders shrouded in billowy clouds. The stillness of the mountain was almost absolute, save for the sound of Stone's car as he, Teri, and Loki drove down the road and out of sight and sound. The cooing of a mountain dove somewhere in the distance was the only other sound to be heard, and it, too, blended with the peacefulness, adding its voice as if mocking the quiet.

Annie stood in the yard beside the cabin looking out over the distance, listening to the serenity and tranquility surrounding her. It made her sad to remember how happy she and Taylor had been for the short time they had together here in this beautiful place. They had shared such incredible dreams for a future together.

For the moment, she felt an elusive happiness at having made new friends through such a sad occurrence. She knew as time passed, she'd feel that happiness deepen and spread as her mourning for Taylor slowly let go of her.

Sensing it was time to get busy doing what she came to do, she walked into the cabin intent on beginning the many cleanup chores that were waiting for her. Instead, she came to a standstill in the center of the living room thinking of Taylor, thinking once again of all the plans they had made for a future of wonder and bliss but now knowing that all their dreams had disappeared like the flash of a shooting star.

She thought about the things Loki had told her about Taylor's work at her dad's firm. None of that made sense. She *knew* Taylor; she knew how he thought and the depth of honest emotions that were such an important part of who he was. If he did the things Loki told her he did—the money, the faked name—there had to be a substantial and deeply felt reason for doing so. Unfortunately, there was no longer anything to go by except her faith and love, but that faith or love would not answer any of the questions.

She couldn't let go of that thought. It stubbornly remained with her as she began gathering up his clothing scattered about. He may have been an honest man, but he was also a very sloppy one. A small smile at that thought served to ease the heartache she felt. Looking around, she was forced to admit he wasn't the only messy one of the two; she did pretty good at creating mess all by herself. Justification or rationalization aside, she recalled with sadness the hurry they had been on that day, rushing to the water with their boat in tow, ready to enjoy a fun-filled day. Little thought had been given to the mundane task of putting anything away before they left. After all, there was no need—they would both be home in time to do that.

Folding the clothing they'd left lying in the living room, she put them on the kitchen counter; Taylor's were in a separate pile destined for the local animal shelter thrift shop in Kahului. Sentimentality had never been a part of Annie's makeup. Everything would go except for one or two small keepsakes, reminders of their time together that she couldn't bring herself to part with.

Gathering up all his things in the bedroom was going to be a different story. Romanticism was deeply rooted in her character, which harbored and controlled such matters. Their lovemaking had always been powerful, almost like a second plane of existence just between them. It had taken on such strong meaning in their lives, and Annie succumbed to emotions as a powerful grief took hold of her.

Kneeling on the floor to continue the arduous task of clearing out possessions, she pulled the handle to one of the two drawers built into the bed frame under the mattress. In her hastiness, she yanked on it a little too hard when it became stuck, as it usually did, and her force quickly brought it all the way out, catapulting her back against the wall; the drawer unceremoniously came to rest on top of her outstretched legs. She impulsively shoved it off, dumping the contents on the floor in the process. Her grieving had morphed to anger, thinned-veiled as it was, but it easily gave way to a speck of humor at the bizarre situation. Her emotions were on a roller coaster. She laughed, but that was quickly mixed with frustration and tears.

With the drawer still turned upside down on her legs, she was looking at it through blurry eyes when she caught sight of something unexpected that froze tears as they fell.

Neatly taped to the back of the drawer was a key and a small piece of paper with a penciled number written on it. Her first thought was that a previous tenant must have forgotten it and left it behind, after all, it was a great hiding place and one easily forgotten. She quickly dismissed that, though, when she realized the tape holding the key and paper looked too familiar. It was the tape Taylor had bought one day, supposedly for some odd job he insisted needing his attention. They had both sat and laughed at his childhood memories and obsessions. It had a series of brightly colored cartoon characters printed on it. The one showing had been Taylor's favorite character from childhood—a caricature drawing of Walt Disney's Goofy, colored in bright reds and blues. The piece of paper had been sold as a package deal along with the tape.

She sat there, on the floor, holding on to the drawer, staring at the key, a thousand questions rolling through her thoughts.

"What the hell?" were the only words that came out.

Looking closely at the key, she saw it was clearly embossed with the words *First Hawaiian Bank* into the head, along with the number *69*. That was the bank they used in Kahului.

Knowing she had no choice but to find out what this key held hidden at the bank, she straightened herself up and pulled the key from off the bottom of the drawer. As she reached for her purse, she remembered Taylor's death certificate and their marriage papers. She was pleased with herself for remembering. If there was a new person at the desk that didn't know her, they'd surely want to see these papers before admitting her to the lockbox vault.

Explorer's keys in hand, she removed the boat from the tow hitch and simply let it drop to the ground, then headed downhill to the First Hawaiian Bank on Kaahumanu Avenue. She puzzled over how she didn't know anything about this box during all those times they'd frequented the bank. *How curious,* she thought.

The signature card that the teller asked her to sign told part of that story. There were two prior dates that Taylor had signed in, and both were a few days before they had moved to Maui. Nothing since. It made sense to her why she knew nothing of this box, but it startled her to know that Taylor had made two trips to Maui that she knew nothing about.

Unlocking the small door marked 69, the teller pulled a small drawer from the enclosure and placed it on a convenience table within the vault.

"Let me know when you're ready for me to replace it. I'll be right outside," offered the teller.

With trembling fingers, Annie slowly open the lid. In it was a shockingly thick, four inches at least, rubber-banded stack of currency. She did a quick calculation, fanning the stack as one would with a deck of cards. She guessed there was ten to twenty thousand dollars, but she had no experience at this sort of thing, and she laughed at her counting actions gained from TV shows and movies. For all she knew, it could be five or a hundred five thousand. This was not the time to be detailed about the amount.

Along with the cash, there was a sheet of white, office-sized paper. There were two columns on one side listing names of people and associated dollar amounts. Many of the names were ones she was quite familiar with through numerous newspaper articles and conversations with Taylor when he'd come into the Perch to unwind. Thinking about those times, she remembered noticing that he'd often seemed a bit nervous.

She felt it wrong to even think of doing so, but she seriously considered taking a thousand off the top of the stack. Her funds were getting low. An influx of cash would be a tremendous help to her right now—her savings were close to nil—but she couldn't justify taking any of it. With reluctance, she lowered the lid.

With the cash back in the box and the lid closed, Annie asked the teller if she'd watch over the box while she go and make a copy of the paper. The teller, smiling politely, had to refuse saying the bank's policy forbid her from doing so but offered to replace the drawer and lock the box. Annie could then make whatever copies she needed at the bank's business station. The teller said she'd be happy to reopen the drawer when she was finished with all her business.

Leaving the bank, the money, and a copy of the list safely secured in the vault once again, Annie stopped in at the Mail, Etc. store next door to the bank and bought two envelopes. Before mailing the two copies she'd made at the bank, she wrote a brief note on each one:

> Please keep this in a safe place. I won't explain now, and hopefully, there'll be no need to later. I'll call in one week to fill you in. Should you not hear from me, call Sgt. Mike Kalama at HPD. He'll take it from there.
>
> Mahalo.
> Annie

She mailed one copy to Stone and Teri; the other, to her old boss at the Perch, Paul Hender.

With this accomplished, she felt better for some reason. She was more at ease than she had felt for several days ever since Taylor died, she realized. She felt it would be her first step toward discovering the truth, of finding the peace she so desperately wanted.

She hurried back up the mountain to her cabin to resume packing. The sooner she managed to get it done, the sooner she'd be able to join Loki in Hawi and sit without distraction and begin making sense out of all the loose ends that were piling up and clouding any clear thoughts about her life.

In the cabin's bedroom, she knelt on the floor and taped the key back where she'd found it and replaced the drawer. While on her knees, she bent forward and rested her body, draped like a blanket, over the edge of the bed. It felt good to close her eyes for a few moments. Ever since she was a small kid, she'd always found this position—half on the bed, half on the floor—very peace-giving. She often did this while her parents proudly thought she was saying her evening prayers. Picking up the sheet of paper she'd brought back from the bank, she noticed she must have put the copy back in the bank box instead of the original. *Same, same. An easy mistake but not a serious one.*

She thought about calling Stone to seek his advice, but she let go of that idea. As far as she knew, Stone didn't know anything about what Loki had told her so that whole explanation bag of worms could get complicated. At least, she didn't think he knew. Her mind had been a jumble the past few days. She assumed all he knew about was Taylor's supposed inheritance, not the name nor the embezzling part of things that were being pinned on him.

She couldn't have known that Loki had already talked with Stone and Teri and confessed the whole truth of Taylor and the money as she knew it.

Still comfortably kneeling on the floor and bed, she saw one of Taylor's T-shirts on the bed in front of her, the one emblazoned with the word *Natatorium* in large letters across the front. She had been so touched to learn he'd gone back the afternoon she saw him sitting there just to buy the T-shirt. He told her he had wanted to commemorate their first meaningful time together. She picked up the shirt and a pair of his swim goggles that were close by and buried her face in the shirt as tears began flowing once again; the easiness she'd began experiencing earlier was gone.

She wanted desperately to talk with Loki, to hear some encouragement, but Loki's phone just kept ringing. By the time the answering machine came on, there were too many questions and emotions flooding through her to talk with much sense. Weeping into the phone, the only words to come out clearly were "Loki, I need your help . . . please—" She couldn't finish and let the phone fall as she laid her head back on the bed and wept; her thoughts suddenly swamped by the extraordinary circumstances she felt imprisoned by.

Unknown to Annie during this time, a pair of eyes close by that were supposed to be performing watch duty, were closed tight. Benny, the owner of them, wasn't doing any watching. In fact, he'd missed her leaving as well as her return. He was tired from having been woken up so early that morning and was fast asleep in the cool shade of some naupaka bushes along the edge of the road just as Milo pulled up beside him.

Milo had been hungry, and needing to charge his phone left Benny to perform the watch duty, hoping he wouldn't fall asleep. He had stopped at Zippy's Drive-Inn and picked up two bentos, a Japanese-type fast food in carry-out boxes. Bentos were Milo's favorite as well as Benny's. The wait for his food took way longer than he'd hoped, so he'd been gone for over an hour, much too long to leave Benny on the side of the road with shade close by.

"Wake up, Benny." Milo kept nudging at him with his foot until Benny came around and finally stood up.

"You been asleep all the time I've been gone? You see anything happening at the cabin?" Milo was annoyed that his friend may have let them down again and let Annie slip away.

Covering as best he could, Benny volunteered that no one had come, and no one had gone. As far as Benny was concerned, she was still inside doing whatever it that she was doing.

"Doing whatever she's doing," repeated Milo, mumbling to himself. He didn't need to ask; he knew his friend had probably been sleeping the whole time. He had noticed the old Explorer still in the driveway of the cabin when he'd just driven past so had to assume Annie was still inside the cabin. Everything appeared to be good.

Together, they sat under the naupaka bushes and ate their bentos—the piece of fried chicken and the slice of SPAM were Benny's favorite.

Quickly finishing, Milo pulled at Benny's sleeve and said, "Let's go," and started walking down the road toward the cabin, leaving their car by the side of the road.

Chapter Forty-one

$\mathcal{A}$nnie was emotionally drained—barely a spark left. Her body remained comfortably draped over the edge of the bed; her face still buried in Taylor's T-shirt. She loved his scent that still lingered, and she inhaled it with each breath. Sensing part of her grief begin to release its grip, she fell into a shallow sleep.

She was so cozy with the soothing warmth of sunshine and the cool breeze streaming through the window that was bathing her back she failed to hear the scraping sound of the door as it opened, accompanied by movement of feet on the wooden flooring. Even if she had heard the sound, she may not have thought much about it since the old cabin was so full of aging creaks and groans, she had become immune to its aging.

On the edge of her shallow slumber, her senses, though, became aware of a subtle change in the room—unfamiliar body odor, air suddenly shifting around her. It was enough to bring her out of sleep. Looking up, she was immediately confronted by two men standing by the bed. One directly in front of her on the other side and the other standing at the end of the bed only three feet away. She was forced to raise her eyes in order to see their faces.

Her first thought was of wondering how long they'd been in the cabin and how it was she hadn't become aware of them being there until now. She'd always thought her cocktail-lounge training had honed her skills of awareness of other people, especially those posing a threat, but it had obviously failed her. Recognition of one of the men quickly dawned.

"What the hell," she exclaimed. "I know you," pointing her finger directly at the large man standing at the foot of her bed. "You're the guy who grabbed me and my friend in Kaneohe." She wished she had something like a baseball bat close at hand. She'd had enough of this guy the first time around.

As Benny moved around the bed to position himself behind her, preparing to take hold of her, Annie managed to get her feet under her and abruptly stood, her right arm already in motion coming around in an arc, Taylor's swim goggles still tightly clasped in her hand, forgotten. She managed to connect with Benny's left eye and nose sending him reeling backward, yelling in pain as a spray of blood erupted like a Roman fountain leaving a pattern on the adjacent wall. He bent over, grabbing his aching nose that had emitted a loud cracking sound when Annie's fist connected. All three knew it was broken. He uttered several loud expletives as a flow of blood, much like a leaking water pipe, began pooling on the floor.

Before she could get herself positioned for another swing, though, Milo, with some difficulty, managed to clamber over the mattress and get her arms pinned behind her. He was struggling having grossly underestimated the woman's strength and determination; he wouldn't do that again.

He managed to wrestle her back down onto the bed and sat on her as best he could, holding her arms stationary behind her back.

Unable to move with the full weight of Milo resting in the center of her back, she did the only thing she could, she yelled. "Who the hell are you two clowns, and what do you want?" she demanded. "We've already gone through this once before." As much as she struggled, she couldn't dislodge the weight of her captor.

Benny, with an anger Milo had never witnessed in his friend, shoved him aside and quickly wrapped his huge arms around

Annie's torso capturing her arms and lifting her clear off the bed. He held her a short distance off the floor, virtually immobilizing her. Blood from his nose was dribbling down the back of her shirt, making him even angrier, but he didn't know what to do with her.

Milo moved directly in front of her, saving Benny from having to do anything, and brought his face in close. He didn't have much practice with this sort of thing. None in fact, but it was the best he came up with.

"All we want from you, lady, is the money. Hand it over, and we'll be out the door before you can blow your nose." He looked apologetic at Benny; his poor choice of words had just slipped out.

"I have no idea what you two crazy people are talking about. What money?" From the story Loki had told her in Stone's front yard and then finding that list of people and companies along with the stack of rubber-banded bills in Taylor's secret safety box, Annie had a decent idea what money they were looking for. These were people of Loki's father—they were the muscle Loki spoke of. From Annie's viewpoint, neither of them looked to be all that tough or fearsome. She decided the big guy could do a lot of damage if he ever decided to, but he didn't come across as all that mean or smart. Actually, quite the opposite.

"You have two million dollars that don't belong to you, lady." It was an overstatement, but Milo figured it might get a reaction out of her. He'd seen that in a movie once. "Your boyfriend is gone, so you're it. We're going to babysit you every minute for as long as it takes for you to remember where he stashed it."

Few things ever totally surprised Annie but that got her. *Two million! Could they possibly be serious? Had Taylor even lied about the amount of money he'd lied about. If that were the case, then it was no wonder Loki's father had coerced her into developing their friendship—that was a huge amount of money for anybody to walk away with.* A spark of doubt wedged itself into her thoughts.

Understanding what they were after and realizing they had no clue as to the whereabouts of the money nor the list she'd discovered, she quickly figured out these men weren't going to do anything to her until they figured out where it all was. She momentarily felt a little more secure until she looked down on the bed cover and saw the sheet of paper she'd brought from the bank with the list of names. She thought she'd put it safely in the drawer beneath the bed. It was certainly an indication of some secret worth hiding.

Unfortunately, it was too obvious lying on the bed, and just as she brought her eyes away from it, the guy not holding her reached down and picked it up. His eyes became bigger as he scanned the listing. He appeared bright enough to know exactly what he was looking at.

"Well, look what we have here, Benny," not really directing his comments at either her or his partner. "Mr. G.'s going to be very interested in seeing this." He waved it in front of Benny. "Let's hope it relates directly to the money the boss is looking for."

She found a little wiggle room when Benny's concentration was drawn to the paper. Acting quickly, she broke free of his grasp, but just as quickly, she realized she had nowhere to run to that these two wouldn't be able to overtake her, so she simply stood still and stared at them.

Taken by surprise and puzzled by her inaction of not running, they didn't attempt to reestablish their hold on her. Even Benny, twice thwarted by her, stood staring. It was a three-way stare-off.

"Listen to me, you two bozos. I have no idea where that money got to, and that sheet of paper is my property, not yours. If I knew where that money was, I sure as hell wouldn't give it to either of you. So it seems we are at a stalemate. She remained stationary, staring them down, unblinking, not moving.

The lull was all Milo needed to formulate a simple plan and act. Moving behind her, he threw his arms around her, being especially conscious of possible kicks and the proximity to his groin to her feet and yelled for Benny to find some rope. He was relieved she wasn't putting up a struggle.

Back on the bed with her arms and feet tied, she was helpless to do anything, but she was not in the least concerned that they would do anything to her. She let herself relax.

"What are we going to do with her, Milo? Do we have to kill her?"

"If we did that, how would she be able to tell us where her boyfriend hid all the money? Come on, Benny, do I have to do all your thinking for you?"

Chapter Forty-two

As relaxed as she could be under the circumstances, she felt her anxiety building moment by moment as her captors talked softly in the living room. It was such a helpless feeling lying face down on the bed like a trussed calf at a rodeo. She heard part of their discussions about killing her, which didn't make her feel any more at ease even knowing, praying, they wouldn't.

She couldn't move anything but her head; her back was beginning to develop a serious pain. *Cheap mattress,* she thought. At least small head movements allowed her to catch glimpses of the men as they shuffled about in the living room. They were mostly just standing in front of the large window, but she had serious doubts they were admiring the view.

They had a problem with her, and she knew that. They also had the other problem of finding out where all the money had gotten to; she knew that as well. She would really like to know the truth of that as well. Were they exaggerating about there being two million dollars involved? She sincerely hoped they were. Was there a second or third page of details that Taylor failed or forgot to put into the bank box? The page she did see and made copies of had a page number noted in the lower left corner. It said, "1." *One of how many?* she wondered.

She was finally willing to accept the notion that Taylor stole an amount of money from Anthony Gravello. The circumstances were too overwhelming to not be factual. Besides, why else would they be doing all this to her? It was a difficult truth to accept.

Why did you do it, Taylor? What did you do with it all? Why didn't you trust me enough to confide in me? We could have returned it all, taken our punishment, and maybe had a chance at the life we both dreamed of having. She was finding that tears came without provocation now. Hell of a thing to get used to it.

She had to get her mind working and come up with some way of solving this uncompromising predicament. Her confidence in believing that she held all the playing cards still held strong, but she had to admit her strength was quickly leaving her, sliding down some muddy slope into a pit.

But what can I do if I don't know anything?

Along with her back, her arms and ankles were beginning to hurt from the coarse rope they'd used to tie her with. It was tied much too tightly. She recognized the rope as the one that had been hanging in the garage when she and Taylor initially moved in to the cabin. She'd had the intention of throwing it away at the time but could never convince Taylor to let go of it. He always insisted it was a good, usable piece of rope, and he'd find a use for it. *If only he had. What would he say if he were alive and saw what his precious rope was being used for now?* More gentle tears to be absorbed as they rolled onto the bedcovers.

So immersed was she in her own thoughts she was surprised to hear the cabin door open and close.

* * *

Milo and Benny walked out into the yard so the girl couldn't hear what they were talking about.

"Benny, you go and keep an eye on the girl while I make a phone call. You think you can do that without me having to tie you to the bed along with her? And don't fall asleep."

"Aw, come on, Milo. Don't treat me like that. I'll watch her real good. You'll see. I won't fall asleep again either. Why am I going to watch her when she's tied up good?"

"I gotta make a phone call, and we can't see what she's up to from out here. Go back in there and keep your eyes open. We can't take any chances on her working those ropes loose and getting away. Mr. G. would not look upon it kindly, if you know what I mean. I'll only be a few minutes."

"Who you going to call?"

"King Kamehameha, Benny. Maybe he can tell us what to do." Milo was in a lousy mood. Things weren't working the way he thought they should, and he didn't know what to do about it other than continually calling the boss, and it was the last thing he wanted to keep doing. He liked when everything moved along easily like an old, reliable clock, no surprises. At present, that old, reliable clock was apparently missing a hand.

He thought of all the perfect beaches on this island. He would give anything to chuck it all to the wind and scrunch his body deep into the cool white sand and let the small waves wash around him and watch the world drift past, but that wasn't going to happen any time soon. He called his boss.

The news that Annie had possession of a list of his clients and notations showing various money totals almost floored him. *That's incredulous. How the hell did Jason manage to come up with all that information?* The news of even having the girl had been overshadowed by that bit of information.

Hearing Milo's news, all he could think of was that perhaps his time in Hawaii had truly come to its end; everything was beginning to turn sour. He sensed that he returned to that conclusion much more frequently lately. The sooner he made the move home, the more at ease his life would become.

He had enough money, with or without the amount Jason had taken from him. He paused a moment as he wondered about the precise amount Jason had actually pilfered. His money was scattered over too many different accounts, both here in Hawaii and internationally. If he were to sit quietly for an hour or two, he would know the exact amount to the penny; he just hadn't taken that hour of time to do so. The truth was that if he never recovered it, it wouldn't make a big difference to him. He'd still live out a life of luxury in his homeland.

First, though, he needed to make every effort doing what he could to find the missing funds and erase the evidence of that list Milo found. His Sicilian upbringing would not allow him to simply walk away leaving such a rock unturned. He needed to talk to this woman face to face and see what force he could bring to bear on her. *She* had *to know something.*

Still holding his phone, Milo almost forgotten, he said, "Milo, go into Kahului, Mokulele Highway by the airport. Find a Dr. Harley Badger. His office is right next to Zippy's at the corner of Mokulele and Kuihelani. You got that?"

"I got it, Mr. G. Even wrote it down." He was lying, of course, since he had no pen or even a piece of paper with him standing out in the yard, but he could trust his memory to remember a name like that. As for Zippy's, he'd been there just a couple hours ago—he could easily remember that as well.

"Dr. Harley Badger will have something for you, along with the instructions of what to do with it. Go do this now," Gravello continued, telling Milo precisely what he expected to take place and how soon. "No excuses, Milo." A further warning ended the call. "Don't you mess this up, or your life won't be worth the price of the dirt under your fingernails, and that goes double for that sidekick of yours."

The call ended almost before the last syllable was spoken. It failed to elevate Milo's mood in the least.

He walked back into the cabin and looked in through the bedroom door. Benny was sitting cross-legged two feet to the left of the girl, his eyes riveted on her, looking as if he dared her to move a muscle. Annie had rolled her head sideways and was watching Benny just as doggedly. Milo felt a tinge of shame after having vented his own frustrations on his friend over things that were out of either of their control. Benny tried hard and always meant well. Milo needed to remember that. He also noticed the bandage he'd applied to Benny's nose would need changing when he returned—a lot of red was showing through. He felt sorry for him and imagined it must be quite painful, yet Benny would never think of complaining.

"Benny, I have to drive into town and pick something up for Mr. G. You going to be okay staying here with the girl until I get back?"

"I'll watch her real careful, Milo. We'll both be right here when you come back."

"Okay, Benny, and remember not to untie those ropes or loosen them no matter what argument she puts up. And if she has to go pee, hold her arm while she hobbles to the bathroom. Either that or take her out in the yard and tell her to squat. You'll probably have to help pull her pants down. You okay with that?"

Benny simply blushed at the thought, and his eyes opened wide. He'd never actually seen a naked woman up close, only ones in a magazine, and he could still visualize the pictures. His curiosity suddenly began running a little crazy as various possibilities began to take hold.

"Yeah, I can do that." His voice was suddenly small and uncertain.

Not believing what she heard, Annie twisted her head in order to look directly at Milo. He thought if she twisted it any farther, it would snap off. He heard the words she uttered and knew for sure they would be capable of frying the hair off a goat. He backed out of the doorway. He pitied Benny if she had to pee before he returned.

Milo thought about the instructions he received from his boss. He didn't fully understand the whole money issue that was taking place other than the fact his boss wanted it back—that he understood well. Nor did he understand why his boss seemed to be going overboard in what he was expecting Milo to take care of. *Maybe,* he thought, *his idea of two million was closer to the truth than he realized.*

He also knew his boss really didn't care what Milo thought about the whole thing. Milo existed on a low level in the pecking order as far as Garvello's family was concerned. He was expected to execute commands and never question the why. Perhaps he'd been with the Gravello family too long already. He knew he'd adopted a good deal of the American way of thinking, and he liked it, but it was not good for his continued health. A cement anchor around his ankle was too close to a real possibility.

Milo had no way of knowing that his boss was also envisioning a move and was deliberating what he might do with Milo and Benny when he leaves—*perhaps take them with him*. Milo was amused with the thought of that.

* * *

Tony Gravello eased back in his chair and looked out over the water and took a deep breath.

Get this money thing and Jason's girlfriend out of the way first, one way or another.

Chapter Forty-three

$\mathcal{M}$ilo was thoroughly confused and more than a little concerned. Mr. G. had never asked him to do anything illegal in all the time he'd been working for him. Shady, yes, that went with the territory, but nothing that would get him thrown into prison for. Milo knew enough about the Sicilian *famiglia*-style of life that he'd considered himself fortunate that his boss hadn't brought all of that ugliness with him. However, now he wondered if the old traditions had finally caught up with him. *I've definitely become too American in my thinking.* An involuntary shudder coursed through him at images of what fate may have waiting for him.

He drove down the mountain, weighing the possibility that this could be the start of something he'd prefer not to be a part of. It went against his Sicilian blood, the core of who he prided himself to be. Refusing to carry out a family order was a death sentence; it just wasn't done. But this whole doctor-medicine business was beginning to feel as though he were leaning on the fringes of a very deep hole. The instructions he'd been given sounded like this may be the final straw that would push him over an edge he didn't want to get anywhere near.

It didn't help his thinking knowing that he harbored a healthy dislike of doctors in general and all the medicines they had within easy reach, willingly dispensed and often without any overseeing authority.

Milo figured his disdain of doctors had a lot to do with an office visit his mother took him to long ago in Palermo when he was very young. It turned out the guy wasn't even a doctor but an out-of-work print-press operator that had printed his own certificates of education and hung them all over his dingy office walls. Milo had come very close to dying that day because the filth and germs that flourished there and in a bottle of crud he'd had to swallow. He'd often wondered how his mother had come to place trust in this man, and where was his father when all this was going down? Questions that would never receive answers.

He'd been told that Dr. Harley Badger would give him what was needed along with instructions on how to proceed and what to expect. He crossed himself and said a prayer to the Virgin Mary as he opened the door to the doctor's office.

After it was all taken care of, he reminded himself that he had to pick up any container the doctor gave him and dispose of it somewhere away from the cabin. Mr. G. had repeated those instructions several times as did the doctor.

It was quite apparent, judging from the conversation Milo had had with his boss, that Gravello and the doctor had a very close bond. It made Milo wonder why he'd never heard of Dr. Harley Badger before now—he knew most of his boss's close associates.

What Milo didn't know, but certainly could have guessed had he given it more thought, was that Dr. Harley Badger was being generously rewarded for his discretion and had been similarly rewarded several times in the past when a medical blind eye was needed. So much rewarded, in fact, that the good doctor had amassed a sizable fortune and was, in fact and unknown to Gravello and to his many other underworld connections, in the process of planning a quick retirement—perhaps to St. Augustine, Florida. He'd heard it was a nice place to be.

The doctor and Anthony Gravello had literally bumped into each other aboard the ship as both young men were fleeing their respective families in Sicily, both headed for America. They had formed a bond and made a pact to help each other whenever needed, and so far, it had been a very rewarding relationship for both—perhaps more so for the doctor. He wasn't about to trample on Gravello's friendship and close bond, not to mention the funding he was receiving to pave way to his dreams.

Milo's instructions from the boss were for him and Benny to bring Annie back to Oahu, specifically to Pohakau, after the medicine was satisfactorily ingested and the effects realized, and they were able to get her to the airport and board a Honolulu-bound flight.

Milo was told that a wheelchair would be required and that Aloha Airlines would provide one. He was assured he would understand it all after talking to Dr. Harley Badger.

At least, he hasn't requested the airline to provide a casket. This whole thing is very complicated.

He couldn't figure out one single reason why they would require a wheelchair unless one of the three couldn't walk, and he knew that wasn't going to be himself. It would definitely be for Benny if he'd let that girl get away from him.

As Milo discovered, Dr. Harley Badger was an intelligent and thoroughly likable individual. He was drawn to him immediately upon meeting. Becoming acquainted with this man and knowing Mr. G. as well as Milo did, he understood why his boss's connection with the doctor was as tight a bond as it appeared to be.

Dr. Harley Badger was a short-statured individual. He was a bit rounder than is healthy with a bald dome fringed by a bit of remaining gray hair, much like an abbot from a previous era. Everything put together, Dr. Badger possessed a personality and openness that would easily allow him to be the center of attention in a room full of strangers.

Milo was at ease with the situation now that he understood better what the small bottle of liquid that was put into his hand was for and what effect it would have. The doctor explained that the bottle contained a high-potency form of methamphetamine, plus a sleep inducer. Milo had the impression there was more mixed into the potion than he was being led to believe but was assured the patient would feel no long-term effects and that it would all wear-off within twenty-four to thirty-six hours.

Beyond that, the doctor feigned ignorance of any other details of what was taking place and simply explained that it would make the patient appear drunk, unable to control the movement of their arms and legs as well as their neck. A wheelchair would be a necessity, and the victim would require being strapped in against the likelihood they would flop, his word, out of the chair with the slightest of motion. Again, Milo was reassured she'd return to normal reasonably quickly.

The last statement the doctor made left Milo with the impression that he knew a lot more about what was taking place than their meeting had implied.

Milo went back to his car feeling a lot better than when he'd arrived.

Heading back up the mountain, he was at ease with the task that he and Benny were now required to perform. He just hoped the girl wouldn't put up too much struggle. He also knew he was kidding himself to even hope that would be the case. He was expecting the worst and was mentally prepared for it.

With a stop at Aloha Airlines ticket office, Milo reserved seats on an early afternoon flight with the request that a wheelchair be at curbside for a very sick and unstable friend. They were instructed to leave it at the terminal in Honolulu when they arrived. There would be an airline representative at the curbside to retrieve it.

He was looking forward to returning to Oahu. He failed to find the slightest enjoyment doing this sort of thing—even in beautiful Maui.

Chapter Forty-four

The whole process of getting Annie back to Oahu turned out to be much less difficult than Milo had been anticipating. He was enormously relieved.

When Mr. G. first informed him of what he was expecting to happen, Milo's first thought was simply knocking her unconscious with something heavy, but then he'd have to find a way to get her aboard the airplane other than throwing her over his shoulder. He was certain the airlines would frown upon that.

Now he had to find a way to encourage her to drink the concoction Badger had provided without setting off her internal warning bells. He'd probably have to wrestle her to the floor and force her to drink it, and he wasn't too sure either he or Benny or even both of them together could manage that feat with any ease or without incurring serious injury.

The doctor did, however, suggest that it could be added to the contents of a can of Coke. He claimed it wouldn't lose any of its potency and would be unnoticeable by taste. It wasn't a bad idea and provided Milo with the remedy he was looking for. He stopped at a food market on the way back to the cabin for the necessary supplies as well as a couple of premade tuna sandwiches for him and Benny. He knew Benny loved tuna sandwiches, the real thick kind heaped with tuna.

Walking in the cabin, he found Benny still faithfully sitting right where he had been. It didn't look like he'd moved so much as an inch from the spot he'd been in when Milo left almost an hour ago. The only thing Milo noticed was a very large and crookedly placed fresh bandage over his friend's nose.

"Nice job at bandaging, Benny. What blind man did you find to do that for you?" Milo had a big smile as he handed Benny the sandwich.

The sandwich had his attention, so Milo's joke was missed. For having sat for so long, Benny wasn't complaining but instead looked smug and pleased with himself. The girl was asleep, which was perfect for what Milo had to do.

In the kitchen, he explained the plan to Benny and hoped they could get Annie to drink the medication without them giving off any warning of danger. Benny returned to the position he'd been in on the bed, trying to get into position as carefully as he could without waking the girl. Milo made all the preparations in the kitchen, then went into the bedroom and sat down hard on the bed, making it bounce.

Annie immediately came awake. She hadn't intended to fall asleep, but her exhaustion apparently took her in its own direction. She quickly refocused on her situation.

Milo wasted no time in initiating his idea.

"You're probably tired of lying there bound up like a handful of watercress," he said to Annie, talking with a soft, almost friendly, voice. "Benny and I are going to fly back to Oahu, which leaves us with the problem of the whereabouts of the money you have as well as the problem of what to do with you when we have the money and leave. You see the fix we're in?"

"Since we're being all friendly like," replied Annie in an even-toned yet no-nonsense voice, "you want to hear my problem? I'm tired of lying here bound up like a pig ready for roasting in someone's *imu*. My arms and legs hurt from the rope. I think my feet are going to fall off from lack of blood, and I still don't have

a clue, nor do I have a care in hell where your stinkin' money is."
The last few words were said loudly, with a lot of intention. "If you
don't untie me right now, I promise to God, as soon as I manage to
get loose, I'll make you two bozos wish you'd never stepped foot on
this island."

Appearing to take her seriously and actually considering her
words, he looked over at Benny and said, "Benny, I brought a
couple cans of Coke back with me, and I'm getting thirsty. They're
in the kitchen. How about you go and get me one? Help yourself to
the other if you want."

Nothing was offered to Annie.

Watching them sip and seeing the cold condensation drip
from the can, Annie realized how extremely thirsty she was. Milo's
seemingly friendly attitude opened the way for her to ask, "You
have another one of those I could have?"

Milo smiled. His plan was playing out just as he'd hoped.
"Sure, no problem. Benny, untie one of her hands and tie the other
hand to the bedpost. Leave her ankles tied so she doesn't try to
make a run for it, then go and bring another Coke. I think there's
one more there that she can have." The words were as sweet as the
soda they were drinking.

Benny brought it in already opened.

Annie either didn't notice or didn't care as she drank deeply,
not realizing just how much she enjoyed the bubbles and foam
created in her dry throat. She took several more swallows since she
had no idea what was going to happen next or when she'd have
another chance to quench her thirst. Taking the can from her lips,
most of it gone, she discovered a slightly different, unusual taste
lingering in her mouth. Within mere moments, her world began
to do head spins. Her fingers let go of the can as her head flopped
forward and her body fell back on the bed into a puddle of Jell-O.

"Your plan worked, Milo. That was sure fast. What do we
do now?" he said, flexing his legs several times to get circulation
flowing again. He'd been sitting on the bed for a long time, and his
knees hurt but he didn't want to mention that to Milo.

"Now," Milo's face holding a look of complete satisfaction as well as relief, "the three of us get to the airport. The doctor said the initial effects would last several hours depending on how strong a person was. We can't let her come out of this before we get her to the boss's house."

Milo bent to the task of undoing the ropes and half dragging, half carrying Annie, got her into the living room. He put her down awkwardly slouched against the cushioned back of the small sofa.

"Benny, pick up the soda can that's on the bed and grab the bottle in the kitchen. We gotta take those with us. We can throw them away somewhere between here and the airport. I'm going to help the girl into the car, so we're ready to get out of here."

It was a good plan and may have worked out all right had Benny not forgotten why the Coke can was there and what had been in it. There was hardly enough left in the can to wet the inside of his mouth, but he was still thirsty, and there was just enough to bring some results. It didn't take but a minute, and Benny was beginning to mentally spin in a circle. He managed to make it out the door and into the car before closing his eyes.

His head voluntarily fell back against the neck rest. Milo was so involved with the girl and getting under way that he failed to notice the odd condition his friend was suddenly in.

The cabin door remained partially ajar since Benny failed to close it all the way. Left lying in the open on the kitchen counter was the empty medicine bottle. The Coke can, with a minute amount of liquid still remaining, rested on top of the bedcovers, forgotten.

As prearranged, Aloha Airlines had a wheelchair waiting curbside outside their ticket counter. When the ticket agent asked about their friend, Milo lied and said they were taking her to Queen's Medical Center on Oahu, to the Kekela ward. Benny's somewhat erratic behavior, the minor impact the trivial amount of drug had created, was still present but rapidly wearing off as he slowly returned to his normal self. Its residual effects, though, added to the believability of Milo's story. He went ahead and explained to the uninterested ticket agent about the Kekela ward, saying that it was a designated ward the hospital had established as a place for patients with symptoms of habitual drug use and minor physiological issues. The ticket agent nodded her head in understanding while looking at Benny. The girl, still out cold in the wheelchair, didn't seem to bring any awareness.

As far as anyone could see, the woman was secured to the chair so she wouldn't fall out and cause a liability problem for the airline. The threesome would be the last passengers off the airplane in Honolulu in order not to inconvenience any of the other passengers. This was just fine with Milo. He'd like to draw as little attention as possible.

Finally arriving at Pohakau, their boss appeared in front of his large, ornate wooden double-doors. He had been anxiously waiting for them and had been alerted to their arrival by entry alarms at the driveway's entrance. He noticed Benny acting very strangely but gave it no further attention; he was Milo's responsibility.

The main doors into the house were recessed in an alcove skillfully created from lava rock and offering a very upscale and wealthy invitation to arriving guests. The handsome doors showed deep relief carving depicting some of Hawaii's popular and quite recognizable fauna. They were the focal point of the main house centered on the sweeping circular driveway.

Chiseled stone bordered the entryway's walls to the left and right, and both sides depicted a pineapple in chiseled relief. Gravello had planned to have them removed when he first purchased the place until he discovered that the pineapple was actually a centuries-old symbol of hospitality dating back to the days of Columbus. Discovering that, he had warmed to the idea of them fronting his mansion.

Milo noticed that his boss held a very intense look as he walked out toward the car. There was no smile, no handshakes. He was all business. Milo knew his boss came out to check to make sure the girl was, in fact, barely conscious before he would allow her out of the car. He wasn't willing to have her suddenly come out of her stupor and start screaming and raising a riot that would draw attention from some of his *niele* neighbors. Milo knew his boss was not at ease having this girl here, yet he had demanded—it was his call.

Besides being a friend of his daughter, this girl was the link to retrieving his money. Milo was sure it wasn't strictly the money prompting all the cloak and dagger; his boss had more than enough resources available. A few more greenbacks meant nothing to the big man. It was the old-country value system of taking back what had been stolen. The main point of Gravello's aggravation and lack of feeling was simply that no one ever took Anthony Gravello for anything and got away clean.

* * *

Annie's eyelids were closed as she was wheeled from the car. She appeared vacant of life; there were no lights on. Spittle had run down her chin and dropped on the dark-red T-shirt she'd put on this morning. A drop was accumulating on her chin and was about to take its place on her shirt. It wasn't difficult to see that not a single muscle in her body was functioning, which pleased Gravello. He'd be sure to mention his appreciation to Badger next time they talked.

A strap stretched taut across Annie's chest just below her breasts was the only thing keeping her upright. More straps were in place around each ankle holding her feet on the chair's stirrups. Her hands and arms, though, rested somewhat comfortably in her lap—not tied in any fashion. If anyone who knew her could see her at this moment, their hearts would break.

Apparently, while manhandling her out of the car and into the wheelchair, no one had noticed the slight movement of her left arm as they refastened the straps. Contrary to what the doctor had said about the recipient of his special cocktail remaining under the influence for many hours, Annie had begun coming out of her stupor during the forty-minute airplane ride. Her awareness had been gaining in clarity ever since.

From the moment she'd been brought off the airplane, she'd been doing her best to remain visibly motionless and lifeless. Her body was leaning to the left for much of the time, putting a lot of weight on her left arm, and it was responding with an increasingly dull pain, but she couldn't dare move it. This was no game, and she knew that. There was a lot at stake, and her life was being threatened. She could feel the unspoken antipathy emanating from the man and instinctively knew he was quite capable of causing her permanent harm. By her stillness, she had full intention of coming out of this ordeal unscathed and intact; she was a very good actress.

Benny was pushing the wheelchair with Milo close behind as Gravello escorted them into the house and down a long hallway—a hallway neither Milo nor Benny had ever been allowed to enter. Gravello stopped them midway to the end of the hallway and took control of the wheelchair. He motioned with hand signals directed toward the two men. The meaning being quite obvious—turn around and head back down the hallway to the entrance and wait there.

Gravello had had a special room built soon after purchasing the house, which was now going to serve as Annie's jail. She would be the first person other than Gravello himself who had ever entered this space. It was his very private domain, and he didn't like having to bring her in here, but he was clueless as to any other option.

He rolled the wheelchair down to the end of the hallway and through the back entrance into his office. Situated on one of the walls was a floor-to-ceiling bookcase. Operating a mechanism behind one of the books, the bookcase noiselessly slid fully open, revealing this special room. He rolled Annie into the center, left her there, seemingly still under the drug's control and went back out, closing the bookcase behind him.

Annie's jail was centered in the house. The room had no phones, no windows, and just the one door. A highly polished wood floor with a plain scatter rug centered the room. The barest of furnishings were placed around the room. Two thick and comfortable appearing brown leather chairs with an ornate wood-carved table taking the space between them. Bookshelves had been built into the four walls but housed a sparse number of books scattered throughout.

The only objects that stood out in the room were several carved busts of ancient theological heroes, similar to busts that were in every room throughout the house.

The odd thing about such a private room was that there wasn't anything of value in it, nothing that would require being kept so secret. The other oddity was that it was double wall constructed with ultra-soundproofing material sandwiched between. The room was essentially Gravello's security blanket. A need he still held from his earliest childhood and had felt compelled to duplicate soon after buying the house.

No one would suspect that the exterior strength of Tony Gravello sheltered this small element of insecurity. This room gave him emotional comfort on the rare occasions he needed to escape.

At this moment, he wasn't about to analyze those emotions; he'd done that many times in the past and usually to no avail. For now, it made an ideal spot to keep the girl hidden from sight until he knew what he would have to do with her. There was an odd sensation lingering within him since introducing this stranger to this inner sanctum. He wondered if perhaps he was slowly overcoming some of his long held insecurities. He wasn't sure how he felt about that.

He was also beginning to understand some of things his estranged wife had often confided to him about many of his responses to situations that affected their lives. That it was often nothing more than his ego not willing to overlook someone getting the best of him. He knew deep down that his current attempts to retrieve the money stolen was just that—his ego not willing to accept having been taken advantage of.

Sitting in his office, he was thinking of Dr. Badger's words about the lifespan of the drug he'd provided and figured he still had a few hours to decide what to do with the girl.

He had failed to realize that Annie was in such good physical condition and that it had already been several hours since Milo gave her the drug.

From what Milo mentioned about their questioning of the girl at her cabin, he had doubts she knew where the money was. She did, however, have that list of his clients that could prove to be disastrous. He was certain she would have looked at it and would have known some of the names mentioned. He prayed to God she hadn't made copies. If that list went public and any authority came to search his books, he'd be spending a lot of years behind bars at Oahu Correctional facility.

His time was very limited; his task, specific.

He sat staring out at the ocean. This was the best place for planning the next step.

In the end, he knew he would have to dump the girl into the water; he saw no other logical ending for her that bought safety for him.

Chapter Forty-five

Hawi, Big Island of Hawaii

*L*oki was feeling anxious, not sure what she needed to do. She had just listened to the message that Annie had left her almost an hour before. The distress in her voice was almost palpable. It was unlike the Annie Loki was coming to know and care deeply for to sound so desperate. Besides the uneasiness Loki was experiencing, she was more distraught with herself for not running to answer the phone when she'd heard it instead of simply letting it go to voice mail. It was a habit she'd developed since moving to Hawi. She needed to work on that.

The only consolation she could allow herself was that by the time she'd heard it ring and realized it was hers and not that of a neighbor's, there was really no way she could have gotten to it in time.

Now Annie wasn't there to answer her phone. It was frustrating to have something that sounded so important left hanging in the air.

Loki's yard was big, almost an acre, and she'd been in the back reaches of her property picking fruit when Annie's call had come in—too far to run and still be able to answer.

She sat down on a deck chair and looked out over her backyard. She loved her yard and often used its visual beauty as a catalyst to a troubled mind like now. Looking around at the various plant life that had been in place when she'd purchased the house, it was apparent whoever had owned it before her had been a fanatic about planting edible plants and trees. There were strawberries, guavas, bananas, papayas, *pipinola*, and quite a few *mamaki* trees, Loki loved mamaki tea, and a lot of other plants that she had no idea of what they were. They *looked* like something one could eat; that was all she'd observed.

The question now was what did she need to do about it? The distress evident in Annie's voice implied that it wasn't a social call but carried the earmarks, albeit quite short, of a plea for help. It was also evident in Annie's voice that she was crying and had sounded close to being hysterical.

When she had left Annie, along with Stone and Teri, on Maui to return home, Annie seemed upbeat and excited to get on with the process of packing so she could get to the Big Island and live in Loki's house for a while. They had both been excited with the prospects.

Then what had happened? Somewhere in the recesses of her mind, Loki once again began wondering if her father had possibly done something to create this panic in her friend. The chances were good that he had.

She tried to call Annie at the cabin again but still received no response. She didn't know anyone on Maui to call and ask if they'd be good enough to drive up to the cabin and check to see if all appeared okay. She knew of two of her father's clients that lived there but asking either of them for a favor would be tantamount to asking a hungry wolf to go in and check on the chicken coop.

She had left Annie and the others in Maui to tend to her mother's broken ankle, but it turned out her mom hadn't been in as bad a shape as Pops had implied. Loki was certain that Pops simply wanted her back home for a bit and had exaggerated a little. She didn't blame him. It had been quite a while since they'd hugged, and she knew he missed having her there. Her mom was a very strong woman, physically as well as willed, and a little thing like a broken ankle was not going to become an anchor to her.

Loki had stayed in Hilo for the night with Pops and her mom and then returned home to begin preparing the way for Annie. *It is going to be so much fun having Annie stay here. There is so much in the area for us to see and do together.*

Now it appeared they had to get beyond whatever had taken place back in Maui that was creating the pothole in front of them. She prayed it was just a pothole and not a sheer drop-off that her friend had stepped into.

The more she thought about everything, the more certain she was that her father was involved in creating the distress she'd heard; he and those two inept gophers of his were entirely capable of creating a crater full of stressful situations. Her father had told her the last time they'd talked that he would take care of things since Annie was becoming a friend and Loki had begun putting up resistance.

She thought about calling Stone and Teri, but they weren't any closer to Maui than Loki was, but she knew that Stone would be able to help in some way.

Chapter Forty-six

$\mathcal{I}$t was another beautiful day, and Stone had nothing that had to be done that couldn't wait for later, so he decided to head for the water. He had his bathing suit on and was out the door with the intention of grabbing one of the two kayaks he and Teri kept on a rack beside the beach when the house phone rang, bringing him up three steps short of reaching for his kayak.

His plan had been to paddle out around Coconut Island, then to simply sit back, and let the current drift him across a few of the many shallow reefs that abounded in Kaneohe Bay. The water over most of the reefs was shallow and clear, and small sea life flourished.

He quickly backtracked to answer the phone. It took a moment's hesitation as he considered not answering but dismissed the idea—there was too much happening lately to let it go. He decided he'd head for the water just as soon as he could dispatch the caller.

Teri was upstairs with her rock samples spread all over the dining room table, busily analyzing various pieces and would probably not like to drop everything just to answer the phone when she knew he wasn't doing anything.

The rock samples she was sorting through had been sent in by a field geologist working in Palau, one of the small islands in the Micronesian group. The department would look the other way when Teri took some of the extra samples home. They knew she was practicing her identification skills, and that made her that much more valuable to them.

The phone rang two more times before Stone managed to pick it up. It was a landline. He liked landlines so much more than cell phones and accepted the need for quick dashes to answer.

He was pleasantly surprised to hear Loki's voice on the other end. He'd been thinking about her and Annie since the girls had spent the two days in his house. He had planned to call her later that evening to see how her mother was doing.

On hearing the urgency in Loki's voice, though, he sat down in a lawn chair close by and listened to what it was that was obviously disturbing her so much. His first thought was something might have happened to her mom, maybe something catastrophic by the sound of her voice.

"Stone, thank God, you're there. No," she answered quickly in response to Stone's immediate question, "it's not mom. She's doing great. So great that she told me she and Pops didn't need me there. I'm home in Hawi and starting to make plans for Annie. That's what I'm calling about." The desperation in her voice quickly became very evident.

"It's Annie, Stone. I don't know for sure, but I think something has happened to her, and I don't know what to do. I am afraid for her. I may be overreacting, but I don't think so." Her mind was struggling, trying to remember if Stone knew about the stolen money and her father's involvement and hesitated to bring it up. The details of their conversation around the dining table about all this had gotten confusing so she decided not to say anything unless Stone mentioned it. "What should I do?"

"First off, Loki, you have to tell me what happened to make you feel Annie's in trouble." Unable to hold back, he had to ask. "Does this by any chance have anything to do with your father and the money Taylor and Annie inherited? The same money you told Teri and me about?"

Good, I did tell him.

"You made the same leap I did. I've been having a difficult time accepting the thoughts I have about all this. Are you always this sharp?" It wasn't said with any meaning, more of a conversation filler.

"No, Teri would tell you I'm dull as a tack most of the time. I've been wondering about that possible eventuality since you mentioned it to Teri and me and then you both getting abducted."

"You've jumped to the same thought that I've been wondering about all afternoon while trying to reach Annie. That's why I'm calling you. Annie left me a message that sounded desperate. She was calling from the cabin, and she had obviously been crying and maybe still was. I tried to call back fifteen minutes after she called, but she's not answering. I'm afraid for her, Stone. Do you know anyone in Maui who could drive up and check the cabin to see if everything looks okay? Could your police friend, Mike, do anything about checking it out?"

"I don't know anyone in Maui well enough that I could impose on them like that, but I'm sure the police can do something. Where are you right now?"

"I'm home in Hawi."

"Stay there. I'll call Mike and see if he can arrange for a patrol officer to drive to the cabin and have a look around. I'll call you back when I have some sort of answer. Sit tight, Loki. Everything will work out exactly the way it's supposed to. It always does."

Stone let out a loud sigh. It appeared his pleasant kayak paddle around the reefs was going to be a bit delayed, and that was all right. There was lots of daylight left for playing.

Chapter Forty-seven

It took a while to convince the desk sergeant overseeing the phone lines at the Maunakea precinct to relax enough to tell Stone where Mike was, but he finally succeeded. As soon as Stone had identified himself and after mentioning that he and the sergeant's boss were Hui O'Kainalu brothers, the desk sergeant told Stone where Mike was. That delay tactic usually meant only one thing: Mike was off duty and was out spending some time with Robin, his soon-to-be fiancé. Mike had only mentioned that bit of information to a few close friends. Time would be the judge of it really happening. Mike had probably told the desk sergeant not to disclose where he was unless the caller was a friend and, certainly, if there was an emergency that he needed to respond to.

Mike and Robin tried to get together whenever their schedules allowed, which was often close to impossible to manage. Either one or the other would get caught up in work, typically with little warning and that would cause their plans to change. Occasionally, though, such as this afternoon, they'd both been able to arrange for the afternoon off and the entire day the next day as long as nothing urgent came up. They were celebrating as they always did when mutual time together materialized.

Robin Jaffers was the radio and communications central clearing person for the Island Coast Guard Station operating on Sand Island, Oahu. The station overlooked Honolulu Harbor and Aloha Tower—primo real estate.

Robin hadn't been trained in active Coast Guard duties, but her expertise with communications were invaluable. With approval, all the way up the chain of command, the Coast Guard wanted her on board and created a special slot for her, bestowing the rank of seaman first class along with the pay and all the amenities of military service that went with that rank. She knew it was an outstanding honor.

She loved the work—constant communications with personnel out on the seas guarding the coastline of Hawaii's many islands, as well as the units assigned to man ground operations. There was talk of a future space-based Coast Guard, and she wanted to be around for that.

As a young girl, Robin had gotten interested in communications, VHF radio in particular, because of her stepfather, Doug Holmes. He'd had a license to operate VHF and had had an elaborate setup in a room above their garage and huge antenna's all over their backyard. She spent hours sitting beside him, provided her homework was finished, listening to him talk with people from exotic countries all over the world. On several occasions, he'd let her initiate a call and talk with a friend of his or allow her to hunt the airwaves for a new contact. She'd then mark the city and country on a special map her stepfather had provided her, and that encouraged her even more.

That experience took her into DeVry University for a bachelor in arts in media art. Following graduation, she moved to Hawaii and earned her masters of science data services degree at the Manoa campus of the University of Hawaii. The Coast Guard caught wind of her accomplishments.

She had met Mike after someone cut a hole in the Coast Guard's security fencing, and the police were called in. Robin had discovered the breach and subsequently met Mike who came to investigate.

* * *

Stone reached Mike while both he and Robin were sitting at their favorite table at the Waikiki Beachside Bistro overlooking the famous beach. It was a very relaxing setting, exactly what each looked forward to during their sometimes-long absences apart.

They were busily planning the rest of their day and their tomorrow with ideas ranging from spending their next day stretched out on the sands of Haunama Bay to maybe flying over to Kauai and scuba dive in the fresh, cool water outside the hidden caves. Those plans were interrupted when Mike's phone came alive with the sounds of Willie Nelson's "On the Road Again." He felt the song was symbolic of his life.

With a sinking feeling, he glanced down at it, hooked to his belt and the indicator light on top blinking. This usually meant he was needed some place—his day with Robin aiming for a crash. As soon as he heard Stone's voice, he relaxed.

"How-z-it, Stone? Since you knew this was my time off, I have to assume you're critically injured, have received a death threat, been bitten by a rabid dog with fleas, or had some appendage cut off."

Whenever Mike got into talking like this, you just had to let him finish.

"Yeah, yeah, yeah. I've heard all that."

"And, Stone, I hope you know Robin is sitting next to me giving the phone, and therefore you, her evil eye."

"Mike, listen. I'm really sorry to mess with your day. Please apologize to Robin, tell her to put aside her evil eye, and give her a kiss for letting you answer this call. If left up to her, she would probably like to grab it and throw it into the closest fish tank."

"She wouldn't dare." He looked up at her sitting beside him and winked.

"If I'm right, I can hear Hawaiian music in the background and waves breaking on the sand, so I'm betting you're at your favorite bistro."

"You're right, good guess, and I bet you're going to mess with that, but tell me, what are we drinking? That's the question, and also are you and Teri going to come down and join us?"

Getting away from the social side and ignoring Mike's question for a moment, he got right into the reason he'd called. "I need you to make a simple phone call to one of your fellow officers in Maui. You think Robin will forgive you the two- or three-minute lapse back into work?"

"I don't know. If you could see the look she's giving you through the phone waves you may want to seek her forgiveness first before asking." There was a friendly sound of humor in his voice, and Stone guessed Mike was aiming that smile at Robin. "You realize this is going to cost you, don't you? What do I need to say in this phone call I'm about to make to Maui?"

"Mahalo, Mike, bless the patrol car you rode in on. You remember the girl Annie, right? Her boyfriend died at Castle earlier last week after the beestings on Molokai?" he added to bring up Mike's awareness in case recent events had pushed it too far back.

"Yeah, how can I forget that poor girl?"

"My niece, Loki, received a distress call from *that poor girl*, as you put it, a short time ago on her voice mail. Apparently, Annie had been or still was crying, and the message gave Loki the distinct impression that it was an urgent plea for help. I'd be grateful if you could manage to get an officer to swing by Annie's cabin off Haleakalā Road and check to see if everything appears to be in order."

"I'll make that call right now. I know just the person to handle this. I'm sure the officer will know which cabin since there's only one other cabin off that highway that high up. I'll ask her to call me back after she's been there and checked it out. May take a little while—there is a manhunt currently in progress around Ioa Needle, and I know a lot of the island's officers are involved in that.

"In the meantime, my friend, since you now owe me for this future call, Robin and I are going to John Dominis Restaurant this evening. Why don't you and Teri come down and join us? We can share a bottle of Dom Perignon and dive into one of their huge seafood platters?"

"That has the sound of a celebration of some kind. Care to share?"

"Only if you and Teri show up. Otherwise, you'll just have to guess what it's like to be simply an ordinary person without privileges like everyone else in Honolulu until you receive the invitation. You coming?"

"If Teri's up for it, yes—wouldn't miss it. I'll give you the answer when you call me back. Should I bring a gift with me or wait for the official announcement?"

* * *

After disconnecting from the call, Stone called Loki to inform her what was being done. He hoped that by now she would have reached Annie and that all was back to normal—*that would be nice,* he thought, but that had not happened. He told her about a patrol car making a stop at the cabin to check things over and promised to call her back when he heard anything.

After checking with Teri about meeting Mike and Robin and receiving enthusiastic response, he went back out and picked up his set of kayak paddles and headed for the beach. It looked like he would have time to indulge. He put his cell phone in a plastic baggie so Mike or Loki would be able to reach him if they needed to.

He was pleased Teri was excited to see Mike and Robin. He knew she liked Mike and enjoyed his company and had mentioned several times her desire to meet Robin. He was looking forward to the evening and the company.

* * *

While Mike and Stone had been talking, getting things arranged for the cabin inspection, Robin had gotten into a conversation with the waitress. Robin and Mike knew her quite well from the many hours they'd spent at the bistro. Mike, not wanting to interrupt their conversation and those around them, had gotten up and walked outside to use his phone again. He called Maui and spoke with an officer he'd met in a classroom discussion a few weeks prior. He asked if she'd mind driving up Haleakalā

Highway and checking the cabin. He gave her the address. She said she'd be happy to.

Robin and the waitress were just finishing their conversation as Mike sat back down. Robin's hand immediately came to rest on his thigh; he loved the feeling and the intimacy implied. He leaned over and kissed her neck.

Chapter Forty-eight

$\mathcal{M}$ike and Robin sat enjoying each other's company as they sipped their second mai tai for the day. They were both avid body surfers and were quietly making comments, complimentary for the most part, on a group of locals riding the waves a hundred yards offshore. The waves on this part of Waikiki, Kuhio Beach, were perfect for body surfing. Mike recognized one of his officers, off duty for the day, entering the water and, with practiced ease, dove under an incoming wave before swimming out.

* * *

While the surfing action was taking place in Oahu, a Maui patrol officer, Sonya Kim, was in the process of turning off the Haleakalā Highway onto the red-cinder driveway leading to Annie's cabin.

Officer Kim had been quite willing to go on this errand even though it was out of her assigned patrol area. She knew and respected Mike Kalama and was quite willing to do him this favor. Mike hadn't explained anything to her about his interest in the cabin, but he'd said he would explain what he could after she'd been there, telling her that he'd rather not influence anything she might notice out of the ordinary. She fully understood this reasoning. He did caution her, though, to be vigilant and not let her guard down, and that spoke volumes about the interest he had in the place.

Getting out of her car, she immediately noticed the cabin's door was ajar as if someone had made the gesture of pulling it closed but had not checked to see if it had latched properly. Her body tensed in response; her awareness immediately alert. If someone were inside, she reasoned, they would have come to the door to see who had driven the length of their driveway. It wasn't as if cinder driveways were quiet. The cinder-covered surface made any arrival, even those on foot, very noticeable, but no one had come to the door, nor did she see anyone glancing out the huge glass window.

Reflexively she placed her right hand on the butt of her gun and slowly moved up beside the cabin.

She was aware of an eerie absence of sound. There weren't even any birds. That was the thing about Haleakalā that she had never liked—it was always too quiet. Kim was the product of a household of eleven brothers and sisters, so noise was a natural part of life. She was comfortable with noise. She remembered that as a small kid, her parents used to bring her and her siblings up here on family outings, crowded into their old pickup truck. She didn't like the quietness of the place then, and that attitude had never changed.

After moving around the exterior of the cabin, she cautiously pushed the door open wider and entered the cabin. She was in the main living space but found it vacant; she looked further. She thought it very odd that there was a car in the garage, but no one inside the cabin. It was apparent the cabin's owner had been picked up by someone; no one in their right mind would choose to walk either up or down the mountain from here. It was too desolate; the sun's rays, too intense; the solitude, too absolute. *It's just too quiet.*

She was reaching up for her lapel mike to call her desk sergeant and ask that he relay a call to Mike Kalama telling him she'd found nothing. The only things out of normal were the unsecured door and a tipped-over Coke can lying on the bed. Before she reached her desk sergeant, though, she noticed the small glass bottle lying on its side on the kitchen counter. It appeared to be out of the ordinary in the otherwise orderly kitchen. Sticking a pencil into its opening, she held it to her nose and was immediately aware of a strange odor, an odor she was unfamiliar with, but one that had the unmistakable smell of medicine.

Going back into the bedroom, she sniffed the remnants of the Coke can. Coke Cola was her beverage of choice, and she was very familiar with its smell. She wasn't too surprised to find a hint of the same smell as the glass bottle. She put both into a baggie and went outside and proceeded to relay the call.

Since Maui didn't have the facilities to analyze the contents of either the bottle or the can, Mike instructed her to use the police department's overnight courier and send them to his Maunakea Street station. He explained, in brief fashion, what had taken place and her part in partially resolving the question of what had happened to the cabin owner. He explained that the owner's dear friend on the Big Island was worried and unable to resolve her deep concern, thus the search.

Ending the conversation, Mike said, "Mahalo, Sonya. An excellent job as I knew you would do. I'll keep you filled in on what we find out. Lunch is on me next time you're on Oahu." He didn't bother telling her the cost of the future lunch would actually be that of Stone's. She didn't need to know that.

Chapter Forty-nine

$\mathcal{T}$he two couples walked through the door into John Dominis Restaurant. It was immediately apparent the restaurant was doing a thriving business—nothing out of the ordinary for JD's. They had known when they walked in that this would be the case. Mike had used his car phone and told his desk sergeant to call ahead for reservations. Even though his brother was JD's head chef, Mike would never ask him to trump other guests just so he would have a table available whenever he walked in the door, that wasn't his style.

The restaurant drew their clientele from the island's locals as well as the many tourists who arrived by the busloads. Tour bus drivers were generously treated to dinner while they sat and waited to return their tourist-guests to Waikiki hotel's and were usually given a gratuity along with the meal in appreciation for bringing their busloads to the restaurant—an accepted way of doing business in most tourist areas.

The restaurant's seafood was superb as well as diverse and somewhat on the pricey side. The restaurant was ideally situated on one of the best pieces of real estate on the leeward side of Oahu. Built on a lava rock promontory, it faced the open ocean on one side with the Kewalo Basin channel skirting its side. Both walls of the restaurant facing the water were constructed of floor-to-ceiling glass. Floodlights were directed outward to light up the water and the close-in surfers for diners. Underwater lights had been installed to add an eerie glow to the view.

The restaurant boosted of having a one-of-a-kind feature. There was a small saltwater stream, just four feet wide and two feet deep, running through the restaurant from one side to the other, hosting a wide variety of different fish, lobsters of varying sizes, complete with a few small sharks—a fascination to many guests. The stream was a constant fish parade. One could order a lobster by simply pointing it out to a waiter, and it would be on the table within twenty minutes, steaming hot. The stream served to divide the cocktail lounge from the main dining area. A short garden bridge, with its simple wooden railings, enabled guests to move from one side to the other.

The four sat in the corner with the ocean view on one side and the Kewalo Channel on the other. The men chose to sit with their backs to the water for the benefit of the women—chivalry, such a good thing!

Stone and Mike had known each other for more years than either cared to admit, but this was the first time Teri and Robin met. Both hadn't had any opportunity to meet up till then, and they hit it off immediately. It turned out that Robin had a keen interest in geology so with Teri's extensive expertise on the subject and her work environment that encouraged such knowledge; they had much to talk about. The men were cornered out of most of the women's conversation, and that was fine with them.

They had their own interests to delve into. They shared a history of competition; both had many years of experience paddling for outrigger canoe clubs and had competed in many races. Stone had paddled with Kuhio Beach Yacht Club while Mike paddled with Diamond Head Beach Boys. They had competed over the years in every race that took place around the islands for a span of many years, including the annual Liliuokalani race between Kealakekua Bay and Kailua-Kona.

It was a relaxed evening as the four enjoyed the food, the setting, and the company. It was a unanimous among them that they needed to do this more often. Teri had invited Robin to spend some time with her visiting the Geology Department at the university, and Robin was excited at the prospect of doing so.

Stone invited them all to Kaikanani for a backyard barbeque the following weekend. They all knew that it would depend on whether both Robin and Mike could engineer mutual time off again.

With Loki and Annie in mind, Mike told Stone about the officer's search of Annie's cabin and what she found. Mike said his officer described it as being *suspicious*. Since their lab hadn't been very busy the past few days, Mike figured they'd be able to make an identification of their contents by early the next day. Until then, Mike said, there was nothing anyone could do except wait and see.

"Wait and see!" One of Stone's frequently used and favorite expressions. It eased most questionable situations he came up against that he had little control over. Some viewed his wait-and-see observation as somewhat blasé, but he'd never been concerned about opinions.

He decided to wait to call Loki until he knew the results of the lab tests. He hoped that would be no later than the following morning. He had a notion that Loki was hanging close to her phone waiting to hear something about what, if anything, had been found. She was also praying for some word from Annie. Stone debated whether he should call her now or not but decided there was no point in disturbing her right then until more was known.

The foursome said their alohas. Mike and Robin agreed once again to do their best to arrange time off next Saturday. Mike promised Stone he'd call as soon as he found out anything.

Chapter Fifty

*T*wo lab technicians were shaking their heads in disbelief at what they'd discovered. Over the years, they had analyzed an enormous number of potions submitted from HPD. Most brewed up by young adults in their continuing attempts to create a super drug better than all others and thereby become legendary, as well as quite rich. The residue found in the medicine bottle and Coke can in the cabin went far beyond what they would have thought a human would have dreamed of putting together.

After reviewing the results, the head of the lab, Joe Lum, called Sgt. Mike Kalama's office as he'd been asked to do as soon as his lab technicians finished the diagnosis. He knew his friend Mike was anxious to get the results. He told him what he knew and informed him that a follow-up formal report would be sent within the hour.

"Oh, and by the way, Mike, I'm sure you noticed, but in case not, the bottle has a doctor's name, a Dr. Harley Badger, printed on an otherwise blank label. My techs thought it odd that a doctor would identify his own bottle that was used for a mixture like this. My guess is that he was in a hurry and didn't think about what he was doing and had probably expected it to be thrown away immediately afterward."

The mixture was a shock to Mike. He'd heard of a lot of oddball concoctions during his career, some extremely dangerous, but this one was a puzzle and one for the books. The doctor's name, though, was a familiar one. The Maui officer, Sonya Kim, had also noted this in her report. The doctor had never had any charges brought against him, but by his record, he'd managed to walk a very tight line.

For now, Mike had all he needed. He called Stone to pass on the information.

"Methocarbamol and tizanidine, both of which would promote dizziness and body fatigue. Mixed together, they make up a super physical depressant. Blended into this cocktail was a substantial portion of THC, the hallucinogenic part of marijuana. This mixture, Stone, must have carried quite a wallop. The lab tech claims that if a person were given enough of this stuff, they would melt like hot butter and potentially could go for days before ever being able to see straight, or ever, if given enough of it. What a cocktail. Let's hope the youth of today don't get wind of this stuff. We'd have stoned, limp bodies puddled all over the streets and back alleys. No pun on your name, of course." Mike chuckled to himself.

"Stone, we have to figure that Annie was given this mix via the can of Coke we found on her bed. What happened to her after that is anybody's guess at this time. My tech people said that she would not have been able to navigate under her own power, which means she was either carried out or wheeled away from the cabin. Her car was still locked up in the cabin's garage. Not sure what to tell you beyond this. We're going to keep investigating. We're looking for a lead to where she was taken after the cabin. Are you going to call Loki and talk to her?"

"Yeah, Mike. She asked me to call her when I found out anything. I'll see if she can shed some light on where she thinks Annie might have gotten to. With those chemicals found in her cabin and the fact the cabin's door was ajar, it sure makes me think something foul has taken place and puts Annie right in the middle of it. I don't think it's voluntary, and I'm thinking you probably agree on that.

"Mike, what about the doctor that brewed up this mess? It feels to me like it harbors on the fringe of an illegal use of the Hippocratic Oath or something. Will he be allowed to get away with this?"

"No, he won't. His name is boldly stated on the bottle, so we have clear evidence he went below the legal line on this. I'm sure he expected the bottle to be tossed after it was administered. We'll wait until Annie is found before taking any action."

"I'll be talking to Loki in a few minutes to bring her up to date. I know she's anxious to learn anything about her friend's well-being. She's got a couple thoughts on what may have happened or, at least, who might have made something happen. I want to get her okay before I mention anything to you about what she's thinking. You okay with that?"

"If it sounds like something I need to know, yes. I'll wait for you to check with her, and then I want to hear it all."

"I'll call you back."

* * *

"My telling you this, Stone, may make you think I'm a very ungrateful daughter, but you need to check with my father to see what he knows about where Annie may have been taken. Like I mentioned to you before, my intuition is screaming that he's got his hands in this somewhere, and you said you were thinking that as well. I don't believe for a minute that he'd do anything harmful to her. That's not the kind of man I know him to be. He can pretend he is and may try to intimidate her, but I know his bark is much worse than his bite. I'm not so sure about those two bozos he uses for goffers, though. They can get off in their own world at times. I'm sure my father would like to scare Annie and see if he can get her to cough up information about where his money went, but I honestly don't believe he'd hurt her."

"Loki, you know if I call Mike back and tell him what you have told me, he may stir up a lot of trouble for your father, whether he's done anything wrong or not. If he must do so, I know he'll try to mitigate any fallout concerning you and your family. Are you okay with that? I'm not sure what else I can do now that you've intimated all this. I know he's waiting for me to call him back. You told me about the money a week ago. Did you mention any of this to Mike? Does he know about it?"

"I don't recall, Stone. I don't think so, but I might have. Go ahead and mention it to him but ask if he can put a soft spin on it. You know I love my father and don't what to see him get in trouble or come to any harm. He had enough of that growing up in Sicily. At the same time, though, I am quite worried about Annie and would feel at fault if anything bad were to happen to her. I sort of feel guilty about all the *pilikia* she's going through as it is."

"Don't feel any guilt, Loki. That guilt isn't yours. Annie's boyfriend, Taylor, did that all by himself. It's unfortunate that Annie got pulled into it like this, but that comes with the territory of being in a loving relationship. Nothing would have changed had you not been her friend other than now she has a caring friendship that she will need to help her get through all this. I think it's our task to see if we can extricate Annie from harm's way and hopefully lessen the damage that may fall on your father if he is in fact involved in her apparent disappearance. I'll need to talk with Mike about all this.

"I'll call you back when I have anything new to report. In the meantime, you're very welcome to come over to Kaikanani and stay with Teri and me if being closer would help you feel more involved. We'd love to have you here, Loki. You know that, right?"

"That's a kind offer, Stone, mahalo. I appreciate that, but I think I'm better off staying right here in Hawi. It's where Annie knows she can find me in case she shows up looking for me."

Chapter Fifty-one

*D*isconnecting the call, Stone sat for a few moments thinking over the many possible consequences of what they'd talked about and the path this could put them all on. It could very well be an irreversible path once initiated, especially for Loki and definitely for her father. He was seriously questioning what he needed to do about any of it and what to say when he brought it to Mike's awareness. He knew he had to do it. If anything happened that could have been prevented and he hadn't done anything about it, he'd feel the remorse for the rest of his life.

He was wishing he didn't know anything at all. Ignorance meant happiness, but he was smart enough to know that rarely helped anyone. He was wondering where his *kuliana* fell in all of this and if he really needed to become involved at all. *But aren't I already involved up to my hairline?*

Still sitting in his swimsuit having come back from kayaking, he was in the cool shade on the lanai outside his and Teri's bedroom, letting his intuition take over; he had always trusted his instincts.

He was mulling over the possibility that Annie had simply gone off by herself because of her depression over Taylor's death or because of fright over what might happen if Taylor's supposed inheritance turned out to be the money stolen from Loki's father, or . . . He could think of ten other reasons she could be someplace else. If she was, he hoped she was having fun. If that was taking place, then it was really her own business and should have nothing to do with anyone else. The exception was that her friends were concerned, and that was important.

The drugs Mike's people found in her cabin certainly implied that something sinister had occurred, and the fear that Loki claimed to have heard in Annie's voice on the message machine implied she was in trouble and needing help. He wasn't at all certain of what he should tell Mike. He wished Teri was home so he could talk to her about this; use her for a sounding board, but she'd left to run an errand. She had a natural way of seeing though the mist of things and grabbing onto the rock sitting in the middle. He loved her for that.

Deep in thought, Stone was startled and jumped like he'd been hit by a Taser when the phone next to him rang. He reached over and picked it up.

"Aloha."

"Aloha, yourself." It was Mike. His voice was very distinctive.

"Mike, this would be a coincidence if I were one to believe in such things. I was just thinking of calling you. You go first, though. What's on your mind if that's not being too optimistic?"

"Very funny, my friend. Remind me not to invite you to my luau next month, and just so you know, as a police officer, I don't believe in coincidences either, but I know we've talked about that before—all things happen for a reason, cloudy as that statement might be at times and as overused as it is."

"Special occasion, this luau you mention? Where are you planning on having it and when?"

"Just wanted to do something nice for several officers in my precinct who have displayed a good head for this hard job. They make my work a lot easier, so I'd like to reward them. I'm having it at your place, by the way, in your backyard next to your beach. Care to help me dig the *imu* and prep the pig?"

"How could I refuse such an invitation, especially since it'll be happening in my backyard? I'm certain I'll be home if I know when it is. Why are you bringing this up this afternoon? There's more, isn't there?"

"Of course, there is. I'm calling about Annie. We've happened upon the names of three individuals who caught an Aloha Airline's flight from Maui to Oahu yesterday. One of them appeared to have been out cold and strapped to a wheelchair. They said it was a wahine, about thirty years of age. She was a local woman and quite attractive, according to the TSA rep I talked to. The two caretakers claimed they were heading for the Kekela ward in Queen's Medical Center and had a note from a doctor, a Dr. Badger as it turns out. The note explained the woman's condition, so the airlines wouldn't get too nervous about allowing her to board the plane. Badger just happens to be the same name that appears on the bottle we found in Annie's cabin. Coincidences—I think not."

"Doesn't sound like it to me either. Got anything on the two guys who were pushing her?"

"That's the puzzling part, Stone. They gave their real names, and we've found out that they are employees of Anthony Gravello. Kidnappers don't usually give out their real names. In my books, that puts this duo squarely on the smart meter down at the *not very* end of the scale."

"All of this falls very close to what I was about to call you about, Mike."

"Oh" was all Mike said. It was a typical Mike response, guaranteed to encourage the talker to divulge more information. Stone knew this as a salesman's technique employed to overcome objections. He had used it himself many times.

"Loki is convinced Annie has been abducted—kidnapped as it appears—and feels strongly that her father has his fingers mixed up in it. Do you know about the large sum of money that may have been embezzled from Gravello's firm? It's probably the money that Taylor told Annie came from some unknown relative of his who had passed away. The amount seems to be in question. It could be any amount, from a thousand to a million or even two million.

According to Loki, her father isn't sure. Seems Taylor's job was keeping financial records straight and updated. It's anybody's guess if the figures recorded are factual or completely fictitious."

"That's getting into a healthy neighborhood. Wish I lived there. No, I wasn't informed of that. Obviously, you were," Mike sounded a bit surprised at not being previously informed.

"That throws some serious blame," he said. "Obviously you know I'm now obligated to investigate this."

"Yeah. All Loki asks is that you walk gently on this until you know more. It's her father, after all, and despite his quirks, she loves him. I think she's praying you'll discover he had nothing to do with Annie's absence. But whatever you discover, Mike, please let me know, so I can keep her updated. She's sitting in Hawi completely freaked out but praying Annie will call there."

After talking with Mike, Stone decided not to wait and called Loki.

As he suspected, she must have been practically resting her hand on her phone. It was answered before the ring finished sounding. With a brief explanation of what had taken place with Mike and knowing for certain that Annie had been taken to Oahu, Loki decided not to sit it out in Hawi, isolated from everything.

"Can I come over there and stay at your place until this is solved? I feel totally useless sitting here in Hawi now."

She was on her way. He figured he would need to leave for the interisland terminal within the next two hours to pick her up. He was quite pleased she had decided to come.

Chapter Fifty-two

As the sliding door closed, Annie heard its lock slide into place. Finally left alone, she became acutely aware of every joint in her body rebelling and causing pain. She'd been holding herself motionless for more hours than she could recall—all for what? To end up alone, locked in a room.

She had a general idea where they had brought her to. She knew the streets of Honolulu so well she could navigate blindfolded—and had been doing just that. The sounds and smells of Waikiki as they drove through were as familiar as her face in a mirror. They had driven up and around Diamond Head, then down a gentle slope toward the ocean. She guessed they had stopped somewhere in Kahala, an upscale community with large homes and manicured gardens surrounding them. She could hear and smell the ocean close by, so she figured it was either the Black Point area of Kahala or Diamond Head Beach Road. The crunch of the car tires slowly coming to a stop told her it wasn't the Beach Park but a private driveway.

It had become quiet in the house, so Annie figured it was a good time to move. Fortunately, they had left her hands free of bindings. If they'd tied those to the chair as well as the rest of her, she would have been stuck. Making fast work of the knots, she freed the chest straps, then reached down, and undid the ropes securing her legs. She sat up straight and breathed a sigh of relief.

Standing up was a different issue altogether. Whatever the drugs that they'd fed her were, they left a lingering and foggy-minded effect that was making her unstable; her balance was off. All the physical conditioning she'd done faithfully over the past was paying off big time as blood quickly spread throughout her body and brought her limbs and joints back to living. The stiffness and some joint pains she had experienced were quickly subsiding as well—*thank God.*

Looking at the sparsely appointed room she was in, she experienced an unfamiliar feeling of being held in a cage; there were no windows. There was only one place on all the walls that could possibly be a door, but there was no handle to open it with. She knew she'd been rolled in from out there somewhere. At least, when she and Loki were imprisoned in the water aquifer, even though they couldn't see anything that was near them, much like this room, there was at least a feeling of space and distance as well as a perceived opportunity for escape. This room gave her the direct opposite feeling, that of being totally closed in a large box that contained nothing but a very simple, square space sparsely furnished. The room radiated the least comfortable and unwelcoming feeling she'd ever experienced. A faint smile broke the corners of her mouth as her eyes took in all the marble busts resting pedestals here and there—the only other furnishings besides a couple of chairs.

She walked the room searching under the cushions of the chairs, looking in all the corners. The place was sterile, too sterile—almost as if no one had ever been in here. There was nothing—not even dust.

She sat back down in the wheelchair, slowly turning in a circle in the center of the room as she thought through her options, which came down to just one. She started making as much noise as possible for as long as possible, yelling, screaming, bumping her wheelchair up and down on the floor. Someone *had* to come and open a door.

Her eyes were looking in the wrong direction, so she failed to see nor did she hear the door slide open. She hadn't realized anyone had entered the room until a part of the rope she'd removed was being put around her wrists and chair so quickly it was a shock. She could only think that some of that drug she'd been given was still dulling her senses and slowing her reactions.

She soon found she was once again secured to the chair, even more tightly than she had been.

"That ought to take care of that urge to freely roam this room and create a racket, wouldn't you say?" As the man spoke those words, he came around to face her. It was the first time either had looked at each other. If it wasn't for that fact that she held the key to his missing money, he might have found his daughter's friend enjoyable to look at and perhaps interesting to talk with. He admired beauty and physical fitness, which she obviously possessed.

"And you're Loki's father. She showed me a picture once while we were being held in a very wet, cold place—a place your hired goons stashed us for safekeeping."

Gravello didn't say any more, but from behind her, he placed a cloth gag over her mouth and tied it quite securely. He then turned and walked back through the doorway, hitting a closing device as he went out. Annie had a fleeting moment before the very quiet closure slid into place, blocking her view, to see into a beautifully appointed room adjoining the one she was in. Obviously an office—his, she assumed.

Chapter Fifty-three

*B*ack in his office, Gravello knew he must do something dramatic either to scare Annie into opening up and telling him what he wanted to know or to convince him that she really didn't know anything. He had a few notions on how to make her divulge what she knew; after all, he wasn't a Gravello for no reason. After seeing her, though, he needed to take a few moments to harden his resolve.

First, he needed to give Smythe and Catena, the butler and the cook, the rest of the day off. He'd never done that before and briefly wondered what their reaction would be, not that he really cared that much. *They'd just think I was going soft.*

That was of little concern to him. He knew that their tenure here was short if he followed through with his plan to return to Sicily. A smile creased his lips at the thought. It would be just like Smythe to voice a comment if he saw anything unusual, and very soon, the entire staff would know, and the police, soon after. That was obviously the last thing he needed. His butler had a memory like a steel trap and a mouth that rarely closed. If Gravello wasn't planning to leave the islands, Smythe would be gone as sure as daylight comes to an end. It was fortunate that that day was the housemaid's and the gardener's regular day off; he wouldn't need to be bothered about them.

The remainder of preparations after the staff finally left for the day was to assemble the various pieces of his plan—fifteen minutes tops.

Thinking over what he was putting into action, he had to caution himself. He knew he had the capacity to be carried away at times, thinking only of the result and overplaying the actions needed to arrive there. He wanted answers, but he didn't want to create any real injury—the money just isn't worth doing permanent harm. That would bring the law to his door too quickly. He frowned knowing his family in Sicily would disown him if they knew just how gently he now viewed life; that wasn't the Gravello way. Their way was to proceed much like a road grader and flatten whatever or whoever stood in their path.

He decided it was time to put his plan into action; there was no reason to wait.

In his office, he manipulated a specific book on a bookshelf, and the entire bookcase quietly rolled over the thick carpet on huge unseen castors that supported it. Now with the bookshelf opened to the side, the interior of his hidden, private room was exposed, along with his prisoner.

Annie sat in the wheelchair squarely facing the doorway, still strapped in, unable to move. She was looking directly at him as he came through the doorway; her direct penetrating gaze startled him.

What he saw, or thought he saw or imagined he saw, was a fire burning in the center of her dark eyes. Since living in the islands, he'd heard tales of a deep anger many Hawaiians harbored that undoubtedly had an origin in the missionary days. That anger could seemingly cause passionately dark eyes to glow red in anger. Any doubt he may have previously possessed in the folklore was immediately erased. He wished now he'd had Milo leave the blindfold on her when they arrived at the house.

He hesitated for only a second before continuing into the room and moving toward the wheelchair, but he kept his distance from it and from her. He noted that her hands and feet remained tied, and that was good. Still, he left a wide gap between them just in case.

Reaching over and pulling the gag down her chin, he said, "I need an answer from you. You have"—making a deliberate show of looking at his watch—"ten minutes to tell me. If you don't, you'll know exactly when your time is up without need of me telling you. It'll be very obvious. Your ten minutes begin now.

"What I want," he continued, "is for you to tell me everything you know about my money that Jason took from me. Specifically, tell me exactly where it is."

"Taylor. His name was Taylor. Get it right."

A flash of anger crossed his face. Without further comment, he began pushing the wheelchair out of the room, through his office, and out through a doorway to the yard.

The choppy ocean was thirty feet away on the opposite side of a beautiful swimming pool. Annie could smell the water; she loved the smell of the ocean. It brought with it a flashback to the last time she'd been able to enjoy the smell—a time before any of her perfect life changed with Taylor's death.

He stopped pushing the wheelchair just outside the door to the yard. Untying both legs, then retying one ankle to a cement block, he hoisted the cement up onto the footrest of the chair and began pushing the whole rig once again toward the water.

It became all too clear to Annie exactly where they were headed. A short, wide pier extended out into the water. A very sleek Sea Ray inboard boat, gleamed white in the sunshine, fastened to the pier. She could see a wooden handicap ramp leading up onto the boat's deck. Waiting for her?

She loved boats and experienced an odd emotional sensation of anticipation mixed with fear—a fear of how all this was destined to end.

Annie heard the sound at the same time Gravello did. He turned quickly and looked in the direction the sound was coming from. He was very familiar with where the sound was coming from and what generated it. He just didn't know who was making it.

Shock registered immediately. He could see just enough through the shrubbery to recognize a blue-and-white police cruiser rolling to a stop on the cinder driveway outside the main entranceway to the house.

Loudly cursing, something he rarely did, he quickly whipped Annie's chair around and immediately began pushing her back toward the door.

He untied the block, leaving it on the grass, and rolled Annie back into his private sanctuary. He left her in the middle of the room and closed the bookcase. He went to meet his unwelcome guest.

The sliding bookcase latched shut simultaneously as the door chime sounded.

Chapter Fifty-four

*H*e opened the door and, as expected and came face to face with two police officers. Both were big men, like the other two who had been here, and could also have been candidates for HPD's Metro Squad and perhaps were. They displayed an attitude that plainly told him this was not a social visit. He noticed their expressions were so similar it might have been something taught at the police academy: *how to intimidate a suspect—make your face look like this.*

He knew that game from growing up in a crime family. He didn't say anything, but neither did he feel any sort of response to the intimidation. He was surprised, though, at their uncanny timing. Like many people, he held little belief in *coincidences*, but their timing, at this particular moment, made him wonder.

He had learned early on that most things in life had to be accepted head-on. The police and their endless suspicions were just one of those things. It was a lesson he picked up as a small boy at home in Sicily. Running around on the family's property as he was wont to do, he often collided with one of the goons, the hired enforcers, whose job it was to keep watch around the house and surrounding grounds. They didn't appreciate his energy and his sudden appearances, and their faces would clearly show just such an expression.

Something he did notice about the two officers standing in front of him was the flash of surprise their faces registered when he'd opened the door. He assumed they were expecting a butler or someone else to appear instead of the man himself. *Maybe I should do this more often—throw visitors a little off balance when they first arrive.* He'd give that some thought for the future.

"Yes?" he said, unconsciously standing a bit more erect, head inched slightly back, taller—a confrontational stance to match that of his visitors.

"Anthony Gravello?" asked the more authoritative-appearing one but not waiting for a reply, he continued. "I'm Sgt. Mike Kalama, with HPD."

The other officer spoke on the tail of Mike's words.

"I'm patrolman Henry Tang, but most people know me as Togo. May we come in?"

The informality of Patrolman Tang surprised him, but he quickly realized the informality as well as the request to enter were purely words spoken without meaning as Sergeant Kalama proceeded to brush past him and walk into the center of the foyer, leaving the second officer still standing just inside the door. *Interesting*, he thought. In a very quick manner, he was boxed between them.

Intimidation ingrained into police training, he thought again. The move, however, again failed to bother him in the least. He'd witnessed the epitome of intimidation growing up. It was an integral part of what made his family who they were—and more than likely still were. He subtly made the officers aware of his calm emotions saying, "Follow me and please," and then addressed the younger officer still standing at the doorway, "close the door behind you." He proceeded to walk around Mike and led the way toward his elaborately appointed ocean-view office, as Officer Tang closed the door and followed them across the immense foyer. Gravello couldn't help but smile to himself.

He sat down behind the desk he was so proud of, rested his forearms on it, his hands clasped together, then immediately asked, "Now what can I do for you, gentlemen? Why am I being honored with this unannounced visit by Honolulu's finest?" He intentionally hadn't offered chairs, leaving them standing, hoping they weren't planning on staying long. He would encourage them to leave as quickly as possible if he could manage that without offending them too directly.

To Mike, the unspoken game had just been initiated. Mike was quite good at this sort of tacit jockeying. He had learned a few techniques in basic police training at the academy, but for the most part, it was the result of his having grown up with three brothers, all just a year apart. He was the youngest of the four and learned early on that he had to rely on outwitting them instead of outfighting them if he were to grow up unscathed.

Even though uninvited to do so, he and Togo settled into the two chairs facing Anthony Gravello and looked over the wide expanse of wood that was a desktop. Mike had been coaching his partner in stall techniques for the past few weeks, techniques to use during an interview. This would be good practical experience. Togo was a novice with the department, so this visit was a valuable lesson.

Mike spent a few moments silently looking around at the many books that lined the numerous shelves in the room along with the crowd of busts on pedestals forever staring into space. He was intentionally ignoring the growing impatience evident on Gravello's face, who was alternating the glare being projected at the face of one of the officers then the other.

Gravello suddenly got quite anxious when he became aware of the possibility that he'd left his prisoner's feet and legs untied when he'd rushed from the room to get to the door. He thought he had retied them, but he wasn't positive. *What if she begins to make noise again?* He hoped for the best as it was too late at this point to do anything about that.

Overriding his concerned about the girl making noise, a bigger alarm gripped him when the officer in charge, Sergeant Something-or-Other, stood and walked over to one of the bookcases—the bookcase that happened to be the sliding door to his private room.

As the officer reached for a book, Gravello's heart skipped a few more beats. The book the officer was reaching toward was the very one that controlled the sliding door.

He could see that, in his haste, he had forgotten to push the book back all the way into its normally locked position—the position it needed to be in to keep the door from opening. The automatic sliding door was built in a way that in order to activate the automatic lock, putting it into its locked position, one had to give the binding of the book a slight inward push. At present, it was jutting out a short distance, making it quite noticeable against the other, evenly lined-up rows of books. It had been intentionally designed that way as a visual reminder that the door remained unlocked. It was a glaring indictment of what he'd failed to do.

Purposefully stalling, Mike had noticed the book out of alignment with the others and took the opportunity to go and give it a gentle push back in place—a play for time. Had he pushed it an additional half inch, he would have heard a loud clicking noise coming from the wall behind the book, indicating the lock mechanism was being activated. To a trained ear, the sound would be telltale of what it was and would have only caused many questions that Gravello would have been hard-pressed to avoid or to answer. Fortunately, none of that happened.

Finished delaying, Mike returned to the chair beside Togo and sat down. They had very few questions, so Mike knew it would be quick, and they could then return to the station. They really needed to talk with Loki first to learn what the suspicions she'd mentioned to Stone were and what they were based on.

Mike explained to an obviously impatient Gravello, why they were there. "A woman is missing, Mr. Gravello. One Annie Gaines. We're just beginning our investigation. Since your daughter is acquainted with Ms. Gaines and since her boyfriend was an employee at your firm, you'll understand that we must begin with what you may know. Your daughter is on another island, and therefore out of reach at the moment, but you already know that.

"Were you acquainted with Ms. Gaines?"

"No. Loki, my daughter, mentioned her once or twice, but I've never personally met her. I believe she works in the cocktail lounge, the Perch, that's on the street level of the building I have my offices in, but I'm sure you already know that as well. Maybe the owner or manager of the place is where you need to start looking."

With that said, Anthony Gravello rose from his chair. "Now, gentlemen, I have a busy day, and time is short, so if that's all, I'll show you to the door." He handed Sergeant Kalama one of his business cards. "Should you have further questions, I would appreciate you making an appointment with my secretary. That's what she's there for. I'll be in my office tomorrow and could possibly squeeze a spare moment for a question or two."

He breathed a sigh of relief as he watched the two policemen exchange glances, stand, and head for the door and their car.

He visually followed them to their car but lost sight of it temporarily as the officers made their way down the driveway, moved behind a wall of *hapu* tree ferns and the carpets of red anthuriums that formed Gravello's entrance gardens and out the open gate. He caught sight of the blue-and-white's taillights as the officers pulled out into the street and disappeared.

He wasn't watching out of curiosity or from the politeness of a host and guests. He had to see them gone, so he could return to the task of scaring the girl into revealing what she knew. He was certain they wouldn't continue around the circular driveway and return at his door with a forgotten question or two, but he personally needed to see them leave, and they did.

As he walked back toward his office, he felt the tiredness of the cat and mouse game with the girl. He was very close to saying to hell with the money Jason stole, to hell with everything. He was mentally ready to be back in Sicily; he just had to take that initial step.

He originally planned on simply scaring her sufficiently to cause her to open up—she had to know something, anything. Now he was thinking it may be much simpler to follow through—let the cement block take her to the bottom. No one would know he was involved, and besides, he'd be gone soon anyway.

Inside his office, he pulled the designated book out, and the bookshelf slid smoothly to the right.

As soon as he entered the room and looked at her, he saw the defiant stare aimed at him. Instantly, he knew it was time to bid this woman aloha, permanently.

Chapter Fifty-five

*A*t that moment, while Mike and Togo's blue-and-white patrol car was pulling out of the driveway, on the distant side of Honolulu, Loki was at the interisland air terminal opening the passenger door of Stone's Explorer and climbing in. She was greatly relieved to finally be here. She would remain here for as long as it took to resolve the uncertainty of where Annie had disappeared to. There was no question in her mind that something serious had taken place. It was the only logical answer to why Annie hadn't tried to make contact.

"Stone," she asked, while in the process of fastening her seat belt, "would it be possible to drive to my old house first? You'd finally be able to meet my father, and I'd have a chance to ask him about Annie and judge his response for myself.

"We'll also have time before we get there to talk about this intuitive notion I have about him and his money that just won't go away. Maybe you can help me gain some perspective. I don't understand the reasoning for what I'm thinking."

"Lead the way, Loki. Twenty-five minutes should give us lots of time to talk. You once mentioned to Teri and I that you lived on Black Point Road, right? You can point out your house when I turn off Diamond Head Beach Road."

"Believe me when I say you won't have any difficulty figuring out which house it is. Just look for the one with a tall moss rock wall surrounding it that resembles a fortress. In a way, I guess that's exactly what it is. My father's protective roots go deep."

They made the journey in twenty minutes. Traffic was unusually light, even passing through Waikiki, which can often be a nightmare of cars and tour buses.

* * *

As soon as the bookcase door had opened, he had to chuckle to himself when he noticed that her feet and legs remained tied. After the worry he'd gone through that she be able to get up and create a racket when the police were here, he needn't have been concerned after all. Even in his rush to meet the police at the door, he must have unconsciously done what was necessary and refastened the ropes. She hadn't been able to go anywhere on her own.

"And now, miss, we'll continue where we left off. Your ten minutes is obviously gone, so we'll move directly into the last phase of your life. If for some reason you decide to spill the beans as the saying goes, please do so at any time before you hit the water. Remember, there will be a point of no return, so by all means, speak up if you decide to."

"I don't know how you think you're going to get away with this." Annie was more angry than afraid. "Loki will be asking questions and so will the police when they see the list of clients you stole money from. If I were you, I'd jump feet first into that boat of yours, aim straight out, and don't stop till you get to China. I'm sure they'll value your arrival."

"You forget, my young friend, my boys took that list you think will be my noose from your cabin. I have it in my office for safekeeping and will destroy it as soon as I'm finished with you."

He rolled her out of the house and began retying the cement block to her left leg.

Annie kept on but was admittedly getting more nervous by the second. "You know, your fault is not giving people enough credit for having brains. I think Loki told me that about you after you dismissed her from trying to find out exactly what you're trying to discover right now. Did it not dawn on you to think that I would make copies of that list and mail them to friends? Oh yes," she continued, "I also included a note to go to the police if I should end up missing or found dead. You ever think of that, Mr. Big?" She was pushing every button that she could.

Her mention of copies being sent out caused him to hesitate as he pulled a knot on the block tight. He had thought of that possibility, but she was right. In his haste, he hadn't given her enough credit for thinking of doing that. A lesson his father had once taught him came back to mind. *Whenever dealing with others, always assume they have done everything you yourself can think of possibly doing and then deal with them accordingly.*

Shamed for having overlooked that advice, he now knew his only way out was to speed up what must be done. His decision had been made to leave the islands and leave quickly; he was wishing Milo and Benny were back, so they could take care of the girl while he tethered up all the loose ends. But they weren't there, so he didn't spend time with empty wishing but instead sped up his own actions.

He silently cursed himself at having such a large property and was only halfway to the pier and the waiting boat, pushing Annie and the wheelchair over the grass as fast as he could manage when he again heard a car roll around the red-cinder driveway. A moment's hesitation and the delay it caused was all it took before he heard a car door slam shut—footfalls quite audible in the distance as they crunched on the cinder. From the sound, he judged that two people were headed for the front door.

He had no idea who it could be this time unless the police decided to return for some inexplicable reason. Unfortunately, it wasn't Milo—Milo wouldn't drive to the front entrance unless he happened to be in one of his moods and was pushing the envelope of his imagined authority. He had been told, more than once, to always use the secondary driveway that led around to the back of the house and into one of the open stalls in the five-car garage.

So who could this possibly be?

One of the voices filtering around the edge of the house was faint but quite familiar. It was his daughter.

Chapter Fifty-six

As quickly as he could, once again, he managed to turn the wheelchair around, coming very close to dumping it along with Annie onto the grass. It was an awkward move to make in the thick, lush grass, and his muscles were unaccustomed to the demands he was putting on them. He knew he was attempting to do things too quickly—he had rarely been in the position of the near panic he currently felt. He was beginning to understand a little more of what he'd put Milo through all these years.

He continued to race toward the house as fast as the wheels and weight and his legs would allow. He was struggling; his body was unaccustomed to such abuse.

Practically running now, an exercise he had never pursued, he succeeded to get Annie into the office, through the doorway into his private room and even managed to get the sliding door closed. He heard the lock slide into place just as Loki and a strange man walked into his office. His hand was still resting on the book that controlled the locking mechanism.

Seeing Loki back home right at this time was unsettling. It was as if she was looking in through a peephole at his private life and seeing all his secrets.

"Hi, Father." She had always been formal with him. "Are we disturbing you from reading?" She went to him and gave him a brief hug. He wasn't a man that encouraged many people to want to do that but silently always welcomed it.

"I was finished what I was involved in and putting the books back in order. How are you, Loki? I'm surprised to see you here. It's been awhile since you were home. And who is this gentleman with you?"

"Father, this is a friend of my mom's family, Kensington Stone. Stone, this is my father, Anthony Gravello." The two men shook hands.

Turning back to Loki, he said, "I thought you were happily ensconced in Hawi and had sworn off coming back to this traffic-congested island."

"I thought it was about time I came to see you. Why are you all sweaty? If you were dressed differently, I'd say you had been out jogging, but I know you better than that. I know that would be the last thing you would consider doing unless the house was on fire."

"Matter of fact," he said, ignoring her jab at his lack of exercising and still trying to calm his breathing, "I was out on the pier polishing some chrome on the boat. It needed some attention, and Milo's not around today. It's quite warm out."

Loki was startled by his excuse but quickly relaxed her expression. She knew immediately that he was lying; she just couldn't figure out why unless it had to do with her suspicions of his involvement with Annie but even that didn't answer anything.

She'd learned early on to watch people's body language. It was a lesson both her father and mother had taught her when she was little and learning the ways of the world—self-preservation, they had called it. Her upbringing had matched closely with the tales she's heard of her father's *famiglia* in Sicily and the ways of survival they employed.

Since being brought in her adopted parents' home, there had always been various employees arriving and leaving, many were immigrants from Sicily. They quietly talked of such things, and she had learned through them that the strength of her father's family came from deception. She had been taught to watch people for those telltale signs, and that included her father right then.

Before arriving in Honolulu, on the flight over, she had carefully planned how she should approach him, what questions she would need to ask in order to determine if he had any responsibility for Annie's disappearance.

She was about to launch into some of those questions when there was a sudden, very loud noise, erupting somewhere around the room. Several books fell from the shelf her father had been standing beside. They had all been standing close to the bookshelf, but Stone had been the closest and was hit by two of the books that fell from somewhere on one of the higher shelves. The sound was like a small cannon being fired off inside the room. They were all so startled that none could react with anything other than startled looks accompanied by a level of fear that something catastrophic had just taken place and may signal impending danger, but they didn't know where it came from or in what direction they needed to move. Thoughts raced through all of them in a cavalcade of various explanations, but none could satisfy their questions.

They were looking at one another and everywhere around them for a reasonable cause when another shattering eruption took place, rattling everything around them. Several more books were ejected from the shelves, some ricocheting off all three of them.

Gravello's mind quickly zeroed in on his unwilling guest in the next room as being the cause, and that paralyzed him. He couldn't conceive of what she had managed to put together to create such a loud disturbance or even how she'd managed to do anything. *She is tied up, so she can't—*

He didn't finish his thought. He realized that this time, in his rush to get the door closed, making sure no one saw the girl being held hostage, he had indeed completely overlooked the ropes. As far as he could recall, she was still tied to the cement block as well as to the chair. Knowing that made answering his own questions impossible.

An ill feeling began to broil his emotions just as a third noise, much louder this time, caused by a part of the bookcase itself exploded out into the room. The sliding doorway had been jarred loose from the ceiling tracks and came crashing to the floor—books, shelving, and all. Fortunately, the three of them had unconsciously backed up after the second splintering noise, so they were safely but barely beyond the range of the crashing bookshelf.

The visual shock at seeing what was in front of them was difficult to assimilate.

Annie stood in front of them, a wide smile flashing relief across her face. Oddly, a carved granite face, that of Archimedes, a rope snuggly tied around his neck and the chair seat, lay on the wheelchair staring blindly up at them. Some of the debris had landed on his face, giving the immortal being a smug-looking smile, closely resembling the one Annie's face currently displayed.

* * *

Moments earlier, Annie had watched from the wheelchair she was tightly tied to as the sliding door closed, sealing her back in the room. She was again imprisoned. She'd listened as the lock engaged and had immediately gotten busy.

Even before the door had completely closed, she realized her antagonist had left one of her legs untied; the other had remained tied to the block of cement that was to have been her anchor.

With one foot free to move, she used it to place downward pressure on the rope between her other leg and the cement and began rubbing the rope back and forth over the edge of the block, like one would do with a dull knife. She knew the cement was rough cornered from experience on a brief job she'd had before becoming a waitress and bartender.

As a gofer for a construction outfit, she'd learned quickly why the job was called *gofer*—her job had been to carry whatever materials the guys on her crew needed. *Go get this and go get that*—an appropriate name. The workmen liked having her around, but they didn't believe she was capable of doing what needed to be done and had lined up the most difficult jobs just to test her. One such job was lifting cement blocks off a pickup truck and carrying them a short distance to the worksite. Besides being heavy, the edges were a rough sharpness that caused her hands to bleed even though she'd been wearing leather gloves.

She had quickly enrolled in bartenders' school and relegated the construction job to the past. Now she was happy knowing what that cement block could do to a piece of rope.

With the rope finally off her leg, she got on the floor and into a practiced yoga position, bringing her bound hands under both feet and up in front of her. She made quick work of the rope on her arms and wheeled the chair over to a marble statue she'd had her eyes on. She was lucky that the head and pedestal of the statue was one solid piece of marble. A small laugh escaped her lips when she noticed the bust's name chiseled under it. It was Archimedes, the greatest of mathematicians and physicists Sicily had ever known—*how appropriate*, she thought.

With the distinguished Sicilian lying across the seat, the top of his head aiming forward, facing up, Annie had transformed him into the perfect battering ram.

She had used the ropes that had bound her and cinched the piece of marble as tight as she could to the seat of the wheelchair. Then backing as far from the deceptive door as she could, butting up against the far wall, she leaned in and pushed the chair along with Archimedes as fast and with as much force as she could muster straight at the center of the door.

The first impact made a lot of noise but was not enough. The second rush at the door was better, and she heard an encouraging cracking sound as the wood weakened.

The third charge drove the top of Archimedes's head and his wheelchair chariot through the wall, coming to a stop in front of three very startled people as the entire bookcase door hit the floor at their feet. She figured it was a grand entrance.

It was an odd scene to take in. There was Annie standing behind the debris-strewn wheelchair with Archimedes, looking up at the ceiling, debris littering his face, leaving the surrealistic grin as if it was the most fun he'd ever had, and Annie standing at the business end of the chair, her grin virtually identical to that of the famous marble face.

She was very surprised to see Loki and Stone standing there beside her antagonist. She was at a loss for what to say to them. It was Loki's father who was culpable for what she'd been through and indeed he needed to be punished for his actions—but he was also Loki's father, her best and only friend. Her immediate reaction, she quickly decided, was that if she and Loki were to remain friends her only course of action would be to whitewash events—let the big man off the hook. She hadn't been hurt by the experience and figured she was probably a stronger woman because of it.

A lot of thoughts raced through her mind in that flash of riveted attention. No words were spoken for several long moments.

Chapter Fifty-seven

For the first time in his life, Tony Gravello was at a loss for words. He'd been caught with his pants down, as the saying goes—a circumstance he'd never thought would happen to him. He was someone who was always in control. He knew it was his show now, his time to take the stage, but he hesitated, and Annie spoke up.

"Well," she began, "I'm so glad you all came to view the destruction of this perfectly good wall." Humor was her thing, and she was very thankful it hadn't been jarred out of her. Making a humorous observation had saved her many times from awkward situations while tending bar at the Perch.

"Mr. Gravello, it seems this play has come to an end." Her eyes had fallen to looking at the floor after briefly glancing at her antagonist to judge his reaction, but her expression was dead serious. She let her mind mull over what she needed to say next.

Anthony Gravello remained silent. He was nervously looking at her attempting to predict if she was about to expose him and everything he had said and done to her—the cement-block anchor, the boat, his final demand of her. If she did, he wasn't at all sure of what he would need to explain. He was at a total loss for what to say that would act to undermine anything she could come up with.

Instead Annie raised her eyes and looked directly at him. "I hold no hard feelings. I feel sorry for you, and I'm very happy we never managed to get to the water's edge."

As Stone and Loki looked at Annie with puzzled expressions attempting to make meaning from what was not being said, Anthony Gravello finally spoke. He was a strong man, and although living on the criminal end of society, he couldn't leave the many questions that must be running through his daughter's mind unanswered. In his own fashion, he loved her as deeply as he was capable of loving anyone. He wasn't concerned with what went through this man's, Stone's, thoughts—that he could care less about.

"This is all my doing," he said, looking at Loki. "Annie's late boyfriend took something valuable from me. Loki, we've talked of this." He was looking directly at her. "I wanted to find out if your friend knew where he had hidden it. It's mine, after all. I figured if I scared her sufficiently, she would open up and tell me." He then looked straight at Annie and said, "I'm sorry, young lady, if I did any unintended harm to you."

He was quite proficient at lying once he got started. It was a family trait.

"I'd like to know just how far you were intending to take this little charade." It was Annie. She had moved away from all the litter she'd created and was standing beside Loki. All three were looking questioningly at Garvello.

"Just until I was satisfied that you'd told me all that you knew, no further. As soon as Milo returned, I had planned to have him drive you to the airport," he was answering Annie but was now looking at his daughter. "He has a first-class ticket for her return to Maui. Maybe you, Loki, could do the honor of driving your friend since I'm not sure when Milo is scheduled to return." He retrieved his wallet from the vest pocket of his suitcoat and pulled out a hundred-dollar bill, holding it out for Annie to take.

She didn't take it but just looked at it, then looked up at him.

"I think your conscience needs that more than I do."

Stone finally spoke. "Annie, why don't you and Loki come to Kaikanani for the night? You can both relax and let this travesty"—he looked accusingly at Gravello—"disappear." He didn't like the man, an emotion that was a rarity for him. "I'll get you both to the airport whenever you're ready to leave, tomorrow, or even the day after."

* * *

In the car, Stone didn't bring the incident up again, nor did either of the girls. In his mind, he was busily charting a course of what had to happen next. There was no way Gravello was going to get himself off the hook this easily. Stone had spent a lot of time looking at the list of companies and associated dollar amounts he received from Annie and had finally figured out what it was all about. He planned to bring it up with Mike at his first opportunity. He was certain criminal charges would be levied against the man with jail time to follow.

Chapter Fifty-eight

After a very relaxed two days at Kaikanani, Annie and Loki flew to Maui and spent the day packing up what remained of Annie's possessions still in the cabin. They then drove Taylor's car, with its aging problems, to Young Brother's Interisland Barging Company and placed it in the lineup for a barge bound for Kawaihae Harbor on the Big Island. It wasn't a great car, but Annie would need one to get around without having to rely on Loki to be her chauffer.

They had packed Annie's possessions in cartons and stowed them in the rear of the Explorer. The old Ford may have its problems, but there was ample cargo space for the few cartons. Young Brothers promised the car and its contents would be available for pickup at Kawaihae Harbor in five days.

They had hauled the boat trailer to the barging company as well and consigned it to Stone. It would be on the next barge bound for Honolulu. He had asked her to ship it over, so he could haul her boat out of the yacht club and find a buyer. It was a given that Annie would make better use of the cash than she would having the boat sitting around collecting dust.

When the cabin was finally cleared out and cleaned up, Annie found it more difficult to simply walk away than she had originally thought. She'd spent the two days at Stone and Teri's house mentally preparing herself for the inevitable, but even with Loki's unending support, she found all her mental preparations inadequate for the real event. She and Taylor had created so many beautiful memories together revolving around their lives at the cabin, with their boat, and the fun they'd had exploring the island. But they had always looked forward to returning to their comfortable nest high on the slope of the famous mountain.

* * *

Landing at the Kona airport at Keahole on the Big Island, Loki retrieved her car from the parking lot, and she and Annie drove the hour to Hawi. It was an emotional relief to finally pull into her own driveway along with Annie. She was home and feeling good about having her dear friend safe. A large potted anthurium plant, flowers galore, rested in front of her door. Her mom and Pops had obviously been by the house. Anthuriums were Loki's favorite flower. She knew the plant at her door carried a lot of love.

They both sat up the first night and talked into the early morning hours, making plans for adventure and exploring the island and hiking the magnificent trails close by and finding a place Annie could consider her own. They both agreed that staying together under the same roof would be fun for a while, but they were independent souls, and both would need their own space in order to thrive.

The one thing they didn't speak of, but both knew the other's mind was agonizing over, was Loki's father. He was in a lot of trouble because of the kidnapping and the illegal drain of clients' cash. They knew Stone would be talking with his friend Mike, who would in turn have to instigate an investigation that would place Loki's father into the Oahu Correctional facility for a good long time.

* * *

Over the next few days, the girls looked at different properties around Hawi and the close neighborhood and decided more time was needed to find the right place for Annie to move into. Renting looked to be the only option for now.

They looked at and fell in love with a house and large property not far out of Hawi that bordered on the threshold of Palolo Valley, with vast views into the deep valley as well as out over an expanse of ocean. Unfortunately, the price tag was unrealistically high so they kept looking.

Frequently during the following days, Annie thoughts returned to the past few weeks' events, the short time it had taken to radically change her life as well as her outlook. She had hoped Stone would call with an update on what was happening, if anything, about Loki's father, but she remembered that Stone mentioned that he and his friend Lloyd had an extended fishing trip planned and was probably somewhere on the ocean around the islands pulling in all the fish they could find and enjoying every second.

She wondered what must have taken place at Gravello's house. She knew from Loki that HPD had gotten a warrant for her father's arrest on kidnapping and embezzlement. She hesitated asking Loki if she knew anything more, but when she finally had a chance to ask, it turned out Loki knew just as little as Annie did. Loki said she'd been unable to contact her father but had spoken to Milo a few days earlier but found him quite evasive, unwilling to answer anything. Even Smythe was not responding to her phone calls, so she was quite concerned.

Chapter Fifty-nine

*T*he warrant for Anthony Gravello's arrest wasn't as problematic to obtain as Mike and a few of his officers had thought it would be. With all the money the man had and the influence he retained within the business and government communities, Mike had thought nothing short of a siege on the courthouse would succeed. He hadn't considered the fact that several judges as well as a few higher-ups in the governor's office, possibly the governor himself, were clients as well as victims of TGL & Company.

Upon learning of the embezzlement charges against Gravello coupled with discovering that their own personal financial accounts had been tampered with, the warrant was issued almost before the ink on the charges had dried. *All too happy to haul the SOB*, as one judge had voiced, *into my courtroom.*

With arrest warrant in hand, Mike, and three other officers, pulled into Gravello's driveway, well prepared for whatever it would take to make the arrest.

The chiming doorbell brought an attractive, classily dressed, middle-aged woman to the door. She tilted her head in surprise as she confronted four police officers, and her well-practiced smile faltered. The callers at the door were not who she had been expecting.

"My, my," she exclaimed, "have you boys ganged up to come look at the house?"

This was Angie Ford's first day on the job. Her freshly printed real estate license was carefully tucked into her purse along with a stack of business cards ready for the giving.

She'd been the star among the other real estate agents in her new office when she announced to them all that she signed a gold-sealed contract to represent a very wealthy client who owned the large prestigious home on Black Point Road. It was a house most agents knew of and were not pleased that a new agent had succeeded in doing something as grand as this—professional jealousy abounded.

"I'm going to go out on the limb," she said to the officers standing in front of the door, her beautiful smile returning. "I'm thinking you officers are not here to look at the house with any thoughts of making an offer on it. In case one of you is, a showing is strictly by appointment, but I'm quite willing to bend that rule just for you."

"No, miss, we're not." Mike took charge of the situation to avoid wasting time. He knew that two of the officers with him would love nothing more than stand and talk to this attractive woman. "We're here to see Anthony Gravello. Is he here?" Mike's antenna was signaling a big problem, especially in response to the woman's sudden hesitant expression. He realized she had no idea who he was asking for. This was certainly not the way he had envisioned this arrest to proceed.

"I'm very sorry, Officer," she replied. "I have not met the owner, Mr. Gravello. I have a contract with an attorney to sell the house and property and turn the proceeds over to him. It's being offered at considerably less than market value, so I must assume the owner is interested in obtaining a quick sale. I expect it will be sold within the next day or two or before this weekend at the latest. Are you sure I can't interest any of you in making an offer?"

"Ms. Ford, I'll need that attorney's name and address along with your business card. Also, I'll need the name of someone my department can contact at your office to obtain copies of any paperwork that's involved."

Although remaining courteous and willing to help in any way she could, Angie's winning smile had disappeared and replaced by a look of great disappointment. She sadly realized that her great achievement in signing this deal may have a lot of leaks in it.

The following morning, Mike was looking at the notes he'd taken from the interview he had with Gravello's attorney. It was clear that Anthony Gravello was back in Europe some place or at least on his way; the exact location was not known, or those who knew weren't telling. The Gravello family in Sicily was listed as the contact and recipient of the funds from the sale of the house and property. When HPD's legal people contacted them for information, they claimed complete ignorance of Anthony's whereabouts.

The investigation that followed showed that Milo Palma and Benny Vitali, known to be Anthony Gravello's employees were no longer in America either. Both had returned to Palermo, Sicily. A third passenger listed on Air Italia roster as traveling with Palma and Vitali was shown as Anthony Paison.

It appeared a lot of ground had been covered in just twenty-four hours. Amazing what power one has if enough money is involved.

The way Mike saw it all was that the whole thing was unfortunately out of his hands. Theft of money transported between countries was now the FBI's problem, not HPD's. Annie was okay with it all and was not interested in pressing charges that would, in all likelihood, take years to clear up, if ever. She chose to let it all go. No one had been hurt, and she and Loki now had a fascinating story to tell anyone who might care to listen.

Loki was her dearest friend, and together, they had wounds they would help each other heal.

Epilogue

Hawi, Hawaii. Two years beyond

*A*nnie, Loki, and Loki's mom were busy arranging Annie's new home for the guests that would be showing up within two hours. Stone and Teri were in the yard by the bluff over Palolo Valley helping Pops set up the rented luau tent and tables. It was the day to celebrate.

Annie had thought of digging an *imu* and roast a pig and letting everyone enjoy a full-on luau, but the effort involved was extensive, and there wasn't enough manpower to manage the undertaking. She decided it was much easier on everyone to cater the food from the Bamboo Garden in Hawi. Since Annie worked there as bartender, the owner had given her the cheapest rate she could manage; she was one of the guests as well.

The rest of the gang from Oahu had already landed at the Kona airport and were on the road to Hawi. They'd be there within an hour. Lloyd Moniz and Pam, Mike Kalama and Robin, along with Paul Hender, Annie's old boss and owner of the Perch, where everything had begun—were all traveling together, first class thanks to Annie.

Annie was taking a short break sitting on a bench that overlooked the immense Palolo Valley. She was thinking of all the events that were culminating in celebration that day. She would have loved to have Taylor here with her to share in how her life had blossomed as an unintended result of his actions—this beautiful piece of property and gorgeous home being one of them.

She had bought the house that she and Loki had looked at two years prior but had walked away from because of the price tag. It had then been sold but had recently come back on the market.

The For Sale sign had gone up at the same time that a strange man showed up at Loki's door asking for Annie Gaines.

As it turned out, Taylor had stashed the money that he had indeed embezzled in a Danish bank. Instructions he'd given said that if a two-year period were to elapse without he, Taylor, or Ms. Annie Gaines, coming to collect it, the bank was instructed to use a portion of the funds to find Ms. Gaines and turn the balance over to her.

There was close to one and a half million dollars in the form of a cashier's check. The representative for the bank presented it to Annie. Taxes would need to be paid, he instructed, but that left an ample amount to buy this house and live comfortably.

She'd immediately contacted the insurance company that had to foot the bill to cover losses experienced by Gravello's actions as well as Taylor's. She would pay them back for Taylor's portion over time; they had readily agreed. She was told the interest she would earn would pay for that.

* * *

It was a delightful, warm new-home celebration. Ukuleles materialized, and music and singing filled the early morning air.

Annie's memories had softened over the two years. Her love for Taylor, she preferred to remember him as that, had morphed into moments of smiles whenever she walked along her bluff and looked out over the shimmering ocean.

PLACES MENTIONED

Ahalanui (*ah-ha-LA-new-ee*)—Northeast coast of the Big Island in the area known as Kapoho. A large warm pond, also called Millionaires Pond, was a favorite spot for many local residents for swimming and relaxing. It succumbed to the lava flow in 2019.

Hawi (*ha-VEE*)—A small town on the northernmost point of the Big Island, resting beside Palolo Valley.

Kahului (*KA-who-loo-ee*)—The commercial center of Maui, on the north-center coast of the island.

Kaiwi (*ka-EE-vee*) **Channel**—The channel of water running between the islands of Oahu and Molokai.

Kalohi (*ka-LOW-he*) **Channel**—The channel of water running between the islands of Molokai and Lanai.

Kaunakakai (*Cow-naw-ka-KA-ee*)—South-central coast of Molokai, and it's the biggest town.

Kekela (*kay-KAY-la*) **Ward**—The special ward established by Queen's Medical Center on Oahu to house and help mentally deficient patients.

Kīpahulu (*key-pa-HOO-loo*)—One of several sugar plantation villages in the Hana area. Its working mill operated between 1890 and 1922.

Kolekole (*ko-lay-ko-lay*) **Beach Park**—A popular beach park on the Hamakua Coast of the Big Island.

Koolau (*Ko-o-LA-oo*) **Range**—The range of mountains running from the eastern end of Oahu toward the North Shore.

Maunaloa (*mau-na LOW-ah*)—A small village of a few hundred people, mostly associated with Molokai Ranch.

Nuuanu (*new-ooh-AH-new*)—A valley on Oahu that runs from Honolulu to the Koolau's. The Pali Highway runs through the valley to Kailua on the windward side of the island. It is the area originally settled by the missionaries. The famous Pali Lookout is situated mid-way on this highway.

Ohe'o (*o-HAY-o*) **Gulch**—In the vicinity of Hana, Maui, Oheo Gulch is better known today as the Seven Sacred Pools.

OTHER **HAWAIIAN WORDS** USED

Auwe (*a-oo-WAY*)—Used to express wonder, fear, scorn.

Halepuanani (*HA-lay-poo-ah-nah-nay*)—House of flowers. Teri's Nuuanu house.

Hapa (*Ha-pa*) **Hawaiian**—Half Hawaiian.

Hele mai (*hay-lay my-ee*)—Come, come to me.

Hui O'Kainalu (*hoo-ee o' kai-NAW-loo*)—A group of men on windward Oahu who gather frequently for fun and fellowship established in 1955.

Imu (*EE-moo*)—A pit dug in the ground and used to roast a pig.

Kahauanu (*ka-ha-Oo-AH-noo*) **Lake**—The lead musician and singer of the Hawaiian musical trio, the Kahauanu Lake Trio.

Kaikanani (*kai-ka-NAW-knee*)—Beautiful. Stone's house.

Kalia (*ka-LEE-ah*)—Passive. Annie and Taylor's boat.

Kawakawa (*ka-va-ka-va*)—Bonito, small tuna.

Kiawe (*key-AWE-vay*)—Similar to a mesquite tree.

Kuuipo (*coo-oo-EE-po*)—Sweetheart.

Mamaki (*ma-MA-key*)—A small native tree with mulberry-type fruit.

Naupaka (*now-PA-ka*)—Native shrub found only in the mountains or at the sea.

Niele (*KNEE-eh-leh*)—Nosy, inquisitive.

Opihi (*oh-PEE-he*)—A limpet found on rock at tide level. Coveted by native Hawaiians.

Pali (*PAW-lee*)—A cliff or steep hill.

Pilikia (*pee-lee-KEY-ah*)—Trouble of any kind.

Pipinola (*pee-pee-NO-la*) - Chayote

Pohakau (*po-ha-ka-oo*)—Anchor. Anthony Garvello's house.

Pupule (*poo-POO-lee*)—Crazy, insane.

Wahine (*wa-hee-neh*)—Woman, female.

Wailana (*Why-LAW-naw*) **Sunrise**—Calm seas. Stone's yacht.

Other Novels by Stone Spicer

Deep Green

As a young geology student explores an ancient lava tube, she discovers two artifacts left by early Polynesian travelers. When they are forcefully taken from her, she is left to drown miles from shore. Kensington Stone, on his yacht's maiden voyage, saves her, and together, they begin their hunt for the thieves and her treasures and are forced to confront a ring of merciless black marketers.

Readers are taken deep into the bowels of a lava tube, get caught in a brutal storm at sea, and ultimately find serenity on a moonlit night on the sands of Waikiki Beach.

Hidden So Deep

A weekend adventure on a remote island is shattered by the daring theft of a boat. Kensington Stone leads an all-island search, but as the search begins, Stone and his partner Teri receive an urgent phone call for help from family. Viane Koa, the daughter of Pops and Leilani Koa, has disappeared on a hike on Mauna Loa.

The search for the boat continues but of primary concern is Viane. Her hat is all that is found. As the search closes in on discovering what happened to her, none of the searchers realize the dire consequence of an earthquake that suddenly rolls across the Big Island, forcing an injured Viane toward certain death.

Unforgivable Deception

The last of three Kensington Stone novels.

Printed in the United States
By Bookmasters